Subject Six

by

William Robson

Dedication

For Josie, Seb, Archie and Milo

Acknowledgements

I would like to thank Josie for giving me the initial inspiration for this story, my Dad for helping me on the first few drafts and Taryn at FCM Publishing for taking a chance on a plucky, (almost) young writer.

About The Author

Will Robson lives in Tooting, London though he hails from Rutland, the UK's smallest county. At the age of five he cried when his teacher said he used the word 'and' too often in his stories. It was then he realised he wanted to be a writer. He still overuses the word 'and', although he sometimes swaps it out for a ';' or a '-'. He works in TV, creating documentaries, though he hasn't done one about a superhero just yet.

On Saturday 22nd June, 2018 the world changed forever. Enosh Blake, a multi-millionaire tech mogul who had been cryogenically frozen and sent into orbit until he could be recalled to Earth and cured of his cancer, crash-landed in the English Channel and half an hour later swam to shore.

No-one noticed him. The beach was heaving with paddlers and sunbathers and in his all-in-one Cryosuit he looked like every other body-boarder. Like every other human. There was no way anyone could know that his body was now invincible. He didn't need food or air. He couldn't bleed, or feel pain. His flesh was capable of re-generation; his bones could meld back together the moment they broke.

And that's how the world changed forever, because on that Saturday the world got its first, real-life, super-hero. Subject Six.

This is the true story of everything that's happened to him since.

HOW TO TELL THE STORY OF A SUPERHERO?

For over three years now, I've been focused on Subject Six, knowing that at some point I was going to have to set down on paper everything I'd seen, heard, discovered and thought. The magnitude of this story became apparent to me very quickly and now, in October 2021, it's become crucial for me to ensure the truth is told. There are so many lies out there about him and what he's done, it's time for me to tell you what has really happened. Rest assured, I'm not taking the responsibility lightly.

From the beginning I found myself on the most in-credible, mind-blowing and hazardous journey I could ever have imagined. Both professionally as a reporter, and personally, as my involvement with Subject Six became so great that even my wife and kids got caught up in what was happening.

I guess you're already wondering how this job fell to me, who is this guy who's taken it upon himself to tell the story? Benji Wilson? Never heard of him. What qualifies him to be able to take on a task like this?

Well, ok, here goes. In terms of actual, technical ex-perience as a reporter, I've been doing it all my profes-sional life. At the age of 24 I became a war reporter in Iraq during the fall of Saddam Hussein.

That job was a lucky break. I had recently graduated from a journalism course and a family connection got me the chance to shadow a paper's most experienced war reporter for two weeks on the frontline. The internship didn't last 24 hours. Too many years on the frontline had frazzled the journalist's mind and on the first night into Iraqi territory she went AWOL. I chose to stay with the regiment we'd been assigned to and that night witnessed some of the most intense combat the army had seen so far. My story made the front-page. I had a knack for making friends with the soldiers and being in the right place at the right time and at the end of my scheduled two weeks I got the job. I stayed for a couple of years, doing things I never thought I'd do, witnessing frontline action and developing a taste for gonzo journalism, where I got to live the life of my subjects as closely as possible.

When I got home I turned down a role at the paper, and a more stable pay package, and began pitching non-fiction book ideas to publishers. I wanted to immerse myself in stories, not just swoop in, get a snapshot and churn out a few pages; I wanted to be writing books about the people and the worlds I'd become a part of. My first was about a gold heist. Having befriended the ringleader who was living a free life in Venezuela, I had some exclusive quotes and some information no-one else had. My next book told the story of the wife and family of a man who'd been an undercover jihadi and became a suicide bomber just a few miles from their home.

At the same time I made a podcast and web-series with my wife, Mina, called 'Let's Get Immortal'. If you didn't catch it - like many people - it was about an aristocrat and his, much younger, second wife, who'd spent a few years doing lots of crystal meth and reading medieval books about how to live forever until they both overdosed. We got hold of the journals and videos they'd made to record their work, Mina's a TV producer so she edited the footage and then together we worked our way through their journey over 12 episodes.

The podcast and books haven't made me famous, or rich, but the reviews and sales have been fine and have allowed me to carve out a good life. A great life really, completely comfortable; until the Subject Six story came along. Since then I've found myself in the middle of a story that's probably as big, if not bigger, than any reporter could imagine. The arrival of the world's first superhero.

In pursuit of the story I have tried to understand the biology and theology of what his appearance on earth means. I've attempted to work out what it must be like psychologically to come back from the dead and have to re-assimilate yourself into the lives of your family, who've already mourned you and moved on. I'm also trying to prove this isn't a hoax, while chasing down rumours that his superhero abilities are the result of military experiments. Over the last three years it feels as though I must have thought every thought there is to think about Subject Six.

After three years of working with him, (because from the beginning he was savvy enough to foresee that one day it might pay off to have someone following him and recording evidence to help fight the inevitable fake news) I've come to know him well. Which is tough with him, because he can be an asshole. But, over time I've managed to get past the fact he is incredibly good at rubbing people up the wrong way and as well as getting to know him, I've come to like him. Not only that, I should say at the start of this book, that I believe in what he's doing.

Another thing I'm not going to dodge is the fact that when it comes to my overall objective as a reporter, I've failed. When I first started following this case I wanted to understand exactly how Subject Six exists and why. Don't read this book if you want a definitive answer to that. There isn't one.

What I do have though, is three years of investigation into Subject Six and three years of unparalleled access to his world and his thoughts, putting me in the unique position to be able to create the most definitive portrayal of Subject Six possible. To do that, I'm going to tell this story using as much first-hand source material as possible. I have a huge archive of emails and social media messages to draw from. I've recorded hundreds of hours of phone-calls. I've got transcripts from countless interviews that I've carried out. I've spoken to people who've played key parts in the defining moments of the Subject Six story, all so I can get their personal accounts of what happened. I'll bring together as many voices as possible to tell this story, including that of Subject Six himself, who has granted me hours and hours of interviews almost from the time he arrived back on earth.

As well as including authentic archive material, I'm going to write as honestly as possible about what it's been like to be in the middle of this. Don't get me wrong, Subject Six is the focus of this journey, not me, but having become increasingly immersed in his world I'm going to try and produce the most real and most immediate depiction of what it has been like to have been an eye-witness to this huge, unfolding story.

HOW DID YOU FIRST HEAR ABOUT SUBJECT SIX?

The first time most people hear about Subject Six is May 28th 2019. There's a big chance you remember it. Some people call it a JFK moment, a 9/11; the moment you first hear there is a real-life superhero, saving people. A massive moment.

By late May 2019, ten months have passed since he arrived on the British shore. In that time, I've played my part in helping Subject Six gain his freedom and have been working with him closely. He's still classified as top secret. Virtually no-one knows about him. Then, one morning, I'm lying in bed, checking my iPad when I read the headline of a story I just know he's involved in. Four hostages have been freed in impossible conditions. And I mean impossible. The more accounts I read of it, the more I'm convinced Subject Six is behind it.

GOT THEM!
The Syrian Four have been freed after three years, and no-one can believe it...

MISSION INSANE
This unexpected raid is one we have to ask questions about. Many want to celebrate, and of course we should, because the result is undeniably positive, but as experts around the world agree that a mission like this had a less than 10% chance of success, we need to start

SUPERHERO SWAT
Tonight I'll raise a glass to the four brave souls who've lost years of their lives to terrorist delusionists. Then I'll raise another to the people who freed them.

(from articles that first appeared on May 28th 2019)

Four aid workers; two men, two women, one from America, one from Japan, one from the UK and one from France. They haven't been seen for almost three years until the group holding them posts a video saying they're going to be beheaded in a week. Then, just three days later, without a shot being fired and without any military intervention from any country, the four hostages are somehow delivered to a NATO base just after dawn. Starving, ill, almost dead from three years of imprisonment, but alive and free.

Normally it's after a terrorist attack that you wait to see who claims responsibility for what's happened. After this escape, everything is turned upside down because it's the good guys no-one can identify. From the moment celebrations begin because the hostages have got home safely, the western allies are looking to each other to see who has managed to pull off this remarkable coup. No-one takes responsibility. Yet someone has stolen into the compound, taken out between 10 and 20 guards, broken into the cells and got the captives to safety. That kind of thing just doesn't happen. Or it didn't.

Poring over these stories from my bed, I know Subject Six is behind their escape since he's been training hard for a few months and weighing up how to use his powers. Logic makes me question whether he has the audacity and skill to pull off something like this, and yet I know he's done it. He's jumped in at the deep-end and picked an almost impossible mission for his first task.

I immediately pick up the phone and call him. No answer. I keep trying. I guess he's probably in transit from Syria, but still it frustrates me. Eventually, on what must be my fiftieth call, the phone doesn't ring through to his answerphone. The following is the transcript of the call I recorded and, be assured, Subject Six knew I was recording everything.

Subject Six

Benji, to what do I owe this honour?

Me

Was it you?

Subject Six

Was what me?

Me

Where have you been?

Subject Six

Here. Where I always am.

Me

Is it really going to be like this?

Subject Six

For someone who makes their living as a journalist, your questioning technique leaves a lot to be desired. Your last three questions have been...

Me

Hey, come on, I've been out of my mind trying to get hold of you. Was it you who helped those guys escape?

Subject Six

What? What do you mean?

Me

The Syrian Four.

Subject Six

Oh my god, has it broken so soon? Have they said my name yet?

Me

Where are you?

Subject Six

On my way home. I thought I'd at least get home before this! Jesus.

During Subject Six's training I've taken a few trips to his base in the north of the UK. A huge gothic pile in the countryside. We've talked about what he could do with his powers, but not too much about the fall-out of what would happen afterwards. To begin with, he hopes to remain anonymous, to save himself a lot of unwanted harassment and for security and legal reasons. To act from the shadows and avoid the light, as it were. Yes, he's got a journalist onboard, but there's an agreement between us that I won't publish anything until he says I can. Before then, if possible, he doesn't want a media storm to get in his way. Well, turns out it's impossible to avoid that when you're a superhero.

The moment he accomplishes his first mission our news-hungry culture starts to devour him. As soon as the headlines break about the Syrian Four being rescued, the 24 hour news cycle whips up a frenzy. By lunch, the freed hostages start talking about the person who helped them. A British accent. Performing incredible feats of strength. Taking a bullet but not going down, not even bleeding.

By dinner time, the main details are out. One channel has someone inside the British government talking. That night the word 'superhero' appears on screens around the globe. They know about how he appeared, the basics of his physical changes, how he was locked up illegally while the government tried to work out what was going on and exploit his potential and how, after a legal battle that was kept confidential, he's free and according to the scoop, playing at being a superhero by rescuing hostages. Again, I call him immediately. This time he picks up first time.

Subject Six

You know what? It's better this way.

Me

How do you figure that?

Subject Six

No-one knows any details about who I was before, no-one knows who I am now. But the world does know I exist now which I think is going to protect me. If I suddenly disappear, which we both know certain people want, now it'll get noticed. And if I do go missing, I'll need people searching for me, won't I?

Me

I'd love to see people try and get you to disappear, I've seen what you can do, remember?

As you can tell from these phone-calls, by the time the world hears about Subject Six, we've already established a close bond. That's because I've been dedicating myself to his story since I first heard about him a few months before. A moment that I remember in detail.

I'm waiting at Kings Cross Station for a train home when I get an email from an old journalist friend. Laura Freeman. She's a freelance reporter who works mostly for the major weeklies. One of the stories she's been working on has been shut-down, for reasons we'll come to, and, knowing that I'm on the look-out for stories that are big enough for me to turn into a book, she sends me an email with all her work on what she's been doing.

When I read what she's written, I grab my phone and WhatsApp my wife, Mina.

Me

You know your dad believed good deeds beget good things?

Mina

Yes... (really annoying message)

Me

Well it seems that me babysitting last night has earned me a very good thing.

Mina

It's not possible to babysit your own children #jackass #thatsjustparenting

Me

Blah blah blah - Laura just got in touch with a story.

Mina

What is it?

Me

On my way home. I've got to share this with you.

Mina

Can you get milk. And bananas.

Me

Always bananas.

As I walk home I have absolutely no way of knowing where the story is going to take me, but I have an inkling that the email Laura has just sent contains a one-way ticket to a whole new world.

Mina

The moment he came in I could see a change in him. Well, not true, the first thing I noticed was that he'd got the damn bananas, but the way he was holding himself, the speed he was talking told me all at once that he'd finally found something big.

'Do you remember a story a month ago down in Brighton?' he asked me, 'A group of armed officers swooped down on a beach bar and took someone away and no-one knew how or why?'

Even as I ask, I know it's very unlikely Mina will know what I'm talking about. Unless you scour the papers every day like me, you would have missed it. The incident hit twitter for half an hour in the local area, with the hashtag #swatonthebeach and made it into the small columns on a couple of daily papers. Then it was forgotten. Why? Because the police didn't say anything about it, or any other authority. Neither did the guy who got arrested, or anyone connected to him. News-wise it was a dead-end. Just another example of UK streets seeing more armed police and heavy duty tactics and nothing else.

Mina

'You won't believe me', he said, 'But the man they arrested that day is still being held. Illegally, in London.'
'What? Why?' I asked.

The words I say next feel ridiculous to be saying out loud for the first time.

Mina

'Because," he began, "Well, he's some sort of super-hero, or mutant'.

HOW DOES A SUPERHERO GET DOWN TO EARTH?

The superhero Subject Six, first arrives on earth on the 23rd June 2018, on the south coast of England. It's a normal Saturday night in Brighton. At 6pm the beach front is thriving and busy. A mix of holidaying families packing up to go back to their hotels. Stag and hen parties ramping up the volume after an afternoon on the sauce. Daytrippers from London trying to fit in a few more drinks before they catch the train.

It's been a hot, sunny day in the high 20s. Even though summer days like this are more regular now, they all feel like they're sharing something special. The sunburn hasn't started stinging, the kids are still riding the sugar wave of their last ice-cream, the drinker's bubble hasn't burst yet, so the bars seem exciting and inviting, not threatening and leering.

Mick Powell

The reason I was filming is my daughter, Alicia. For as long as I can remember she's been obsessed with sharks and even though I'd told her that the recent sightings of Great Whites in Cornwall didn't mean we'd see them as far east as Brighton, she'd spent most of the day looking through her binoculars to try and spot them.

Mick goes on to say that just before six o clock, as the family are about to head back to their hotel, Alicia jumps up, beside herself, saying she's seen a shark's fin. It's not the first time she's managed to get Mick to stand on the deck-chair pointing his phone out towards the sea. This time though, Mick starts to think that maybe Alicia is right. Because there is something out there.

Mick Powell

I'm standing on this deckchair trying to get higher, more for Alicia's benefit than mine if I'm honest. But then I catch a sight of something. I've no idea what at first. Except it's not a person, it's not a lifebuoy and I don't think it's a boat. I know that if I stretch up any higher I'm going to do myself a mischief - so instead I hold my hands up as high as possible and point the camera in the direction of what I'm seeing.

Mick's footage isn't fantastic. I don't mean to sound cruel, he's a guy being a great Dad and playing along with his daughter. He has no idea what he's filming as he wobbles on a deck-chair, straining to get a clean shot of the dark object he's seen in the sea. I've watched it a few times now and every time I do, it teases and frustrates me. Every time you think you're going to get a steady shot, so you can process what you're seeing properly, the image blurs, jerks in a different direction, or the waves cover what you're trying to look at.

The moment Mick himself starts to wonder whether what he's filming is important, is when two old guys and one women, run past his deckchair and down towards the sea. Mick hears them shouting excitedly. They all have cameras out too and they're trying to film something out at sea. It crosses his mind to talk to them, to find out what they're so excited about and then something stops him in his tracks.

Mick Powell

Alicia saw the group too. She looked up and asked me if they were shark-spotters. I was about to reply when the helicopters arrived and the police vans with armed rozzers. Loads of them.

We didn't hang around. You know what it's like when that kind of thing happens and you're with your kids; you scarper as soon as you can. I didn't think about it again really, until I saw your advert in the paper looking for witnesses. If I hadn't seen those three people I don't think I would have given your appeal a second thought, but they'd made me think Alicia had seen something.

So what is it that Alicia sees? What does Mick then film, and what gets the three other people so excited? Quite simply, it's Subject Six's pod. And when I say pod, I mean a CryoPod-4. They don't know that as they hurry away from the beach front as armed police swarm towards a man about 100m further down the beach. In fact they don't know that what they see is a CryoPod-4 until they meet me during my research.

A CryoPod-4 is made by the Genix lab. Genix is the company that made its owner, Fabian Tree, a billionaire. And while for the last five years or so Fabian Tree has been delighting viewers of reality TV - or not, if you're like me - by playing the role of an evil mogul bullying people who are less well-off than him, in the background Genix has been flourishing. What does it do? Well, it mostly operates in the UK and US (although it's now doing very well in Dubai, China and India) and since the 1990s has offered people, rich, sick people, the chance to freeze themselves cryogenically.

The CryoPod-4 is their latest design. It's top of the range - not only does it freeze you, it sends you into space.

Here's what Fabian said at its launch:

Fabian Tree

The CryoPod-4 is for the truly long-sighted customer. In an age where climate change, terrorism and weapons of mass-destruction are all too commonplace, who knows how long life on earth is safe or sustainable? The whole idea behind cryogenically freezing yourself is to keep your body secure until medicine and science have advanced to such an extent that you can be woken-up and cured from your illness. Yet what good is that, if before we get to this stage, a natural disaster or bomb destroys the pod in which your body is being kept? For this reason, we have created a way of making sure our clients can wait in the safest place known to man until medicine is ready - space.

Now the idea of freezing your body and having it sent into space isn't one many people instinctively have. I guess because money, and quite frankly sanity, get in the way. But figures from the Genix lab say since the launch of the CryoPod-1, 1356 people have been shot into space in the hope that one day they'd be recalled to Earth to start life again. Or, if Earth has been destroyed, the brochure goes on to suggest that if the human race relocates to a space station or another planet, then the pods can be sent there; allowing the occupants to join the party wherever it is in the galaxy.

These pods measure 8 foot by 3 foot. I've been to the Genix lab and seen one, I've even been inside one, and they're exactly how you'd imagine them. A sleek, silvery grey metal that looks futuristic and incredibly strong, designed specifically to make the person who's going to be paying millions for one feel they'll be safe forever. Yet, despite his huge bill, this wasn't the experience Enosh

Blake had. His pod fell out of orbit. It re-entered the atmosphere and plummeted into the sea. Not the red carpet treatment that Genix promised.

For a variety of reasons, Genix have never fully engaged with me when I've asked them about how and why the pod ended up in the sea between England and France. But not to worry, because we have all the evidence we need from other sources. Remember the three people Mick saw on the beach in Brighton? They're Eileen and Dan Raymond and Nicholas Singh. The three of them come from Swindon and make up DEBRIS, which, as I'm sure you can guess, is short for Defenders of Earth Battling Rubbish In Space. They're what most people would call crazy and they won't mind me saying so. How do I know? I asked them.

Me

Eileen, I just described DEBRIS as crazy people in my book, I know I said it to your face but I feel a bit bad, is it ok?

Eileen

I'd prefer nuts, but we are a little crazy.

Me

You guys are good crazy

Eileen

Dan says as long as you get our message out it's fine. The world needs us even if it laughs at us.

The message they want to get out there has been their mission since the three of them started in 2012. DEBRIS is founded on the belief that the end of the world as we know it will come when something from outer space hits the earth. Hearing that, most people think of asteroids and meteorites; of the end of dinosaurs; of the films Armageddon and Deep Impact. But that's not what DEBRIS is worried about. To them the threat is man-made.

Eileen Raymond

Us humans aren't very good at keeping things tidy, are we?

Dan Raymond

Take the earth.

Nicholas Singh

Yes, that's the best example because people can relate to that.

Dan Raymond

Now, it's accepted, isn't it, that we're ruining nature by dumping rubbish and waste everywhere.

Eileen Raymond

We're polluting it.

Nicholas Singh

Like that film, Wall-E, you know? When people have had to leave earth because it's so full of rubbish.

Dan Raymond

Exactly. Well said.

Nicholas Singh

But it's not just Earth we're covering with junk. Ever since the 1950s when we started to go into space, we started ruining that too.

On their website DEBRIS point to a whole bunch of stats which back their fears up. Apparently there are over 100 million pieces of man-made debris in space right now. Of these, 30,000 objects are over 10cm and are classed as large and, astonishingly, at least one piece of space debris falls to the earth every day. Many bits of debris burn up on re-entry, but many manage to make it down to us. I've double checked these facts. They match those of NASA and other authorities. And as more and more of this space junk builds, DEBRIS believe the risk does too. Sooner or later something is going to fall from up there and hit something important down here.

Nicholas Singh

By the time something comes back down it's travelling fast.

Dan Raymond

Imagine if that hit a nuclear reactor?

Nicholas Singh

It would go up!

Eileen Raymond

Yes, that would be a nuclear event and we have no defence against anything like that. We've created 30,000 ticking time bombs that orbit us 24/7 and could drop anytime.

Me

But what about what NASA and other people think? Don't they say that because the planet is mostly water we have nothing to fear? The probability of anything hitting populated land is apparently…

Eileen Raymond

It strikes me that an argument that says we shouldn't worry about this now because it hasn't happened yet, is a little thin.

Nicholas Singh

One we're likely to regret.

Me

Really? This stuff has been there for years and yet no-one has been hurt.

Now is not the time to get into this argument but DE-BRIS are adamant they're right and have vowed never to stop fighting. When, in 2013, Genix propose sending the CryoPod-4s into space, DEBRIS file a motion to stop them. They lose, inevitably, because that's what happens when three people take on a huge corporation. But during the case, they demand to know what might happen if a recall goes wrong. What will happen if a CryoPod-4, designed to not break-up on re-entry and certainly big enough to cause damage on impact, comes back down to earth when it isn't meant to and lands where it isn't meant to?

In response to this, Fabian Tree and Genix produce a long line of experts and scientists, some who work for them, some who are supposedly independent, who say this will never happen. There are safety checks, fall-backs, contingency plans and the ability to control every pod from Genix HQ to ensure that every pod stays on course. On this slew of evidence, Genix get the go-ahead. Their first launch is on December 8th 2013, the mother of one of the richest men in the world. After her, many more follow. Genix's profits rocket.

DEBRIS however, furious at how Fabian Tree has ridden roughshod over them, don't give up. Nicholas, Eileen and Dan all work for Hewlett Packard in Swindon. Their day jobs don't have much to do with space, but all three of them are technophiles. Or mega-geeks, and mega-geeks with a mission. As soon as Genix get the greenlight, DEBRIS begin working on methods on how to track the CryoPods.

Since they formed DEBRIS, the three of them have been building their own systems to track space junk. NASA has a program that tracks debris, as do a few other bodies around the world but DEBRIS aren't convinced that any of them is good enough. So, in Nicholas' home, on the outskirts of Swindon, they create their own home-made trackers for space junk. I've seen it myself and it's very impressive. I have no real understanding of how they do it, but one machine actually uses FM radio signals to track junk; another more complex one utilizes an optical tracking system through a telescope.

In 2014, after losing to Genix, Dan, Eileen and Nicholas decide to try a new piece of technology - they build a remote sensor that uses laser technology. On a day-to-day basis it can be used to track lots of different types of space junk, but its primary focus is to track all of the pods that Genix sends up. They want to be sure that when one of the CryoPod-4s goes wrong, they'll know about it. Genix obviously don't know about this but every time a CryoPod-4 goes up DEBRIS gives it a number and starts to monitor it.

Me

So that's why you went to the beach that day?

Nicholas Singh

Right, because we'd been tracking pod #1221 since it went up in 2017 and then the moment it deviated from its orbit, well, we went to super-red alert.

This is from the first conversation I ever had with DEBRIS. Only Nicholas is on the phone.

Me

Super-red alert? What's that?

Nicholas Singh

Well, when anything we've been monitoring deviates from the path we go to amber alert. When a piece of junk starts falling back towards earth we have a red alert, and when we have super-red alert, well, that's something we introduced for when the CryoPods went up.

Me

Why super, what makes that so different? Because of who's inside?

Nicholas Singh

No, nothing to do with that, I mean we always believed if a pod crash-landed the body inside would just… well, stay dead.

Me

The logical thinking.

Nicholas

Exactly, the whole super thing was because of how dangerous we consider Genix to be. Don't get me wrong, we weren't hoping for a catastrophe but we were concerned that something with their system would go wrong and we were determined to make sure that if their systems failed we'd be able to prove it.

Me

So what does this super-red alert entail?

Nicholas Singh

We all had to get back to HQ, turn as many of our detectors towards the falling pod as possible and make sure we tracked it. We also got some of our affiliates from around the world, you know people who are into

this stuff too, to try to lend a hand. We needed to have the evidence so they couldn't cover it up.

Me

Did you call any authorities?

Nicholas Singh

Like who?

Me

I don't know. NASA? The government?

Nicholas Singh

Trust me, those guys won't take our calls anymore.

Me

Ok, so you're tracking the pod, and then what's the plan?

Nicholas Singh

Well, we project where it's going to crash. If it could harm anyone, or anything, we try and warn people. If not, then we follow it, we record it and then we get Fabian Tree.

So the three member of DEBRIS, sit and watch Subject Six's pod as it falls. The first thing they want to know is whether it's been recalled deliberately. Once it gets close enough to the ground will its homing-tech kick in to take it back to Genix HQ where the techs are waiting for it? Or if it has diverted from its course accidentally, is there any sign that the engineers from Genix are trying to control the pod remotely, to either try to get it back into orbit or to guide it somewhere else so that it can land?

They see nothing. I've looked at the flight path records and it's true. Once it drops out of its orbit, the only thing it does is to continue dropping. When it enters the earth's atmosphere it simply carries on plummeting, then lands in the sea. DEBRIS believe they've finally got the proof they've been after - the Genix pods are fallible.

Back in their Swindon HQ, DEBRIS believe that while some other space junk watchers may have seen the pod fall, no-one else will be aware it's a CryoPod. This is because out of 30,000 pieces of junk, unless you were tracking a CryoPod from the start like DEBRIS, it would take a lot of work to be certain about what the thing was until it landed. Which gives Nicholas, Eileen and Dan a head-start.

They enlist the help of a friend who's an avid sailor, they look at currents and predict where the CryoPod might drift to now it's in the water and how long it might take to reach land. They arrive in Brighton two days before the pod is sighted by Mick and Alicia. They spend those two days looking out to sea, driving along the coast for different vantage points, desperate to catch sight of the fallen pod.

It's Dan who first sees it. Along with Nicholas and Eileen he rushes down to the shoreline to get a closer look. They have their cameras out, they're convinced it will soon wash up on the shore. They feel - sorry for the pun - like the tide is really turning in their war against Genix. And then the sirens go off. A few, 100m from where they are, from where Mick Powell and his family are too, armed police swarm onto the seafront.

As the beach is cleared and the three members of DE-BRIS are herded away, the CryoPod-4 disappears from sight. Dan, Eileen and Nicholas try to spot it again but don't manage, and by the time the police have disappeared and the beach is re-opened, it's dark. That night, in their hotel, as they review their footage they start to talk about what to do next. How can they use their evidence to hurt Fabian Tree the most?

Bringing it back to Subject Six, I've since asked them about that night and they all agree on one thing. Not one of them connects the CryoPod-4 with the armed police. This is the age of terror after all and it never even cross their minds that the man they saw being bundled into the police van could have come from the pod they're so obsessed by.

WHAT'S IT LIKE TO WAKE UP A SUPERHERO?

JOURNAL ENTRY 1

Things I know.

I don't remember anything before four days ago. Most of what has happened since is jumbled.

I am being held in a cell.

My heart is not beating.

JOURNAL ENTRY 2

Back from more tests.

My head is so scrambled.

I can tell my situation is serious, yet I feel no worry.

What I do know is that no-one knows what to make of me and the guards are fighting over who's in charge.

These two extracts are the first entries in the journal that Subject Six is told to write during his initial imprisonment. The human rights group I worked with to try and free Subject Six from the government, requisitioned the journal and passed it to me.

JOURNAL ENTRY 3

I haven't got used to not having a heartbeat (how could you?) but it has become a murmur in the background compared to everything else.

Two issues dominate my thoughts

Why can't I remember anything? What's happened to me? I'm fine in terms of thinking and speech, I just have no memory of anything other than a few days ago. Not my name, age, where I come from. The guards are British but other than that I have no idea where I am or how I got here. A doctor, the only one with a semblance of humanity, suggested writing this journal as it might help my memory start to re-engage with the rest of me. I don't want to do anything these people tell me, but I'm doing this because it will be worth it if it helps.

At first I thought this might be me going crazy, that it had something to do with me being locked up and alone too much, or even my messed up memory playing tricks on me. But not anymore, now I know this is real - I have a number tattooed on my right wrist. Which changes. Actually changes. Every morning (and I know it's morning because there's an air vent I can see daylight through) the number has changed and it's counting up.

So these are Subject Six's first thoughts, or as close to, written down on paper. Remember, he doesn't know what he is yet. What you can see from these journals, I think, is a sense of deep confusion and disbelief. But there's no panic, there's no overburdened sense of despair or a sense he's going to come apart at the seams. Maybe that's because he's forgotten everything? Perhaps not remembering who he is helps to deflect the fear of his new physical form? No heartbeat, no breathing, perhaps that's nothing compared to not knowing who you are?

It's this confusion I want to explore when I first speak to him. By the time I have my first phone-call with Subject Six, I've already read his journal quite a few times.

I'm excited as I pick up the phone. I mean how many times do you get to talk to someone who is, to all extents and purposes, back from the dead? How do you get your head round that and the fact that your physical make-up has changed? I struggled when my eyes stopped working properly and I had to get glasses, so how does it feel when your heart stops? I want to know what it's like to wake up and at first, not be able to remember anything and then, once it comes back, to realise you're completely different and have been part of some kind of miracle.

But as well as getting straight to the subject, I also know I have to get him onside. I need him to like me, I need him to agree to us meeting, I want him to let me follow his story. The difficult thing I have to deal with is that from the first moment we speak, he makes it very clear he's not going to suffer fools.

Subject Six

Let me guess, Benji, you studied arts?

Me

History.

Subject Six

You're wearing black-framed glasses, a lumberjack shirt, jeans with the bottoms rolled up, sneakers.

Me

Boots actually.

Subject Six

You like Dylan, The Stones. You got into hip hop and pills in the years straight after uni but now your only vices are single malt and an increasing predilection for porn that strays into S and M.

Me

I've read about you doing this - before you became Subject Six.

Subject Six

The names of your kids would fit right at home in the Victorian era.

Me

So would yours.

Subject Six

You're a middle-class government-bashing leftie, the opposite of me. Tell me why I should speak to you?

Me

Because it's only government bashers like me who are going to take up your cause.

Subject Six

Go on then. First question?

Me

Tell me what it feels like to have no heartbeat.

Subject Six

Tell me what it feels like to have one.

The more we talk, the less overtly confrontational Subject Six becomes. Yet he's never far from switching moods. If he thinks I'm being lazy with my questions, or narrow-minded with the avenues I'm investigating he's quick to call me on it. While that might make you think he's a constant bore to be around - always being earnest, always demanding, never at ease - the fact is, he isn't. Yes, he's testing. He's frustrating. He's volatile. But he's bound to be isn't he, with everything he's got to deal with?

Me

Can you put into words how it felt, how it feels, to wake up transformed like you did?

Subject Six

I don't see it like that.

Me

Like what?

Subject Six

I didn't just wake up in one instant. It wasn't like I was nothing one moment, asleep, frozen, dead, what-have-you, and then pop, the next second, I'm conscious and fully aware of what's going on with me. It was a gradual process.

Me

You thawed out.

Before we move on, I think it's a good time to address some of the accusations that Subject Six has faced in relation to his journals since they were leaked to the press by one of his critics. Some people claim that the poise you see in his writing proves he's lying, about where he's come from, who he is, what his plans are.

They think the writing in his journal is methodical, almost dispassionate. And some people say, how can that be? How can a man who finds himself in a cell, with no heartbeat, be keeping it together? They claim he's not suffering from memory loss, he's not worried, he knows exactly what's going on and that's why the journals are so coherent. He's lying to us about his origin, deliberately feigning ignorance to hoodwink us so that he can carry out his masterplan.

What this masterplan is his critics don't ever say with any clarity, but that's beside the point. All they care about is trying to cast him as a liar and to stop people seeing him as a force for good.

When I've asked Subject Six about these claims, he rejects this train of thought outright. He says the first days in the cell were the hardest, most draining days he's ever faced, but the fact of the matter is he isn't driving himself mad for 24 hours a day every day. He says no-one can do that and survive with their mind intact. Yes, the days are dark, but he fights hard to salvage some moments of peace. On most days, he reckons he is able to achieve some mental equilibrium and that keeps him sane. And, it's only during these moments of relative calm that he's able to write his journal.

Do I buy that? Yes, I do and I also believe that he woke up with no memory of who he was and what had happened to him. It's important to note, I've not just taken his word for this. In investigating this story, I had to look at every angle and chase down every lead. If, for instance, Subject Six had some evil plan he was intending to carry out once he got back to earth only to find himself captured the moment he stood on land, then wouldn't playing dumb and pleading memory loss be the perfect cover?

The answer to that is yes. But as soon as you start looking at it in detail the idea falls apart. Logistics aside, just from talking to Subject Six, hearing his voice, looking into his eyes, going over everything he has to say, it seems obvious to me he's telling the truth.

Me

Ok, so your understanding of your transformation came gradually. But what about now? How do you deal with it now? Do you ever think 'why me?' Does it ever get too much, you know, wondering what the fuck

is going on here? Because it's huge this thing, and you have to deal with it.

Subject Six

Have you ever known anyone who's got terminal cancer?

Me

Yes, my mother.

Subject Six

Ok, now that's life-changing news, isn't it?

Me

The very definition of it.

Subject Six

And how did you cope with it, say, at first?

Me

Terribly. I was a mess. I remember Mina found me crying in the garden once in the pouring rain. I had no idea how I'd got out there.

Subject Six

And then later? Did you stay out-of-your-mind like that for long?

Me

No. Of course not. She lived for a few months, we had some good times, some great one's even.

Subject Six

So you recalibrated. And that's something we humans are very good at. It was the same when I was diagnosed. At first I felt like I was in the middle of a tsunami, I kept asking why? Why? What? What? And then after about a month I'd become a man who had cancer, who had accepted it, and of course the scale of

what that meant still blindsided me from time to time, but my brain had accustomed itself and I could deal with it.

Even though he learns to accept it, during the first days and weeks of his time in the cell, Subject Six says he often loses himself in a black hole of questions and torment, oscillating between wild disbelief, terror and rage. Then his memory starts to come back and he begins to get a firmer grip on things.

JOURNAL ENTRY 4

My name is Enosh Blake. I know this because after 10 days of questioning (the number on my wrist now says 14) the people who are holding me started answering my questions.

My name is Enosh Blake. I was born in London in 1981 which I'm told was 37 years ago. At the age of 20 I made my first million pounds when I founded an online insurance company. It is now worth billions.

I know I have a wife and two children but not their names. Why not? Because the people in charge are testing me still. They've already tortured me with the physical tests and now they're messing with my mind. They think by withholding important information I'll force myself to access my memories. That hasn't happened, I don't feel like my memories are about to come back, I feel angry and impotent.

JOURNAL ENTRY 5

Yesterday in my cell a psychiatrist spoke to me. She asked if I had anything on my mind that was making me so hostile and I laughed. When I saw she was serious, I said I was being held captive against, my will, illegally, so why should I help?

She said no-one was, and could, deny me my rights and handed me a document. It listed a number of places she said who would answer my letters and work on my behalf if I felt I was being treated unfairly. The first was a company called AllFree and I joked and said I'll just write them a letter then and be gone in a week. She didn't seem to get I was messing her about, but before we could say any more the door opened and one of the head guards came in and led her out. Snatching the paper from me and then I heard shouting directed at her.

For a bit I found myself feeling hope.

JOURNAL ENTRY 6

Ok, I have my first memory. In a white, blank room. A brown-fringed woman turns to me. My wife? I feel deep down she is. She has tears in her blue eyes. Another woman is talking to us. Calm but serious.

That's all.

It came to me minutes after they started piping music - a song which seemed familiar - into my cell. The moment I started writing it down the music stopped. So they're manipulating me. Trying to spark my memory into life.

Well, I guess I just have to go with it.

JOURNAL ENTRY 7

Another. Although this is more like a cascade of memories. Like water is being poured over my hands and I can only hold a few and only for a moment. Here we go.

I'm holding a baby. It's asleep but I wake it when a toddler runs into the cubicle and I start shouting at it to be quiet

I'm in a bar on the side of a snowy mountain. Dancing. Music pulsating. A beautiful, tan-skinned woman wearing a three piece suit walks up to me and kisses me.

On a beach, a Frisbee comes flying at pace towards my head. I pluck it from the air just in time and hand it to a little kid who tells me what a great catch it was.

Someone pushes me from a chair, I reach out my hand to break my fall but a chipped china bell is on the floor and a sharp edge slices into my wrist. After a few seconds blood starts running out.

A masked man, breathing heavily, with terror in his eyes, holds a gun to my head and shouts. All I do is chuckle.

It's a slight diversion, I know, but let's stick with the last entry for a moment. By speaking to Subject Six, and people like his ex-wife, and closest colleagues, I've validated all of these memories and they help piece together Subject Six's backstory. They tell you a lot about who he was when he was Enosh Blake and therefore who Subject Six is now. The first memory in the list is from when his second child, Oscar, was born.

Despite the fact Enosh wants to use some of his huge personal fortune to go to a private hospital, his wife Michelle insists they use the NHS like everyone else. On the second evening after Oscar is born they are meant to go home but the ward is understaffed and an error means Michelle and Oscar are going to have to stay an extra night. Riled, and frustrated after a day spent in the hot, clammy ward waiting to be discharged, Enosh starts to lose it.

Before Enosh has to go home, Michelle gets her first sleep in over 24-hours leaving Enosh holding the baby. Eventually Oscar stops crying and falls asleep in his Dad's arms for the first time, when Tuppence, their three-year-old finishes the cartoon she's watching and starts running around screaming. Unable to control her Enosh erupts in anger, and he's the one who wakes up Michelle and Oscar.

The bar he remembers is one he co-owns with a Michelin starred Swiss chef, Jules Benitto. Enosh is often in Switzerland because it's a centre for insurance and where his company has a lot of business. One evening he's just had the mother of all arguments with Michelle and he's drunk, so drunk he's dancing on his own. We've all been there, haven't we? But we haven't all been reasonably famous millionaires with a reputation for partying - even if by this stage Enosh is a married father of two who hasn't cheated on his wife since they had kids (according to him, not according to her). As Enosh sways, Indigo Greene spots him. She's a super-model, she's met him before and partied with him at a few events. And she tells me he looks so sad that the only thing in the world she can think of doing is giving him a kiss to put a smile on his face. She does. They start an affair.

Catching a Frisbee is actually not one of Enosh's memories, it's one of the first he has as Subject Six. Even now, three years on, he can't remember any detail about being in the pod and crash-landing in the sea but his memory gets clearer the moment he steps onto land. He's literally got one foot in the sea, one out, when a Frisbee almost knocks his head off. Instead, instinctively he catches it. Passes it back to one of the group of boys who're playing with it. They don't give Subject Six a second thought, they think his Cryosuit is a wet suit and he's just one of the many people who's been in the sea that day. They say he doesn't look strange or weird. Just a guy heading up the beach after a swim who pulls off an amazing last minute catch.

Falling off a chair and cutting his wrist is a childhood memory. I've dug into it but I can't be sure whether Enosh was three or four at the time. The cut was never deep but the effect was long-lasting, Enosh was always squeamish about blood after this and was known for fainting during injections, or if he saw anyone get cut. For instance during the birth of both kids he went down at least twice. And, in case you're wondering, Subject Six does still carry a mark of that memory on his wrist with a small scar. As Subject Six he can't be scarred, he heals if he gets injured and his body always reverts to how it was the moment he was frozen - tattoos, scars and all.

This last memory on the list comes shortly after the Frisbee catch. Having caught the Frisbee, Subject Six walks straight up the beach. He says the only thing that is clear in his mind when he walked up the beach is that he wanted a drink. So he finds his way to a bar. He orders a rum and lemonade. Not a drink he's ever wanted before, but it's what takes his fancy. Patting himself down he realises he has no money, orders a beer as well and starts a tab. Then he sits. For a reason he can't place, even though his mind is set on a drink, he doesn't physically want to have one. After about five minutes of sitting watching the beach, with two drinks in front of him, the bar is surrounded by armed Police and Subject Six has a gun pointed to his head. He says he laughs, once, because things feel so surreal and then… well, we know what they do to him then.

Just jumping back to the first memory Subject Six writes down, in Journal entry 4. At first I took it for granted that this is the moment he's first told he has cancer. His wife in tears, the consultant looking serious. But by the time Enosh is diagnosed, Michelle and he are divorced and she's banned from being in the same room as him. So the first memory isn't him being told he's going to die, but it is bad news for him and it's also directly linked to why he and Michelle become so estranged. You see, this is the moment that it's confirmed that Indigo Green's baby is the son of Enosh, despite what he's been saying to everyone, especially to Michelle.

Just on first reading, you can see why those moments are significant enough to bubble their way to the top of Subject Six's consciousness once his memory returned.

Some we'll come back to later because they truly are key, others are just a good signpost to where Enosh is at the end of his life and Subject Six is at the start of his.

HOW THE GOVERNMENT TRIED TO UNDERSTAND SUBJECT SIX

As well as his memory coming back, during his imprisonment Subject Six starts to become fully aware of his new physical attributes. Leading this education are the government scientists who visit Subject Six virtually every day of his captivity with a mission to investigate him. This begins with simple, non-invasive procedures. They spend a few days simply trying to prove for 100% that his heart isn't beating. The scientists know it isn't, but it's such an unprecedented thing that they spend a long time making certain. And as Subject Six watches on, and hears them talk about him, he begins to learn what he is.

Is he a willing guinea pig? Well, not really. He might not know his background, but he does remember being arrested by armed police. He does know he's being locked up in a cell for most of the day. This life he finds himself in is not a free one and his instinct is to dislike his captors. A feeling that soon becomes far more acute, as the government scientists ramp-up their experiments.

JOURNAL ENTRY 8

The atmosphere has changed.

Before, no-one seemed to be in charge and everything seemed unfocused and confused. All they did was fuss

and test and re-test and it didn't seem to have any direction. Now that chaos has a purpose, I think. And it's to test me to… well, to destruction.

When I'm in the lab, rather than thinking of new ways to check for a heartbeat, they're talking about how to get definitive proof about my limits.

Their focus has moved to trying to fulfil targets. To get empirical evidence from their tests. The scary thing about it, is I'm no longer a curiosity. It feels as I'm something to be mastered and conquered.

What exactly does he mean? Well, I'm going to lay it down straight even though it's pretty shocking. Our government, who claim they observe all of the international human rights laws, soon start treating Subject Six in an inhumane, frightening way. Having satisfied themselves - though without seriously consulting him - that he is immune to normal physical pain, one morning they run tests on him in the lab to make him bleed. He's strapped down and they make cuts and open veins all over his body. They get nothing. No blood leaks from him. They can see it in his veins, but it doesn't run, it doesn't move.

That afternoon they broaden the search. Saliva, tears, semen, mucus, puss. Their scalpels and needles excavate every part of his body. To no avail.

It sounds horrific, doesn't it? Nightmarish. To be pricked and cut, probed and picked apart, your body sliced and diced and the whole time you're awake.

Subject Six

By then they essentially knew that my nervous system was down. That somehow I wasn't feeling physical pain and that as soon as I was injured my body would begin self-healing.

Me

How did they know that?

Subject Six

Next time you get forcibly arrested by a 30 strong team of armed police, keep an eye out for how many times you get kicked, punched, hit. And hit hard.

Me

They treated you rough?

Subject Six

Of course. These guys are so hyped-up nowadays, they do take-downs all the time and they're trained to expect suicide vests and to be faced with automatic weapons… when they get you, you are nothing but the enemy. A threat they've stopped. A target they've downed. So as soon as they have you, they let you have it.

Me

They did that on the beach bar, in front of all the witness?

Subject Six

By the time they got to me, there weren't many people still around, but yeah, sure. Like I said, they're well drilled and following orders.

Me

Orders which are to neutralise you at all costs.

Subject Six

Sure, and that's how it should be. They are the public's first line of defence against terrorist fuckheads. They're not playing, and the country needs it that way.

Me

If they'd beaten me up, I don't know if I'd be feeling so forgiving.

Subject Six

That's maybe to do with the fact they couldn't do any lasting damage to me and the fact you're a soft leftie while I'm a realist who knows what price has to be paid to keep people safe.

Me

So that was when they started to see you were different, physically? Because they'd beaten you and you hadn't turned into a bloody mess?

Subject Six

Basically. Obviously, I hadn't bled at all during their attack, and apparently they were all surprised at that and that I hadn't shown any pain or reaction to what they were doing. But they could see they'd broken my arm and that my leg wasn't working properly because they'd smashed in my knee. By the time they got me into my cell I was in a pretty bad shape. And then the following morning I was as good as new again.

When I talk to Subject Six about the tests to see if he can bleed, his voice levels out to monotone, his eyes glaze over. His mind takes a step to the left of reality as he detaches himself from the memory. Which is, he tells me, his main coping mechanism when he's in the lab. He focuses every ounce of his being on moving his consciousness 10cm to the left of his head. Trying to keep himself there and wait it out.

Reading about these tests makes me sick. How can anyone do this, and how can anyone who supposedly works for the government think it's ok? Now, I've never been so naïve as to think that governments only ever obey the law, but doesn't this seem a bit extreme?

It takes me a long time, but in the end I manage to find one of the Subject Six's guards who is willing to speak to me. As it turns out, she never actually worked for the government; back then, in 2018, she was studying in London and working part-time as an employee for a private firm who had the contract to run the place Subject Six was detained in. Her name's Issy and here's what she tells me about what it was like working in the detention centre at the time.

Issy

At first, when he arrived the atmosphere around him was really odd. We didn't really know what to do. Everyone else in the centre was a home-grown terrorist, more-or-less, and we treated them the same. Didn't let them get close, made them follow every rule and took them from the cell to the interrogation rooms and back as quickly as possible.

He was different. He was highly classified, secret, but not a threat in the same way as the terrorists. Everyone wanted to guard him, everyone wanted to find out about him... at first.

When I asked her for specifics about what changed, she explained she'd never even been close to having high enough security clearance to know details.

Issy

All I can say is that after a few weeks, someone high up, from the government or military I was never sure which, started coming to the centre virtually every day.

I don't know what the trigger was, but suddenly the scientists had a deadline and they were being pushed to do more tests and experiments and something that had been fascinating, became frightening. I mean I was aware that with the terrorists, the agents sometimes crossed a line to get information, but compared to what started going on in the lab that was nothing. It was all because of whatever the person from the government was saying.

Having looked closely at what was happening to Subject Six, I think I have a handle on what's going on in the government at the time and why things take a sudden and sharp change. For whatever reason, at first they take a few weeks to get their act into gear. Possibly because of how busy the government is and how many different people there are in different departments on different levels of authority are involved. Then suddenly, the magnitude of his arrival hits home across the board. He becomes a priority. What is the potential of Subject Six? Immune to pain, able to regenerate. Could he be the ultimate soldier? What secrets does he hold and what future advances can he help with? Having figured out he's big news they start to push to find out how big.

Hand-in-hand with the government's realisation he could be truly special, I presume came a fear of losing him. It's around this time that Laura is digging into the story and when she's stopped from working on it, it falls to me to carry on. Simultaneously a human rights group finds out about him and starts to try to get him released. What happens if they're forced to release him on humanitarian grounds before they've worked him out? Worse yet, if a leak has told a journalist and a human rights organization about Subject Six, how long will it be before foreign governments start getting interested?

All together these motivations get the government worried that they might not be able to keep him captive for much longer. The response is to put their foot on the accelerator and demand answers.

Subject Six

I'm a new frontier, essentially, and they've been ordered to understand me. Fast. So they start taking things further and further.

Me

Didn't it shock you?

Subject Six

Shock me?

Me

How brutal they could be?

Subject Six

That's only shocking when you live in the sheltered world, like you do. Brutality isn't consigned to history. People are still acting like Nazis all over the world, every day.

Me

Just mostly not near Britain.

Subject Six

Mmm, if you want to think that.

Me

I do. But ok, if you weren't shocked, how did you feel about it?

Subject Six

I wasn't shocked and I could understand them to an extent, but that didn't mean it wasn't hell. Sure, I was

**always ok after, but during the tests I... I thought I
wasn't going to make it through. My body was still
new to me. I didn't trust it completely back then and I
kept thinking I wasn't going to recover this time. So as
well as trying to fight them and stop their tests from
working simply out of defiance, I was also fighting the
fear that I would actually die.**

In the detention centre, the scientists take things to
extreme levels to try and make sense of Subject Six. One
thing I keep asking myself how could these people treat
him like that? How could they live with themselves? They
can't be monsters, they're government employed scientists and I know Subject Six referenced the terrible crimes
the Nazis did in the name of science, but Hitler's Germany is very far from Britain today. And I don't say that
lightly. So why did they act like that?

In the end I guess it comes down to two things. One,
is that on a practical level perhaps they knew that they
weren't causing him physical pain, so it made it easier for
them to experiment on him. Did believing he was some
kind of superhero, and therefore not human, an 'other',
make it easier for them to act inhumanely? Then comes
the other reason, their orders.

Subject Six says the two main scientists who lead the
experiments - whom he terms Glasses and Blondie because they never reveal their names - at first seem to hold
back when the escalation begins. But as what they're doing becomes normal, as the pressure from above them in-
creases they seem to become more inured to the cold-
heartedness of what they're doing. Soon he can see
they're so detached when it comes to him it's frightening.

They start getting excited about what they call his
'potential'. Both start getting giddy and overlook the cru-
elty of what they're doing. As if they're scientists in the

middle of pioneering discoveries who will go down in history for the breakthroughs they'll make by studying Subject Six.

JOURNAL ENTRY 9

More tests. More torture but they will not break me.

They cannot. If they think they can, they don't know Enosh Blake even though they say they do.

JOURNAL ENTRY 10

Their words keep swirling round my head 'Work with us, we want to understand you, don't you want to know what you are? It'll be easier if you don't fight'.

Today I did fight. They wanted to test my skin regeneration. To see how long it would take to heal. I was strapped down onto a chair and forced to listen to them discussing what part of my body they were going to cut, what with and how deep they were going to go.

We won't hurt you, the one with the glasses said. We can't hurt you, the blonde woman said. Work with us.

The moment they came at me I struggled. Every-time they tried to get a camera close-up to me, or set up a microscope so they could track the regeneration I kicked out.

In total it took 10 guards, with Glasses and Blondie looking on, before they managed to make the cuts they'd agreed on.

I was left with no choice but to sabotage their tests in the only way I could - opening and re-opening the cuts as much as I could by struggling against my harnesses. One of the worst cuts covered the number on my wrist, they wanted to see the process of the recovery - would

the skin come back first, then the number? Or vice versa?

One morning they start burning him to see how his flesh reacts to fire. Strapped to the chair Subject Six is reeling, his mind turned to ash, when he hears Glasses talking about bones. His bones.

In front of him, as if he's not there, they start planning how they'll test how Subject Six's bones heal after breaking, then how they'll escalate that and see what'll happen if they remove one of his bones entirely from his body. Will it act like any normal bone and just exist outside his body? And if so can they then start using it to grow more people like him? Or will it somehow disappear and re-form back inside his body? And what about Subject Six? Will he grow a new one? Or perhaps something has changed about his whole skeleton and they won't even be able to get the bone out?

Aware that the scientists have lost all sense that he is an unwilling partner in their experiments Subject Six finds his fear forces a moment of clarity on him. A thought pops into his head and he knows where the conversation is going. He knows what the next question is going to be because it's one he's thought himself during one of his many hours staring at the cell wall. It's a horrible question, but it's the natural one to ask when you take the experiments to the nth degree.

Blondie asks Glasses a question and says that if they answer it, it could be an experiment on a par with the first Atom bomb in terms of the possibilities it could open up as to how we could change the human race.

What would happen, Blondie asks, if you pack Subject Six's body with explosives and blow him up? If they do that, not only will they answer the government's key question, which is whether he's indestructible but they'll also be known as the first people to discover an immortal.

WHO ELSE KNOWS ABOUT SUBJECT SIX?

Being tested to destruction is not something Subject Six wants to be part of so he begins to formulate a plan. At the same time, unbeknownst to him, there are people outside the detention centre who are doing everything they can to get him free. For the time being, therefore, let's leave him in his cell, so I can give you the lowdown on what's happening with the Subject Six story in the wider world.

I told you at the start of this book that I was first told about Subject Six by the reporter Laura Freeman. A few hours after I get her email I give her a call. One of my first questions to her when we talk, is who gave her the lead?

Laura

A journalist never…

Me

…gives away their sources. Very funny.

Laura

I guess seeing as I've had to give you the whole goddamn story, after all my fucking work I may as well spill the proverbials… have you heard of AllFree?

Me

Only from what's in your email, I haven't had time to look them up.

Laura

They're a Human Rights organisation. I know a few people there and I've dealt with them a few times.

Me

How?

Laura

You know how it is, either they've wanted some publicity to help a case along or because they've won a case. And then a couple of times I've called them to see if they could get me access to a story, or to a member of the government they were lobbying. One of the things that helps AllFree stand out is they've got fantastic links to MPs and Whitehall.

Me

So that's how they found out about Subject Six? A leak in the government?

Laura

Typical, Benji, jumping to conclusions.

Me

What do you mean typ...?

Laura

No, they got in touch with me at the start of August. At that point they didn't have much that was concrete evidence and they wanted me to help them find out if there was any substance to the story that someone had been arrested on Brighton Beach and not heard of since.

Me

And what did you find?

Laura

**Nothing really, but a few days later AllFree got back
in touch. They'd managed to find a leak, someone who
was working at the illegal detention centre who was
promising to give them information.**

At this point, my pen is in my hand. Poised. Ready to
start writing. It's obvious the leak is a key player in the
whole story and I know I need to get their name.

Me

Who was their leak?

Laura

Nobody knows

Me

What? That's…

Laura

**I'm serious. I've dug. Got nothing. Someone in the
centre is passing information to AllFree, that's how we
know this guy is in there, but no-one knows who the
leak is. Or why they're doing it. Man, woman? No
idea. Government employee or private contractor? No
idea. Someone who has long hated the way the British
authorities flout human rights, or someone who just
doesn't like the way this particular captive is being
treated? No idea.**

And, drumroll please, we still have no idea. We don't
know who first alerted the outside world to Subject Six's
predicament in the cell. AllFree never knew, Laura
couldn't find out in the few weeks she looked at the story
and I'm no closer three years on.

Does it matter? Well, the thing is, it might do. In a
major way. It's one of the many missing pieces in this

ever-changing puzzle and I have no idea how it fits. If you'll excuse me really stretching a metaphor here, I don't know if it's an edge piece that would help me give form to other parts of the story; a rogue piece that's not relevant at all to what I'm trying to see; or could it even be central picture piece that could lead me to discovering who's behind Subject Six? Because one of the key things to the Subject Six story is who's orchestrated it? Is it an accident, a freak occurrence, or is someone behind it?

Now, say there is a person. I'm not going to call them Mr X, for obvious reasons connected to the fictional world of superheroes. So, I'll call them Miss Q. And let's say Miss Q creates Subject Six and brings him back to earth so he can be put to work using his new body and skills. And then, disaster! As soon as Subject Six arrives back in town he's captured by the government. So, what does Miss Q do?

Well, she's powerful enough to have advanced science enough to create a new form of human, so surely she has it in her to be able to activate a mole she has working for the government? Not wanting to bring attention to herself by doing anything directly to get Subject Six free, she uses her person on the inside and gets them to contact a human rights organization. Becoming Laura's leak. Now, that's conjecture, but is it too far-fetched? Maybe, but it's not as outlandish as Subject Six himself (in the sense he's actually an immortal guy who's dropped from the sky) and as far as I can tell it's one of the most workable theories as to who the leak is and why they're doing the leaking.

Much as it could be important to find who this leak is, for now we'll park that train of thought. Mostly because I haven't found the answer yet. Instead, let's get back to how people outside the centre are trying to help Subject Six.

Laura's first plan is to break the story that Subject Six is being held illegally as a way of getting public opinion to help get him free. The government are saying they're no longer holding people against their will without due cause, and yet this guy proves they are. She's close to getting her story ready to publish when she's stopped.

Laura

It's like there's been an injunction, without an injunction.

Me

How do you mean?

Laura

You get media blackouts all the time, a footballer boffing a friend's wife, an actress with a heroin problem, a married politician being caught shagging a dog. The media gets gagged by the courts a lot.

Me

But in this case… there's been no court case?

Laura

No. Which is bad news for me, great news for you.

Me

How so?

Laura

It proves the government deems this highly important. They wouldn't risk silencing so many papers without using the proper channels without reason. Seeing as you can play the long-game, in time, this could make a great story… you know that.

Once the government prevent anyone publishing her story, Laura can't place her piece anywhere. Which is why she passes the reins to me and why I start working with AllFree in her place to try and get Subject Six out. I figure that if there is a superhero guy being held in central London then freeing him will help me twofold - one, it will give me something tangible to write about and two, if I've played a part in helping him get free, it stands me in good stead to get access to him in the future.

Now, so far, in the main, my experience with charities and NGOs is negative. Staffed by people who mean well but don't have the means to do it. From my first contact with AllFree however, they prove to be astoundingly good. They know, as I do, that this could be a very high profile win for them and a few days after I've initially got in touch I find out they've made a major breakthrough since they last saw Laura.

After gathering all their evidence, AllFree have petitioned the courts to get Subject Six's case heard and get him released. The government may have been able to keep Laura's story out of the papers, but they haven't been able to get AllFree's petition thrown out of the courts. With the help of a high-ranking judge with human rights sympathies AllFree get a date to be heard. Which will give them a chance to prove the government are holding Subject Six illegally.

Me

How will that work exactly?

(This is me, talking to Larry Bonner who heads up AllFree.)

Larry

It means that for the first time they're officially acknowledging that this person exists.

Me

What have they been doing?

Larry

Denying all knowledge. Refusing all questions. But not anymore. We've been able to pull together enough witnesses and evidence to show someone is being detained - and yesterday a judge agreed with us.

Me

So what now?

Larry

Now? We fight. We try to prove he's being held in contravention of his human rights.

Me

And what will the government be saying, now that they've had to admit someone is in the centre?

Larry

I don't know for sure, but from what we know we guess they'll argue he's being held on the basis that he's a threat to national security. It's my job to debunk that.

Me

And can you?

Larry tells me our best hope is the fact the government can't risk the bad publicity that would be involved if it ever got into the press they were detaining someone illegally in London. The government got elected by saying they wouldn't abuse their powers to imprison people even with the rising threat of terrorism. They've already taken a huge risk by getting Laura's story pulled which means now that the judges have ruled there has to be a court case, the government might decide they have to back down. If they don't, it could get out of control and cause a scandal.

Jumping on this, and eager to help, I suggest leaking the story online. I know Laura thought getting the story out there might help get the detainee out, so how about I do it? Having published a few books I have a decent-ish following on twitter. I could give people a sneak preview of what I'm writing. I could announce the book, hint that I'm working on a story about an illegal detainee and open the floodgates. If anyone gets angry, I can plead that I don't know the media ban exists, but by then it will be too late and public opinion will be on our side.

Larry

No, that could have worked if the government were still flat-out denying he exists, but our thinking is that now we have the court date, we could actually harm Subject Six's case if the press find out.

I'm just going to pause for a moment, point out that this is the first time I ever hear him called Subject Six. The reason? Because according to AllFree's source on the inside of the detention centre, he's being held in cell number six and that's what the guards and staff call him.

Me

Harm him? How?

Larry

We don't know everything about this guy they're holding, except he's unique, yes? Physically, he's different. Now if that story breaks, it's going to interest every single government in the world, isn't it?

Me

Or course. But couldn't we use that? International pressure would help, surely?

Larry

Ok, think of it this way. You're a judge. In one version of this trial, everything is super secretive, there's no pressure from the press. We admit this guy is unique but follow on by saying that's no reason to detain him, why not let him go and monitor him because he has right to his freedom?

Or, in another version of the trial, the case happens against a completely different backdrop. We've leaked the story and every news agency in the world is suddenly in London, talking about him. The TV, the papers, online. Everyone demanding to see him, get a piece of him. Is the judge really going to let this guy walk out into a publicity storm when the government are saying we need to keep him secret?

Me

Well, when you put it like that, I'll keep my tweets to myself.

Having been firmly put in my place about my leaking-the-story-to-the-press idea, I decide to leave Larry and his team to the case. The date for the trial is 18th September, 10 days after this chat with Larry. And if AllFree win, it could be the day that the government is forced to release Subject Six.

WHAT POWERS DID SUBJECT SIX USE TO ESCAPE?

Back in his cell, Subject Six is unaware that the effort to free him is gathering pace. In his mind he's still on his own. If he wants out, he has to do it himself. It's time to mobilise everything he's got to get himself out of the centre.

So, as Enosh Blake would have done, Subject Six starts working on a plan. From talking to a few people who knew Enosh at the height of his powers, it's pretty obvious he was a force to be reckoned with.

Clarke Lemon (business partner)

Enosh was a 110% nightmare. Luckily he was my nightmare, fighting on my side. If I'd ever gone into a boardroom to battle against him, I would have hated it. I saw him rip people's plans up countless times all because Enosh saw every angle. Every time someone tried to come at him, Enosh had already seen their play and was ready.

Jade Gora (finance director)

When I first started working with Enosh I knew he had a reputation as a hothead and playboy and I went in expecting things to be ad hoc and done on the run. His company had grown so fast, was making so much money, I presumed it would be a mess he hadn't bothered to get a handle on and my job was going to be to tidy it up. I was amazed. It was the tightest run finance department I'd ever seen and it was all him. He didn't leave anything to chance.

Scott Gary (mentor)

If I was a dog trainer, Enosh was my killer staffy. I knew from day one that without doubt, even though I was training him and helping him, that one day he'd fuck me over. I was right, he did. The only thing I got wrong was how soon he did it.

I guess it's no real surprise that Enosh, a millionaire at 20, was an exceptional guy and a pretty ruthless businessman, right? That's par for the course for an entrepreneur playboy, but I just wanted to set the scene. To show you exactly the type of mental powers Subject Six is putting to use in his cell when he starts thinking about how to escape.

But before we can fully understand what he hopes to pull-off, we need to understand what he's capable of physically. Mentally he's got the same ability as Enosh Blake, but what can his body do now? Shortly after Subject Six is free, after I've met him a few times, we're talking on the phone and I try to dig down into his physical transformation.

Subject Six

I'm not a specimen.

Me

Of course not. But you can see why I'm asking.

Subject Six

Then you can see why I'm not answering.

Me

Sure, what they put you through was…

Subject Six

Look, Benji, I don't talk to you so you can investigate me. I talk to you so you can find out who did this to me and why.

Me

I know but…

Subject Six

You won't get anywhere if you spend time playing at being scientist and focusing on me. You need to start looking everywhere else. Find out 'how' not 'what'.

Subject Six is adamant. I am too. Eventually he comes around to my argument that for me to work out who has done this to him, I need to know as fully as possible what exactly has been done. He gives me two days. He's in training, but marks out a weekend on which he's willing to put everything on pause so I can travel up to his country retreat and put him through what is essentially a medical.

He's right though, there's no point in me playing scientist, so I immediately start looking for someone who'll be able to carry out the check-up for me. I need someone with medical expertise and experience of dealing with the unusual. I've always found there are two types of scientists: those who get excited about the unknown and embrace the chance to explore it; and those who get scared by what they can't explain and seek safety by hiding behind logic and existing theory. Naturally I need someone who's going to be excited by Subject Six and my search doesn't take long.

Step forward, Dr Carly Lillane. She's half-French, half-Kiwi, lives on Sanibel Island in Florida. Born into a ridiculous amount of wealth, she chooses not to follow in the family footsteps of inhumane property development and drug addiction and trains as a doctor. After working in A & E in Miami for almost a decade Carly decides she wants something more to her life. She quits.

Carly

Benji! Hi there. So sorry I keep missing your calls, you know? I only just got back from Kazakhstan.

Me

Kazakhastan?

Carly

I heard about a town there where people are falling asleep for days, sometimes weeks or months. I've just got back.

This is a recording from our first call and this is what Carly Lillane does. She finds medical mysteries and then using her expertise and limitless resources she travels to ground zero to gather evidence. If she needs to she brings in other experts and scientists to help her find out what's happening and then, depending on what she discovers, she'll write an article or book, or even do a documentary about it.

The moment I tell her about Subject Six, she starts asking questions. She opens up her laptop and books her flights while we're talking. Mina picks her up from the airport and drives her up to meet me at Subject Six's country retreat.

Mina

I seriously think Carly talked at me for the entire drive. Five and a half hours. I remember when Benji and I got to bed that night, even though we hadn't seen each other alone for over a week, we can't have said anymore than five words to each other. It was like Carly had done all

Don't think for a second that Mina is exaggerating. I think Carly is brilliant, she's been integral to this story, but oh-my-god can she talk. All weekend she asks questions and asks questions. That's what she's there for, obviously, but as soon as she gets out of the car and somehow manages to talk more face-to-face than she does on the phone, I start to get worried. Subject Six, remember, is only doing this begrudgingly. He doesn't want to be a lab rat, a freak to be investigated. So how is he going to react when it turns out the person I've brought to do the tests is a loud-mouth from Florida who won't shut up? If she acts like a toddler who's just learnt the word 'why', isn't he just going to act like a grumpy dad and shut the door on her?

Luckily, for me, the answer is no. Carly and Subject Six get along like a house on fire. How come? I think because of how completely over the top Carly is. When Subject Six speaks of the tests he's forced into by Glasses and Blondie, the atmosphere in their lab is secretive and stressed at best; tortuous and tyrannical at worst. He's treated like he's not even human, a material to be tested and nothing else.

Carly couldn't be more different. She's in awe of him, she's inspired by him and the weekend the four of us spend in the lab is surprisingly light and funny (Mina's in charge of filming everything so we have it on record). Every test she does she explains. Every cut or incision she makes, she checks with him first. She makes him feel like he's in control of what's happening, or at the very least like he's a majority stakeholder. As for Subject Six, to become a teenager in the playground for a second, I can tell he fancies Carly from the moment he meets her. He wants her to like him, he loves the attention she gives him, so he goes out of his way to help her. More of that later.

One of the first things Carly does is tell Subject Six, and me and Mina, what her plans are. We're in the kitchen of Subject Six's place on the Friday night after she arrives. We're starting at 6am on the Saturday and I half expect everyone to be on edge and for no-one to want to hang out. But Carly's bounce and energy hits us all and soon I'm cooking dinner and Carly is outlining what she wants to do.

Carly tells us the story of a young girl from England she met the year before. As a baby this girl is different, but not really, really different. She hardly ever cries and when she does it's when her mum leaves the room, not because of hunger or tiredness. She drops all naps at two months having slept through the night from four weeks. Now any parent, Mina and me included, will tell you that's astonishing, but I doubt if either of our kids had slept so quickly we would have gone to a doctor. We would have smugly congratulated ourselves behind closed doors and professed to everyone else that we're just really, really lucky. Which is what this young girl's parents do. Nothing bad is going on, so why seek help? She puts on weight because her parents feed her at set times, and she grows like everyone else.

The only odd thing is that the few times she falls over as a toddler, she doesn't cry. At all. At three, she cuts herself on a piece of broken glass in a pub. She bleeds a lot, but again she doesn't cry. Weird, the parents think, of course it is. But then they look at the whole picture and rationalise it - they're in a pub with lots of people, so maybe the girl is embarrassed to cry? Or they're always telling her two brothers to be brave and not cry, so maybe she's just taken it to heart? And anyway, after a nasty accident, who's going to go to a doctor and complain that their kid isn't crying? Your focus is on the cut healing, on the kid being ok and so, perfectly naturally, they think no more of it.

Until, when she's six, something awful happens. She's playing football in the park and kicks it over the hedge. She sprints onto the pavement to get it. A supermarket delivery van is driving by. Changing playlists on his Spotify. Sees the ball out of the corner of his eye, then sees her running as fast as she can towards it. The girl gets the ball before it goes onto the road, but the distracted driver thinks she's coming straight for him. He swerves, loses control of the van. Hits a parked car, deflects off it, mounts the curb the girl is on and hits her. Horrifically, she's dragged 20m up the road. Her dad leaves the park and sprints behind the van until the driver gets it under control and brings it to a halt. When he arrives, expecting the worst, having had to run over a streak of blood, he's dumbstruck. 'Dad', she says, 'Did you see that?'

Her Dad's in shock. So is the driver. She just offers out a hand and tries to stand up. It's plain for the two adults to see that her leg is broken, the bone is exposed, and yet she still tries to walk. She's taken to hospital. She's operated on and makes a full recovery and by the time Carly meets her four months later she's back to normal. Except she's not normal, is she?

When Carly tells us this, all of us have our mouths hanging open. I've never heard anything like it. That's because it's not been reported yet, or before. What the experts, including Carly, think they've worked out is that this girl has a chromosome 6 deletion. Lots of people have chromosome disorders, they have either missing or re-arranged genetic material and this is often seen in those with conditions like Down's Syndrome. Some people with these disorders might not feel tiredness, hunger, or pain, but as far as Carly knows no-one has yet had the mix of characteristics that this girl has. She's not got Down's, or anything else, and yet her chromosomes have turned her into someone with superhero abilities - and saved her life. Because if she could feel pain, Carly says her body would have tensed up as she was dragged up the road which would have made her injuries far worse and probably fatal.

The point of this story, Carly says with a laugh as I lay down four plates of food - Subject Six doesn't eat but still says it's good for his soul to taste the idea of it - is not that she wants to tie him to a car and drive around, but that she wants to start by testing his genetics. She won't have the results on these tests during the weekend, but she says they could be the key to what's happened to him.

Throughout the weekend, Carly keeps hitting us with theories and ideas about Subject Six that she's taken from the natural world. Another one that's stuck in my mind is the immortal jellyfish, which she says can turn back into a baby once it's an adult - normally when it's under threat. It then matures again and can then, you guessed it, turn back into a baby. Incredible right? It could theoretically go on forever because age isn't going to stop it, hence its name, but in nature the fact is they normally die of disease or get eaten. Apparently this is a case of transdifferentiation where cells change into another type of cell, and Carly wonders whether Subject Six might be doing this in some way.

At this stage, during the 16-hour-days of tests, she says she's not going to focus on the why but rather the what. Once she has all the data and Subject Six is back training, she can start looking at the cause.

About a week after Carly had got back to Florida she sent me an email - heavily encrypted of course - with her findings. I'm going to let that do the talking:

Benji! So I know you said not to, but I have decided to spoil those adorable kids of yours. Presents are being sent as we speak, watch out for that mail man! Say hey to lovely Mina too, tell her I've been making that nu-tribullet recipe of hers every single day. I'm an addict already.

So here we go. I wish you'd give me more time to put this into proper shape but I know why you're impatient. I'll write this up properly asap, adding in all the results from my gene-testing etc, and get you something I'd be happy to share with scientific colleagues. Digest this then lets Skype. I've sent it over to SS too and we've already chatted. I wish I didn't need sleep like him, jeez I'd get so much done! As discussed I've laid it out straight-up, breaking it down like we said to help us make sense.

WHAT HE WAS - ENOSH BLAKE COMPARISONS FROM BEFORE - ENOSH BLAKE vs SUBJECT SIX

Cancer - no sign of any tumours, the affected areas are now clear but the scar tissue from his first unsuccessful cancer op is there.

He used to wear glasses - no more.

He had bad back and liver pain - no more. Everyone carries around a few physical issues, like a house needs a few fixes, but he doesn't have any gripes or niggles.

Dog allergy - no more.

Age - his biological clock says he hasn't aged at all since he was cryogenically frozen; his physique is also the same. When he was frozen the cancer symptoms hadn't taken effect yet whereas three months of clean living and exercise had - he was in above average condition for a man in his early 30s and he still is.

Summary - Essentially he's stayed the same as he was when he was frozen - scars, tattoos included - apart from one major thing - all his physical imperfections, health issues have gone. Almost as though he's gone back to default, factory settings.

WHAT HE IS NOW - SUBJECT SIX
NB. Benji, This part is trickier, less easy to categorise. You said you were happy to keep it general at first, so here goes, please forgive my very basic headlines!

MR VAC-PACK MAN
This is my terrible name for him. You know how in science books you get cross-sections of our bodies? Layer by layer. In the picture the epidermis, blood, muscles, sweat glands, collagen, bone everything just sits there still, obviously, as it's a 2D image. In life, obviously not. Apart from Subject Six. Cut a slice down his arm, bend the two parts away from each other and everything you'd normally see in a person is there except it's all solid. Like he's been Vac Packed.
I carried out tests on this. The cells are all what they should be i.e. the nerves are nerves, the capillaries have everything they need to be capillaries... and in a way they are. They hold blood. It's just that blood doesn't move or flow.

CAN'T TAKE ANYTHING IN
Food, drink, he doesn't digest anything or need to.
I tested whether he could, gave him a small amount of water. I scanned him. Gravity had taken the water as far as it could go and then it just sat there in his intestine. You know that kids game, the wooden labyrinth? You have a baring ball in a box and you have to tilt the box to get the ball to move to the right holes? I guess the water inside him is like that. With all that training he does the water will slosh around inside him, moving up, down sideways until it one day, maybe, falls out from whichever end it's travelled to.

NB it's unlikely to evaporate in there, because his internal temperature is the same as the atmosphere he's in.

DOESN'T PRODUCE ANYTHING #1
I'm guessing because it's all solid, it means he doesn't produce or emit anything - no fluids, blood, mucus. It's all inside his body, it just doesn't move.
As for breath, no. He doesn't breathe. His body shows no sign of oxygen deprivation, his lungs are perfect... and I can't believe I'm just going to leave this HUGE medical first as is for the time being but I have to.

HE. DOESN'T. BREATHE.
Pain - in normal humans, in a sense, our nerves produce pain. His don't.
Brain - looks perfectly healthy, able to function, to send signals throughout his body and yet in all the scans I did I detected no brain activity whatsoever. So it's working, yet not displaying it...

DOESN'T PRODUCE ANYTHING #2
Linked to this not producing trait is one of the hardest things to get my head around. Nothing about him makes sense, not really, but this is the toughest one.

SPOILER ALERT, BENJI - so far I have no explanation. AGAIN!!
My tests have shown he can't visually be picked up, seen, recorded, by any type of camera - film, digital, photos, videos, radar.
If you shine a laser at him he stops it.
If you shine light on him, his body stops it.
Dracula check - he can be seen in a mirror and he does cast a shadow.

Lens check - I wondered if it was a lens thing that stopped cameras, but telescopes see him, binoculars, spectacles etc. GO FIGURE.
Infra-red - he doesn't appear on, but as his body has no core temperature I'd expect that.
So is it he doesn't emit anything? Is that the rule? No - because you hear him, you DO see him AND, perhaps paradoxically, you can record his voice and the sound he makes.
Is it that he leaves no stamp, like is he a ghost? A spectre? Well, no, because he also has 'weight' - if he hits you, you know it. He can pick you up.
Ok, so how is this possible?
It's not
Seeing as it is, can we deduce any rules to investigate? TBC!!!

Let me add in a bit of texture here because I like the story that Subject Six tells, about how he figured out he can't be seen on cameras. At first when he's in the detention centre he's kept in what is essentially a hole. I'm guessing the centre - because we don't know exactly where it is - is a renovation of an old London prison and he's kept in an old cell. But after a week or so, around the time he starts to remember things, he's moved to a much more modern cell.

About an hour after Subject Six has been locked in, the door bursts open and in pile five guards. Guns drawn. Frantic. Subject Six is on his bed. He's been there the entire time. In a kind of slapstick stupor, the guards point their guns down and start whispering. Then they back out.

Ten minutes later they're back in. Again, although who knows why, their guns are drawn. They see he's still on the bed. One of the guards pulls a face at the CCTV camera and then they back out.

Twenty minutes later, unbelievably, it happens again. During this twenty minutes Subject Six has been able to hear the CCTV camera in his cell moving non-stop. Once it's confirmed that Subject Six is still on his bed, Blondie marches in past the guards. He grabs Subject Six and pulls him up. Then turns to the camera. Glasses waves at the camera. His phone goes. He answers it.

'You can see me, you can see me?' Glasses demands over and over again.

Subject Six says Glasses' voice takes him right back to a French class he took at school. One day Subject Six gets a watch that is also a TV remote. Every time the French teacher tries to play a video, Subject Six uses his watch to stop the tape. Or rewind it. The teacher knows he's being fucked with, but has no idea how it's being done or who by.

In the cell, Glasses sounds exactly like Subject Six's teacher and now Subject Six knows he can't be seen on cameras.

REGENERATION

Tests (mostly done by us, some Subject Six has told us about during his imprisonment) have shown that he re-generates skin and bone. We're trying to find out if his cells/chromosome have been altered.

Teeth - if one is knocked out will it grow back? Agreed with SS that if it happens he'll let me know.

Hairs/ Nails - not growing. We all know that after death these apparently carry on growing, but like the rest of him these seem vac-packed. After a lengthy dis-cussion I cut some hair to see if it grows back. Vain as ever he didn't want his head touched, so it's on his groin. We await results.

Question - (not answered yet) to what extent can he regenerate? We know surface wounds, small injuries heal - as they would with anyone, but his process is hours not days… but what would happen if he got peppered with bullets, or exploded, would he still regenerate or does he have a limit? Is he Terminator 1 or 2? Dracula or a Zombie?

Ok, so if I'm honest, when I first read Carly's email I'm a little underwhelmed and frustrated. I know it's incomplete and rushed because I've asked her for a report too soon, but the fact is it doesn't really tell me anything new. It's handy to see what we know in a list, that's all. Until that moment I've been in no doubt that Carly will be able to tell us something about what's happened, but now I'm not so sure.

When we Skype that's what's bugging me.

Me

Hey, Carly, how are you? Thanks for…

Carly

You're disappointed, aren't you?

Me

No, it's… it's early days.

Carly

Early days, early schmays. It's ok to feel flat. That's all part of the process.

Me

I know it's just… well, all of that, it's all amazing…

Carly

But known.

Me

Yes.

Carly

I thought that. You gave me a brief, and on the Sunday night when I went to bed, I did kind of feel all I'd done is confirm, confirm…

Me

And then what happened?

Carly

What?

Me

I can tell from your face, something changed your mind? You're blushing, oh my god, you're blushing!

Carly

Am I? Am I really? Did he tell you? I can't believe it! He did! What was it like a boy's night after I'd gone, was it? Him giving you all the details? Jeez, you would have thought with all he's been through, he might not be such a teenage boy about stuff!? Bragging about girls.

Me

You slept with him? Fuck me. That's not what I was thinking!

Carly

What, he didn't tell you?

Me

Hang on. Back-up. Let's ditch the teenage chit-chat.

Carly

More than happy to do that.

Me

But... I mean, how can he? Is he physically capable?

Carly

More than. Let me tell you.

Me

But he can't… emit.

Carly

He can't cum no, but ask women what they'd think about spending a night with a guy with a body like his who can literally go all night, and I'm sure they're not going to miss the pearl jam moment too much.

Me

Jeez. Too much info.

Carly

Ask Mina, I'm sure she'll see the appeal. He's like a perfect human with a dildo instead of something that goes floppy.

At this point Mina joins the call, having heard her name. Eventually, after a whole load of chat which makes me feel like I've landed in a Sex In The City themed hell, I get us back on topic.

Me

But how does he get it up? I've seen his… it's flaccid. And he has no blood flow.

Carly

That's what got me excited too. So he comes to my room once you and Mina are in bed. He says there's one experiment he hasn't tried yet.

Mina

What a line!

Carly

I know. We both laughed hard at that. But then we started thinking about it. Like hunger, he still gets horny. He still feels lust, and he said he'd been reading about how men with erectile problems can achieve a level of hardness, despite blood flow issues.

Me

Can they?

Carly

It's all in the mind, having control over your body, over your muscles. And one of the things he's been training for the last few months is power of the mind. You know, all of the martial arts he's doing. Anyway, long story short, by getting into a kind of meditative, karmic state, and focusing on some of the things I'd started doing, and channelling his lust... he got there. Not as full as he wanted, but enough.

Me

Ok, ok... lovely image, truly. Now, before you go, one last question.

Carly

Hit me.

Me

Do you think we'll ever find out how this has happened?

There followed a long pause.

Carly

Look, I hate to say this, and I know there's loads of work to be done, but this case seems to defy logic so much, so goddamned much, that if I was you, you

might want to start looking towards something as mad and unsubstantiated as...

Me

As...

Carly

Oh, god, am I really saying this? As... religion.

Hearing Carly say that shocked me, but it was also something I'd thought about myself and something we'll look at. Just not at the moment. Because now that we know, mostly, what Subject Six is capable of, let's go back to him in the detention centre as the need for him to get out becomes even more pressing.

HOW SUBJECT SIX BREAKS OUT

One morning in the lab he's strapped down to the chair. He feels sick the moment he hears the bone-cutter turned on. The assault, because that's what it is, is quick. They cut into his bone but not through it as they're going to spend the day seeing how quickly his skeleton re-generates.

As he lies there, Subject Six hears Blondie and Glasses telling their team about their schedule. They say that someone from the government is visiting in five days' time and by then they need answers. Looking at what we know, I believe the date of this visit is planned for the 17th of September. The day before AllFree's hearing in court.

Subject Six fights the nausea that's threatening to swamp him so he can keep listening. To cut a long overhead conversation short, the scientists wind up their briefing by saying that while the VIP is there it's likely they're going to perform the explosion. They'll spend the next four days building up to that moment, making bigger cuts, chops, incisions and measuring everything. Then, with their superior watching, they'll go for the big one. If he does survive and piece himself together then they'll have put on a show; if not then they'll have a definitive answer to what he's capable of and have enough of his DNA, genetic material and body parts to start trying to make someone else like him.

Back in his cell Subject Six knows that his preparation is over. He's been paying close attention to the security measures they have. Every time he's been led to an interrogation room or a lab he's watching everything. Memorising which guard's fingerprints open which doors, who has which swipecards and what the codes are. He's learnt which guards are stationed where and starts to work out who the weak links are and when they're on duty.

Subject Six knows he'll have one shot. If he tries to escape and doesn't make it then he's in no doubt he'll soon find himself chained up every minute of every day. So he can't mess it up.

Subject Six

Leading up to my escape, I start doing more yoga.

Me

More?

Subject Six

Yes. From the early days of being locked up, I've been doing yoga. I took it up after I was diagnosed, and in that cell, when you have hour after hour on your own with nothing but the same four fucking walls to look at, yoga is a pretty good way to stop going crazy.

Me

Ok, so why more?

Subject Six

I know they can't see me on the CCTV. So whenever they come and get me, they're on red alert.

Me

In case you're ready to jump.

Subject Six

In case I'm ready to jump them, right. So, I start doing yoga, in a spot that's just out of sight of the peep hole in the door and I make sure for about two weeks that every single time they come in, I'm in the same spot.

Me

Rocking a bird house?

Subject Six

You mean a bird nest?

Me

Do I?

Subject Six

Undoubtedly.

Me

So, guru. Continue.

Subject Six

Naturally, once I condition them to this, the guards start to relax. Or relax enough for what I need to do.

Me

So you pounce?

Subject Six

Fuck yeah. I pounce hard.

Two days before the explosion is scheduled, he acts. It's morning. The door opens. Four guards come in. He's not in his yoga pose. Instead he's crouched, ready to spring.

You know the scene in Fight Club when you see Tyler fighting himself on CCTV? He's throwing himself around the garage as if he's being hit but no-one else is onscreen?

I imagine the scene in Subject Six's cell to look like exactly like that. Within seconds the four guards are punched, kicked, thrown and knocked to the floor. To the security guard watching the cameras it looks like they're simply flinging themselves around like madman.

That's if anyone's watching Subject Six's cell when it happens. Because once he takes all four down and steals the keycard he needs, he looks up ready to face a second wave of guards. Luckily for him, no-one's coming. The alarm hasn't sounded. He has a few seconds' head-start.

Subject Six knows the beginning of his journey to freedom by heart. He's been visualising it in his cell for days and he's been pushed and shoved along the corridor countless times. He walks quickly, taking pains to be as quiet as possible so anyone who's walking towards him around the corners won't know he's coming. There are six corners for him to turn before he gets to the first manned door. He's just about to take the fifth corner when behind him another cell opens.

Subject Six

I spin round. It's one of the guards. One of the nicer one's, she's brought me food a few times and during the days when my memory was coming back, and I started to remember about my kids, she and I had a couple of nice chats. Her name was Issy.

Yes, the same Issy I managed to track down later - precisely because she's the only name I had.

Me

So what did you do?

Subject Six

One of the things I've thought about before my escape is how far can I take things? You know? I don't want to escape only for them to be able to bang me up anyway on the grounds that I've beaten their guards to hell, or even killed them. And yet I know I have to do everything I can to get out.

Me

A dilemma.

Subject Six

A big one. The rule I set myself is self-defence. I can't be seen on camera, but they can. If everyone attacks me first during my escape, then everything I then do to them can be…

Me

…justified.

Subject Six

Exactly… so in my cell, once the four guys realised I'd surprised them, I let one of them make a lazy lunge for me before I set about them. And the same for Issy. She double-takes, recognizes me, draws her taser, reaches for me. That's her mistake. What's a taser going to do to me? I grab her wrist, push the taser back onto her, press her thumb down, it gets us both… it only hurts her.

After Issy goes down, Subject Six has a moment to decide whether to hide her or leave her. Then the alarm starts. Complete with the kind of red lights you see in a film. That makes the choice for him.

He rounds one more corner. As he expects, there are two guards manning the exit from his cell block. They've heard the alarm. So they're standing up. Watchful. But they're thinking it might be a test, or a prisoner kicking off somewhere else. They're not expecting to see him charging towards them down the corridor. Panicking, one draws his taser. The other fumbles his. Subject Six, now believing he's acting in self-defence, smashes into them.

The guards are taken by surprise, but they are professionals and they are big guys. They won't stop him by hurting him, but they could overpower him, hold him down. So he has to keep moving. He connects a forearm into the man in the front, knocking him back into the wall. He feels the man behind hit him with the taser. But the shock doesn't even register. Subject Six throws his whole weight into a kick, cracking into the knee of the guard who crumples, screams.

The first man is back up, smashes a fist into Subject Six. His head cracks back as the force of the punch hits home. Subject Six turns the power back on itself as he snaps his forehead up with all the force he has, butting the guard square in the nose. Blood sprays. The guard goes down. The way opens. He grabs the keycard, swipes open the door and doesn't look back.

Now he's in unchartered territory. He's never been in this part of the building before. There's no time to think. He has to keep going. Behind him guards are after him, ahead he knows they must be too. Subject Six pockets the taser he took from the last guard and slides his key-card through the next door he comes to.

He steps into the prisoner processing room. Instantly, he thinks he's finished. In front of him are lots of guards. They've heard the alarm and look like they're getting ready to pile into the cell block to find him. He's just made their job a lot easier.

To the left is a door. He lunges for it. Whipping out his taser - the self-defence rule no longer feasible - he uses it as a club to lash at the two guards closest to him. Connecting, they both roll back and stop the other guards rushing at him. He throws the door open. Goes through. Puts every ounce of force he's got into launching himself at the door to slam it shut. Trying to keep it closed, keep them out, give him some time.

He's in a bathroom. Luckily it's empty. Unluckily, the number of people trying to get in outweigh him. His feet slip. He roars to summon up more force. Fails. Two guards squeeze their way through. Is this the end? Subject Six slams his body against the door and for the moment gets it shut. Flicks the lock on the door. Turns and faces the two who've made it through. Can he take both? He's going to have to. Even if he does, what's his next play?

"You're done for," the older one says, "Make it easy on yourself. Give it up before you take a beating."

Subject Six doesn't care about the beating. But considers giving up all the same. He's got this far, but even if he takes these two out, what then? He can hear the door being pummeled behind him. The lock won't hold for long. The guard who's spoken lashes out. Subject Six blocks. Takes a step back. Out of the corner of the eye he sees the other guard move.

Before Subject Six reacts, this young guard smashes his truncheon over the head of the other guard. He doesn't say a word to Subject Six. Just grabs him, spins and drags him to the cubicle. Above the toilet is a window. It's the guard's toilet so there aren't any bars on it. The guy offers Subject Six a leg-up.

Subject Six tries to speak to him. There's no time. He looks back once he's almost out the window and watches the guard taser himself.

This is the guy we think is our mole. We can't be sure until we find him, but it's got to be, right?

Subject Six finds himself outside. Surrounded by sky-scrapers. There's a perimeter fence, a battery of CCTV cameras but no obvious guards. He hugs the building as he walks round, trying to spot the best place to climb the fence. Trying to keep focused, even though the fact he's breathing fresh air and seeing the sun again is distracting him. He hadn't realised it, trapped in the cell, but he's longed for this moment.

The last time he was outside - he doesn't count being on the beach in Brighton because he's out of it when he walks in from the sea - was walking from the taxi into the Genix lab on the day he was frozen. Then, he thought he might have seen the last of the world.

Now, here he is. He vaults the fence. Finds himself caught between two skyscrapers and looks up and see the sun high in the sky between them. Subject Six is free.

A SUPERHERO ON THE STREETS

Subject Six says his childhood was as perfect as anyone could have hoped for. He doesn't think he's ever met anyone who got more moral or financial support than he did. His father made big quiz shows on TV, his mother owned a classic car dealership, and they had enough money to send him to one of the best public schools in the country.

But unlike many of his classmates, whose parents thought that caring how your child grew up meant paying lots of money for their schooling, Subject Six reckons his mum and dad were always on his side. They were perfectionists and as an only child he was one of their most important projects. When he became interested in coding as a teenager, their only reaction was to encourage him. They got him lessons from one of the best in the industry and if he needed an upgrade on his computer, he got one. Which is why, the day his insurance aggregator website made him his first million, the first people he celebrated with were his parents.

Subject Six

There were my best friends back then. I remember vowing I would be the same to my kids.

Me

And were you?

Subject Six

Nowhere near it. But you know that already, don't you?

Me

Well, I…

Subject Six

Don't pussy around, Benji, you're better than that.

Me

Ok, so how come you got it so wrong?

Subject Six

It's complicated.

Me

Is it? Isn't it because you were pussying around?

Subject Six

Is that what she said?

Me

Who?

Subject Six

Michelle? Or Indigo? I was accused by both of cheating.

Me

And were they right?

Subject Six

This isn't about how I treated them, which was bad, I admit, this is about how I treated my kids. The moment I was free, they were my first thought.

In the middle of London, at eight in the morning, Subject Six starts moving. It doesn't take long for him to work out he's in Canary Wharf and to start churning through his options. In the weeks before he was frozen he says his thoughts were dominated by the flattening truth that while he was failing his children by spending too much time at work, partying or avoiding their mum, he'd always thought he'd have time to make it up to them. His cancer changed that. As he got into his Cryopod, he knew that unless medicine advanced quickly enough for him to be unfrozen soon - which he knew was virtually impossible - that he'd failed as a father and there was no way to change that.

As he puts as much distance between himself and the detention centre, his thoughts keep zoning in on his kids: Tuppence, Oscar and although he's never actually met him, the son he had with Indigo, Fergus. How can he begin to make it up to them?

Subject Six

I mean, what would you do if you were back from the dead?

Me

See Mina, and the kids.

Subject Six

Exactly.

Me

So how come you didn't go straight to them?

Hustling through the streets, Subject Six tries to keep calm and balanced. It's impossible. His emotions are peaking, his paranoia is off the scale. Every time he hears a siren he flinches and hides. He's constantly on the look-out for how to find some clothes so he's not just wearing a blue jumpsuit and looking like either an escaped prisoner - which he is - or a doctor in scrubs. He's also imagining, then discarding, multiple ways to get himself out to his old house in the suburbs, where Michelle, Oscar and Tuppence were living when he was frozen.

Then he hears a helicopter. It didn't exactly surprise me when I found out Enosh Blake got his helicopter license young. It was a 21st birthday present to himself.

Taking as much cover as he can against the wall of the skyscraper he's next to, Subject Six knows from experience that the chopper he can hear above him isn't for passengers. He's flown over Canary Wharf countless times and can tell just from the speed of the blades that this isn't a helicopter delivering the rich to a helipad of a banking HQ. This helicopter is looking for someone. Him.

This is when he realises the obvious. A moment of clarity arriving after a frantic hour. The people searching for him know everything about him. They'll be watching all the places that Enosh Blake used to go to. His offices, the member's clubs he used to drink at, the home he had with Michelle, the flat in Mayfair, the Surrey Mansion he briefly shared with Indigo. His friends, his lawyers, his family, they'll all be being watched.

Which means he can't go to his kids now. He can't try to intercept Tuppence and Oscar on their way to school, attempt to get to them in the playground between lessons, or sneak in to see them once they're home. The last thing he wants is for them to see their Dad again, whom they think is dead, only to be seized within minutes by armed police. Yes, he has an overwhelming urge to see them, but he has to do it properly. Even if he manages to evade his captors, turning up unannounced would be a massive trauma to them. It becomes crystal clear to him that there's no way he can possibly just rock up and say 'hi'.

As the helicopter veers away and Subject Six starts to move again, he pushes his emotions away and focuses on finding a smarter plan of what to do next. This Plan B doesn't take long to think up, simply because he has so few options. The only place he can think of going is All-Free. He only saw the name once when the psychiatrist visited him in his cell, so they won't be looking for him there. But if he goes there, then surely he'll get help, because that's what they do. Protect people who've been imprisoned illegally.

Even though he only saw the letter from AllFree for a couple of minutes, he can still remember their address. He says that while he doesn't have what most people tend to call a photographic memory - because he gets words and numbers not visuals - once he's read or heard something it stays in his head.

Larry, from AllFree, gets a call from the receptionist just before midday. He tells Larry that there's a man demanding to talk to someone in charge, that the guy says he was arrested in Brighton and has been detained in a centre close to the AllFree office ever since. Larry goes down to reception. He's wary, on guard. Five minutes later he's on the phone, calling me.

Now, I know what you're expecting. That this is the news I've been waiting for, so I drop everything and jump on the tube and within the hour I'm meeting Subject Six for the first time. Well, it doesn't work out like that. Mostly because I'm in Italy on a four-day break with Mina for our anniversary. But also, when Subject Six hears Larry talking to a reporter, he starts to get jumpy, so Larry agrees to keep me in the loop and I spend the next two days of our trip at Lake Como desperately trying to pay attention to Mina, not this guy who could be a superhero or mutant who's apparently just broken out of jail.

Larry

Having him escape, and out, I didn't know if it was good for the case.

Me

In what way?

Larry

When he was inside, I felt I had a strong chance of being able to prove he was being detained illegally and force his release. The government were so scared of a bad human rights story that I thought we'd get him out. But having him on the streets? What if they said his escape was proof he was a threat, and use that to arrest him and keep him locked up?

Me

Did he understand that? When you told him?

Larry

Of course. But he hadn't known we were already helping him… all he needed was to get out. And stay out.

Me

True, bad for the case or not, he wasn't exactly going to try and break back in, was he?

At AllFree, while I'm fretting by the side of our hotel pool, it's Subject Six who comes up with what to do next. During his walk across London, he's focused on not being caught and walking the four miles to AllFree as soon as possible. But nagging at his consciousness is a growing feeling that by breaking out he hasn't become more free at all. In fact, what he's done is triggered a tsunami that's gathering force on his horizon and he's not going to be able to stop it breaking. Helicopters looking for him are just the beginning, the first ominous ripples. It's going to be a long time before he can stroll down the street like a free man, if he'll ever be able to do that again.

Knowing this, Subject Six decides to take himself somewhere safe before it's too late. He wants to hole up, try to let things calm down and balance out, both in the world at large, and in his head. The government torturers have gone, but he's savvy enough to know he's going to have to work hard to come to terms with what's happened to him. Within an hour, Subject Six rents out an Airbnb somewhere in London using some simple hacks to make it completely anonymous and untraceable. He agrees with Larry that AllFree are going to keep the case going, not letting on that they know Subject Six has escaped the centre.

WHAT DO YOU DO AFTER COMING BACK TO LIFE?

At this stage I just want to say this book is not going to turn into a courtroom drama detailing Larry's struggles with the government. That would bore me to write and there are pages and pages of documents. So, instead of that, I'm going to tell you what Subject Six is up to while he sits alone in a flat and waits for Larry to help get him free. Or officially free.

One of the things Subject Six does, is start talking to me. But responding to a reporter is far from his priority. That's trying to get in contact with Michelle.

Subject Six - first email

M,

I know you heard from my lawyer last week and I know you told him 'I could go to hell'. Well, I actually kind of have. Or maybe it's purgatory.

But please don't bury yourself away from this - I know you do that (and I know you'll hate for me pointing that out) but I am not going to give up.

I'm going to send this email every hour of every day until you answer. Trust me, I have the time. I know this is weird/difficult/scary/confusing/the-last-thing-you-probably-want but it is happening. For whatever reason I am back and I know you know I won't give up

Michelle - 278 emails later

You know? Fuck you, E, you know nothing!

Subject Six - 8 minutes later

You know nothing, Jon Snow.

Remember when we read that book aloud to each other on the California road-trip? That was the best trip we ever took and I know I ruined it on the last night, and that I never said sorry properly for doing so. Just like I've never admitted to you I messed up everything we had.

Michelle - 1 minute later

Too right you did.

SS -1 minute later

If you're going to respond in one line emails, and so quickly, can we talk on the phone? Or go on instant chat?

M- 5 minutes later

Aren't you even going to ask about your children? Don't you care about them at all? This is so typical of you E and I hate it! I thought it was over! What the hell is even fucking happening! How is this HAPPENING? LEAVE ME ALONE

SS - 3 minutes later

Of course I care about them. Oscar and Tuppence are my every thought at the moment. That's why I got in touch with you. For them. And their wellbeing is the reason I did it properly, through our lawyers, not just turning up and scaring them.

Don't think that's me being cold towards you. I know I've done enough to make you hate me for 50 lifetimes

and I'm aware you can never forgive me for what I did to you, so I'm not after that. I'm not.

What I want is to see my children again and to work out the best way of doing so. Which means I need your help.

SS - 1 hour later

M?

SS- 3 hours later

M?

M - 26 hours later

Stop this.

SS - 1 minute later

Why have you stopped contact? Please M. I'm dying here. I have to see them. I know you're mad at me, but please, for them?

M - 25 minutes later

This is from my lawyer:

Enosh has no legal right to see your children. Your custody agreement ended on his death. He is officially deceased. While there is no precedent at all for this current situation, the fact he is insisting his circumstances are kept confidential means that he has no recourse to fight you on this.

M- 32 hours later

There's a car outside. Is that you E?

M- 40 minutes later

E? They're still there. The kids have noticed and think it's funny, like they're in a movie. The same two people have been in it for most of the day. It'd better not be you.

SS - 6 minutes later

It's not me. But it could be for me.

M- 1 minute later

Why are they here?

SS - 2 minutes later

We should meet. Let me tell you what's happening, let me try to explain what happened to me - as best I can.

And no, this is not a trick. I haven't sent people to spook you out so you'll come back to me. I swear on Oscar and Tuppence's lives.

I'm going to cut out the next, well, 100 or so emails. In them Subject Six tells Michelle as much as he knows about how he's changed - this is, in case you're unsure of the timeline, after the tests by the government and before the weekend with Carly, Mina and me - and how he arrived back down on earth. As you can imagine Michelle asks countless questions, moving between incredulity and outright refusal to believe.

Even though she'd hated him for a long time before he was frozen, this is still the father of her kids and the guy she'd once hoped to be with forever, so it's a huge amount for her to take in. Since he'd been frozen, she'd grieved for him in a complicated, confused way and then moved on. Perhaps more importantly, she'd helped her kids to move on. And now, suddenly, everything she knows is turned upside down and he's back.

The one part of exchange I am going to include here, before moving on with the story, is when she asks him why he'd been frozen in the first place. Which is not a question I'd personally spent much time on. But, it's a question she dwells on and comes back to and seeing as she could well be the person who knew Enosh Blake the best in the world, then I think it's worth considering.

M

What did you want to happen, though, when you signed up for Genix?

SS

How do you mean? Why did I get frozen?

M

Yeah. I mean it's not exactly normal, is it? Most people, I'm sure, couldn't even think about affording it - but even if I could, I don't think I'd do it. And I have to admit when I heard you were, I was surprised. It didn't seem like the Enosh I knew (but then did I ever really know you!?!) Don't you remember I read that book about the guy who lived forever who hated the fact he was always left alone every time he got attached to people? When I told you about that, you said you'd hate that, that you'd never want to be the last person at the party.

SS

I don't remember saying that - but if I did, I had no idea how early the party was going to end for me!

I find it odd you're surprised about Genix. I've always loved tech and what man can achieve, and beating death, having been handed a death sentence when I was so young, what Genix and Fabian Tree (I met the guy a few times) were offering became impossible for me to resist. The idea of waking up at some point, free from cancer, having got one over the Grim Reaper... that just sounded so cool. A way of saying fuck you to the tumours inside of me and it gave me something to cling to... a project that had a future, rather than spending my last days on earth wrapping up the past like most of the people with cancer I knew seemed to be doing.

And then there were the kids. Being diagnosed woke me up to how much I'd fucked things up. And dying, knowing that I'd forever be known as someone who lost their kids, was too much. Genix was a way of postponing that judgment - it gave me hope that I wouldn't be signing off forever with the knowledge I'd failed them, it allowed me to think I could one day put things right.

M

So, you thought you'd be woken up by Genix and then find Tuppence and Oscar and make things right? Really?

SS

100%. Not as kids, but as adults, yes, I hoped I'd meet them again.

M

I don't believe you. I did my research when I found out about you and Genix and everyone who signs up for it is told there's only a 5% chance that they'll be woken up in the next 100 years. Which meant you knew that there was a 95% chance, which is essentially a certainty, that when you did come back everyone you'd ever known would be gone... including them! So don't lie and say you did it for them, you didn't do it for them... you did it because you had money and power and vanity. That's how you've always been, you just hid it from me at first...

Michelle goes on to vent completely at Subject Six. Which he admits he deserves. But even in her anger and in her distrust, as the emails progress you can start to see an old familiarity creep back in. Michelle never truly lets her guard down yet it's possible to see a past tenderness and at times a shared affection between them.

By the time Subject Six has finished telling her what he knows about himself, there's a renewed bond between them.

Subject Six

The real worry I had for Michelle, was what if someone decided to use her and the kids against me?

Me

Like the guys in the car.

Subject Six

Right. I needed to see Michelle, I was desperate to see Oscar and Tuppence, but I couldn't let anyone know I was in contact with her.

Me

In case they tracked you through her.

Subject Six

Not that so much, because she didn't know where I was. It was more that if they discovered how much I wanted to see the kids then they might use that against me and then the two of them would be vulnerable. As Enosh, I'd never really cared for them and I wanted people to think that was still the case.

Me

And what about your other child, Indigo's baby?

Subject Six

Well, that was different. I'd never met him.

Me

Did you want to?

Subject Six

Yes.

Me

Were you trying to then?

Subject Six

No. That had to wait. I couldn't risk it, not with Michelle.

Me

What do you mean?

Subject Six

Michelle knows when I'm lying, I gave her a lot of practise. I knew that if she found out I was talking to Indigo and trying to see her baby too, then she'd shut everything down. She has no perspective when it comes to Indigo... let's not go there now... but I didn't want to be caught in a lie, and Oscar and Tuppence were my priority. So back then, no, I didn't contact Indigo to tell her I was back.

As Subject Six emails Michelle, he's essentially back in solitary confinement. Living alone in his Airbnb flat. He doesn't need food or drink, all he needs is information and he borrowed a laptop from Larry - so he has access to virtually everything he needs. This gives Subject Six a lot of time to think and he says that as the ice breaks between him and Michelle his thoughts focus on two main areas (there is a third one, which is what to do about me and my requests to interview him and a fourth one, which is how's Larry doing with his case). One priority, as we know, is how to re-connect with his kids without hurting them; and the other is what is he going to do with himself?

From the flat he can see the Tower of London and he says that one sunset, after a stormy autumn day, as a fiery and bruised sky turns seamlessly into dusk and then night, he finds himself fixating on a kind of mantra: 'I used to have everything, now all I have is a chance.'

The thing he battles with, is what to do with that chance and how long has he got to play with? Because ever present in his mind when he thinks about his chance is the number on his wrist. What does that number mean? Is it counting up to a set number, and if so what to? The number of days he's got left? Could it be a measure, a number to see how long it will take him to do something - whatever that something might be?

Subject Six has no idea, only theory after theory, and he decides the only thing to be done is to be aware there could be a time pressure on his chance, but not to let that define him, or to interfere with his thinking. He can't be paralysed by the unknown; he has another chance and he's going to be positive about it.

Subject Six

What would you do Benji?

Me

If I came back from the dead?

Subject Six

If you came back from the dead.

Me

I don't know, erm, go to the pub?

Subject Six

Who with?

Me

I don't know, I was being facetious.

Subject Six

Yes, but it was still your first answer... so there's some truth in it. Would you go on your own?

Me

**No, course not, I'd have a fucking big party for every-
one I know, knew. Mina, the kids, my mates... everyone.**

Subject Six

**So, your first inclination would be to focus on yourself,
the microcosm...**

Me

**Well, ish. I mean I almost said I'd work for world
peace and try to find ways to stop hunger.**

Subject Six

Like Miss World models?

Me

**Exactly, but that felt even more facetious, and much
less do-able.**

Subject Six

Is it?

Me

Yes.

Subject Six

Sure about that?

He isn't joking. Subject Six goes on to explain some
of the thinking he'd done staring at Tower Bridge. Now
of course booking a pub and getting everyone you know
to rock up is easier than creating world peace - especially
if on the invite you point out that you have actually come
back from the dead. It's pretty likely that most people will
cancel other plans to turn up for your big 'I've been Res-
urrected Party!'

But that, he argues, is the problem. That party isn't
going to be the party you want. Everything has changed.

You've died, these people have grieved for you, then moved on and changed. They've created a headspace in which you no longer exist. For your loved ones it will have been devastatingly hard to do, but they'll have managed it - because eventually that's what humans do. We recover and move on. And then, suddenly, you come back and fuck everything up. You invade their new headspace and try to drag them back to a place they've worked very hard to get away from.

That party is going to be great for the first hour of re-introductions, then weird, and terrible, and confusing and ultimately a complete let-down. Because, Subject Six says, he realises even though he's back he can never get back what he had. Not fully. For his kids, he's going to make an exception - but everyone else? Will it really be that simple? He decides no. He believes that if he uses this second chance to try to get back what he's lost then it's only going to end in failure.

Me

But world peace? Stopping hunger, inequality, that's achievable?

Subject Six

I've got fucking super-powers, haven't I? It's worth a shot.

Me

And?

Subject Six

And what?

Me

Well, you just gave me 10 minutes of chat about how you decided you shouldn't bother trying to get your old life back...

Subject Six

Yes.

Me

So, isn't there another 10 minutes on why you might, or might not, be able to solve the world's problems?

Subject Six

No.

Me

Now *you're* being facetious.

Subject Six

Listen, the way I figured it is, if I'm not going to be able to use this second chance to get my own, small world back to how it was, with some improvements, then I may as well go big. Focus on the rest of the world. And jeez, does it need someone to focus on it. I used to be one of the main players in the problem, a billionaire who was only after the right thing for me. Not anymore.

Don't start thinking that this is a quick decision and that shortly after deciding not to book out the function room of his old local, Subject Six is on the phone to a costume designer to get himself a superhero costume.

But by the time he speaks to me, it's all done and dusted in his head. It takes him time to come to his conclusion, then once he comes to it he turns his not inconsiderable mind to how best he might tackle the problems of the macrocosm.

If you were aiming to solve world hunger, what would you do? If you were trying to stop wealth inequality, or eradicate terrorism, how would you do it? Obviously, people try to answer these questions all the time. So for the weeks he's holed up in front of Tower Bridge, Subject Six reads every single credible solution to these issues, and lots of other not-so-credible ideas. Once he's seen what people have tried before he begins to formulate a plan that someone with the powers that he's got might be able to implement.

At the same time, Larry is continuing with the case. Amazingly, or not, depending on how cynically you view the government, no-one officially admits that Subject Six has escaped. All the time Larry is expecting them to announce it and for him to have to shift his petition so it focuses on barring them from detaining him again, instead of getting him freed. But no-one mentions it. Larry has to carry on fighting for the release of a man he knows is no longer held captive. Nuts, isn't it? And as Larry ploughs on, it makes me ask two questions.

Firstly, does it ever cross his mind that he's been had? That the man he met in his office isn't Subject Six, that perhaps there is someone still being detained but someone wants Larry to think otherwise? Like could the government have sent someone in as a decoy? Sure, it's a bit of a conspiracy theory, but one worth considering, right? What if they want Larry to give up because his job is already won, so they got a lookalike to rock up at the office and pretend to be Subject Six?

As it turns out, just as that theory occurred to me, it also occurred to Larry. But the thing is, who's more intelligent than both Larry and me, even put together (we both agree this to be true, grudgingly)? That's right, Subject Six. And he'd thought of this theory way before we did. So, the moment he senses Larry's doubts are building, he slips out of his flat one night and surprises Larry at home, where he blows Larry's mind by displaying some of his new abilities. This move is a risk, but one worth taking seeing as it gets Larry completely behind him.

The second question is why does Larry keep doing it? Subject Six isn't official. Anywhere. There are no warrants for his arrest, nothing that means the government can legitimately detain him again. So, there's an argument for letting the case drop and for Subject Six to just stay out of the authority's way.

Yes, it's likely he's a high priority for them, but on the other hand Subject Six is becoming more and more certain he wants to keep a low profile. He's not planning on hitting the London party scene or going back into business, so why does he need to be officially released? Added to that is the fact he's been able to get access to the trusts he set up when he froze himself. He's dipping into them about 100 years earlier than expected, but it means he's essentially got unlimited resources that are very hard to trace because of how they've been set-up. And it's not just his money that's hard for the authorities to track, because he is too. He can't be picked up by cameras. So, with his money and his superpowers, it's feasible he could stay on the run without too much trouble for a long time.

Larry and Subject Six talk about this a lot. Because if they do go to court, and lose, then they might create a lot of pain that could be avoided. A ruling against him could result in a high-profile man-hunt; it could be disturbing the viper's nest when you don't need to go anywhere near it. But, in the end, they decide to fight the case. How come? Because Larry is the kind of guy who likes to believe right and wrong exists and this is a case that needs to be fought. Because Subject Six says one of his mantras in business was never to back down from a fight. Because

Subject Six thinks that if he wins his freedom in the courts it will legitimise his future endeavours.

On November 14th 2018 Larry and his AllFree team, who've been financed handsomely by some donations you might be able to link to Subject Six if you look hard enough, go to court. I'm barred as a member of the press, but Larry nails it. The judge orders that the government have to release Subject Six, on the condition that he has to visit a police station once a month. Larry doesn't contest this decision, even though he has good grounds to argue that this is essentially like putting a free man on parole. Neither does Larry risk upsetting things by asking when Subject Six will be released.

The government's legal team are incensed. From Larry's accounts, Blondie and Glasses are there too and they're not happy. Which isn't surprising.

That night, Larry and AllFree hold a party and Subject Six braves his first public event and joins them. That's where I first meet him face-to-face and while he doesn't give me a full interview, he does tell me that now he's won the case he's going to put his first mission into operation. The target? Tuppence and Oscar.

SUBJECT SIX'S FIRST MISSION

PC Janet Homes - On patrol at the time

It was my first time. Doing the Regent Street Lights, that is. I was quite excited, I remember that. I'd worked the turning on of the lights when I was still up in Skegness. Back in 2016. We got some ex-footballer to do it who I'd never heard of, and there were only about 2000 people there, so it wasn't anything like the Regent Street Lights in 2018. That was crazy. That was massive and when I clocked on and they got us all down there, we knew we were in for a tough shift.

Most of everything we do now, when we're on the beat, is foregrounded with what to do if you see a terrorist, or potential terrorist. Which is fine usually. I mean I don't like it, but you get used to it. But when it's dark, and there are tens of thousands of people in a street that normally only has about two thousand people in it, and there are commuters and tourists and families and kids, how do you police that? How do you look after that?

Magdeline Janda- Michelle Blake's Housekeeper

The children were very excited, you know. They always were of course, both of them have always been full of energy all of the years I've known them. Always bouncing and shouting and talking. That day they'd been taken out of school early to go and see the lights being turned on. I think Mrs Blake, because of the charity work she does, had been able to arrange for them to meet the pop singers who were turning the lights on.

Honestly, I don't think either of the children liked the music, but we all like celebrities don't we? And I think they were looking forward to being able to tell their friends about them. When they got home from school, their granddad dropped them off, their father's dad, I gave them some food, made sure they were dressed and we waited for Mrs Blake to get back to take them into London. That car, the one that had been near the house was there again, and I remember the children both staring out the window and saying silly things about it. They were very over-excited, very giddy.

Larry

I'd been calling him all day. After the party, we'd agreed to talk again in the morning, but he didn't call so I started calling him. No answer, but you know that because I called you, Benji, to see if you'd heard from him, didn't I?

Anyway, I had a meeting outside the office which was near where he was staying, so afterwards, when I'd still got no word I thought I should go and see him. I wasn't worried. Not really. It wasn't like I needed to make sure everything was ok in terms of was he in danger, or had we been fucked over by the government after all and actually they'd known where he was hiding all along, that wasn't on my mind so much, but more to find out what he was thinking.

I guess over the time I'd been in contact with him I'd become fascinated by him. I'd spent all of my working hours on the case, and the rest of my waking hours thinking about him. About the very fact he was here. I mean what was going on? I was dreaming about him, for Christ's sake. I was addicted to him, and all of a sudden I was cut off from him? I had to go and find out what he was thinking, doing, planning. I had to.

He wasn't there.

Anonymous - Contractor for RSG Security who wishes to remain unknown

It was one of my first jobs since leaving the army. I didn't really think about the details, because that's not how it works. I was told to watch the house, so I watched the house along with this other guy who'd worked for the firm a while. We had a photo of a guy we had to watch for. That was it. We didn't know what he'd done, or what we'd have to do if or when he turned up, we just watched. There was a decoy car out front, and we were stationed around the back. It's a clever trick, because it makes the people do everything important away from the car and they don't know, don't even think about the possibility, that it's not just the one car watching them.

At first I didn't see why we were on the job, not really. They were a pretty normal, boring family. Single parent, Milf, two posh kids. The only thing interesting we saw was that she was banging one of the family friends. When this guy came over and the kids were there he was just a mate, maybe an uncle, but he'd also come over at night, occasionally during the afternoon. Because of the car out front he'd come around the back, right past us.

Then after five weeks or so we got a call. Urgent. We had to go into town. The Milf and the kids had left the house about half hour before. So, I guessed we were chasing them.

Michelle Blake

Tuppence and Oscar had been looking forward to the evening for a long time. We had a picnic hamper on the train, they were going to meet that terrible band Twisted and I'd promised them we could look at Hamley's too. What I didn't tell them was what I'd arranged with their Father.

Why didn't I tell them, and why had I agreed to what Enosh wanted? Because I thought it was best to bite the bullet and just do it. They are his children.

Hallam Walker - CIA whistleblower

At the time we didn't know the target. We were told that it was high level. That we had to be prepared for all eventualities and that we'd face resistance. From one or more sides. Back then I was already aware that our command was failing, especially in Europe and quite frankly I had no faith in the people directly above me. They were fine if things were going smoothly, but I had serious doubts about how they reacted in a storm.

We met in Golden Square. Four of us. We knew there was another team that would head towards us from the other side of Regent Street. So, eight of us converging on the same spot where we'd pick up the target and get them to the designated location.

Now obviously, the target had planned well. The last thing we wanted was all hell breaking loose at a big event like this. We knew that now more than ever headlines about our work being too brutal and over-zealous might mean we soon wouldn't be in work. But apparently the target wasn't one for getting out and about and this was our one shot. Intelligence said the target would be wary and on guard, but would have no reason to believe we knew where he was. There was no way he'd know we were coming, which was exactly how we liked it.

PC Janet Homes - On patrol at the time

By about 4.30 it was all quite wonderful. The type of scene you get in a film, you know? The sky was black and dark, lit up by the shopfronts which were all full of Christmas goodies and displays. I could smell those lovely roasted chestnuts; you could hear how excited everyone was. I know I was on duty but I was actually, really enjoying myself. The atmosphere was so warming I could feel it.

Even by 5 o clock, when I began to feel like the street was too full and couldn't really take any more people, everything was still bubbling along nicely. We'd had one woman who was pickpocketed and down at the Piccadilly Circus end of Regent Street I had to give a warning to an idiot of a cyclist who had headphones in and had run a red light and was trying to cycle into a crowd of people. But apart from that, nothing. It was the perfect pre-Christmas occasion. One person even gave me a mince-pie!

Anonymous - Contractor for RSG Security who wishes to remain unknown

We'd taken the motorbikes right into central London. Our orders were to find the woman and the two kids and keep watch. First and foremost, we weren't allowed to lose them but we were also to keep an eye out for the guy in the photo.

At first the difficult thing was spotting them. We knew they'd be coming above ground from the tube at Oxford Circus, but there were four exits and the road was closed so the whole four-way intersection was just a crush of people. There was no way we could stand in the middle of the road and try to find them. So how do two people cover four exits? Not an easy question to answer, not when you have no time to work it out. I was in my motorbike leathers, clutching my helmet, sweating buckets and thinking that in all my time in Afghanistan I never felt as ill-prepared as I did then. And yet all we were after was a mum and two kids in Oxford fucking Circus!

Michelle Blake

Enosh said his email was encrypted, and we'd been emailing on a laptop he'd got to me through his lawyer, so there was no way that anyone could know we'd been in contact, let alone know we were planning on meeting. Yet he didn't want to risk writing the details down. All he told me was to go to the lights and he'd meet us there.

So, if he was going to find us, as far as I was concerned my role was to make sure Tuppence and Oscar were in a great mood when they saw him again. It was going to be a huge thing for them to process so obviously if they were feeling good when they saw him, it might start things off on the right foot. And it was working. They were loving the whole occasion.

We got to the VIP area in plenty of time before the lights were to be switched on. I did a bit of mingling with colleagues while the two kids kind of hung around near the celebrities, desperate to be noticed but too shy to say hello.

PC Janet Homes - On patrol at the time

Just before the lights were turned on I was told to position myself by the VIP tent. Because of all the selfie-hunters, we knew there'd be a crush when the celebrities came out so we had to make sure we kept our line so no-one was mobbed. As I was standing there the cutest two kids came out of the tent with their Mum.

I'd just checked my watch, it was 5.19pm, and I said hello to the little boy who was absolutely over the moon to be so close to where they were going to be turning the lights on. He looked like a little angel with red cheeks, all wrapped up in a scarf and hat. Now, I'm very good at faces and it was definitely the same little boy I saw then who was involved in the incident later.

Hallam Walker - CIA whistleblower

The funny thing was I knew my own wife and kids were somewhere among the crowd. Obviously, that's not what you want personally, and is way beyond anything that's professionally acceptable, but by the time I knew we were going for the take-down on Regent Street it was too late for me to pop my hand up and start creating problems. Anyway, my wife is an ex agent and the best I ever served with so she could handle the kids and on top of that the whole operation was about using non-lethal force so it was unlikely anyone would get hurt.

The weirdest thing would have been if my kids had seen me! Me and two others were wearing Chuggers' outfits, you know those annoying guys who stop you on the street, try to be your friend and then sign you up for a charity. They mug you, as the Brits say, hence Chuggers. I was dressed from head-to-foot in charity branded clothes and a bright green and red hat as we were going for some Christmas style thing. I'd always been a bit cagey with my kids about what I did, so imagine if they'd seen me and thought my job was standing on the goddamn street and conning people into charity!

Michelle Blake

There was a moment, just after the lights were turned on that I got this shiver down my spine. Something inside telling me we were being watched. I looked around, but didn't see him. Because I thought it must be him, but I didn't catch any sight of him. I had the kids in front of me, my hands on their shoulders and I pulled them closer to me.

From being sure about doing this, I suddenly changed my mind. This wasn't right. I didn't, at that stage, feel in danger, and neither did I have a change of heart about Enosh and how we should break the news to them, it's just something was telling me it was wrong. Maybe it was because we'd had such a good time, a perfect time, one they should always remember and yet soon it would be completely overshadowed by what was to come.

A shock I'd planned for them. But even though I was feeling that, I didn't do anything about it. Mostly because I couldn't. The plan was he would approach us and how could I stop him doing that?

Subject Six

I can't really begin to tell you what I felt when I first saw them again. Little Oscar's eyes were beaming, his goofy teeth poking out through his smile as he sucked hard on a lollipop, his head moving every which way as he tried to see everything all at once. Tups, as ever, wasn't quite so open with her emotions but in her own way she was taking it all in, her face shining with a touch of wonderment, that funny mix of excitement and anxiety she's always had - as if she's so desperate to enjoy something she can't quite trust it, maybe hoping that everything will turn out ok.

Overwhelmingly I felt full, flooded, it was too much. Seeing them again. In the past weeks since my escape, I'd watched them 1000s of times on videos online. I'd spent hours poring over photos. But now to see them, in the flesh: I was at their mercy. I was bursting.

Once the lights were switched on they started to move. I was behind them, about six or so people in between us. It took a lot for me not to push through then and there and go and hug them both, clutch them to me. I was even desperate to see Michelle too; something deep inside of me wanted her to see me, for her to recognise me. I'd been on my own too long, I hadn't realized how much I needed someone familiar to see me and acknowledge me. As if I needed confirmation that I was here, that it wasn't all some sort of dream.

What stopped me going to them wasn't reason, or patience, it was seeing a guy, the other side of Michelle and the kids, doing exactly what I was doing. Following her, and looking around... for someone.

A million things started running through my head. I'd been so careful, I thought everything had been completely secret. All our messages were encrypted; Michelle had been going out of her house for weeks and not been followed by the people watching the house which meant they were at her house only to look for me.

I knew this because I'd had a team of my own investigators watching - so why now? How did they know? Was it chance? Was I being overly concerned, was this guy in biker's leathers really watching her? I was certain he was.

Magdeline Janda - Michelle Blake's Housekeeper

I'm not proud of it. I had no choice and also, at the time, I didn't know I was doing anything wrong? I would never have wanted to hurt Mrs Blake or the children, I'd known them forever. I'd been there when she split up with Mr Blake and in a way, I felt very close to them - I spent more time in that family than I did my own!

When the men told me they could get me deported I was very afraid. I felt I had no choice but to let them in the house one morning while Mrs Blake was out. They found the lap-top and phone she'd been hiding but I don't know what they did.

Subject Six

I wrestled my mind back on track, gripping hard onto my composure. The very reason I'd picked now for the meeting was because it was perfect. There were so many people around, as long as things went our way we'd still get into the car and get away.

I sent Michelle a message to the encrypted phone - it told her where the car was waiting for us. The driver was idling, in a side-street just next to the crowds. We'd slip away, jump in and drive off before the guy knew what was happening.

Anonymous - Contractor for RSG Security who wishes to remain unknown

What I didn't need was panic. It was already close there, carnage, but when I went online to tell them I'd seen the

guy, what was needed was a calm head. Instead, when I asked what to do, as I hung back, eyes fixed on him and trying to stay fixed on the Milf, all I got told was to hold my position. Wait for orders. Well, that's no good is it? Not really, not if you're going to have to do something quick. You want to know your endgame with as much lead-time as possible.

Subject Six

As we got closer to the car, I was on red alert. More than that, if that's possible. I couldn't see anyone else to concern me. Just the one biker guy. The only problem I had was at one point I almost lost the kids when a crowd of people opened up and my view was blocked. I found myself staring directly at one of those Chuggers who seemed desperate to talk to me. Instinct made me swerve past them, knowing this was no time for me to be told I wasn't doing enough to help the world. I ducked behind a woman with a buggy as the Chugger was heading right for me, strained up on my toes, spotted Oscar and I soon caught up with Michelle.

The next moment her head turned. Our eyes met. Hers instantly welled up, mine did too. I almost gagged, losing my breath.

Michelle saw the car and got the idea. She rushed forward, opening the car door. I broke from the crowd, pleased the engine was running and the street ahead was pretty clear so we could get away. Then a hand grabbed me. The Chugger.

That threw me. How much commission was the fucking guy on? I pushed him off me and backed away.

Michelle screamed. I jumped back against the wall. Oscar was in the car. Tups was rooted in fear. A woman in the same Chugger outfit had Michelle pushed against the wall. Who were these guys? Were they with the biker?

PC Janet Homes - On patrol at the time

It all happened very quickly. The teams on the CCTV said there was some trouble brewing and sent me and four others over, mobilising an armed team too. I was the closest there when they upped the alarm and said a gun had been seen. I was terrified, yes, but you just have to carry on don't you?

You don't want anyone to be hurt on your watch, ever. Not with all those children about.

Subject Six

The first Chugger and now a couple more guys were facing me. Fight-ready. Then I heard a scream, the biker was running towards us, shouting, barrelling through the crowd. The people around started shouting. That's when I saw the biker guy had a gun. He was trying to raise it at me but kept getting pushed aside, creating mayhem.

I stepped closer to the car. A gun wasn't going to hurt me, but the crowd rushing everywhere like headless chickens were preventing a clean getaway.

Tups and Oscar were screaming. I caught the look on their innocent, terrified faces. They hadn't recognized me yet.

I saw a Police woman pushing through the crowd. Grabbing her Taser. More cops were behind her.

Michelle was still being held against the wall.

The three people surrounding me were pushing for-wards.

I could probably have grabbed Tups and Michelle and got them into the car. We might have had a chance of driving away without being hit by the gun, or hitting pe-destrians. But it was only a chance and there was no way I could expose the kids to that.

My only option was to bolt. They were trying to guide me away from Regents Street. I could see that now. I needed the invisibility of the crowd.

I powered forward. The three guys were strong. They wrenched my shoulder out, but they weren't expecting me to be able to ride an attack like that.

I carried on going with a fury. I made it. I was gone.

Hallam Walker - CIA whistleblower

Firstly, I'll never be able to explain how he made it through us. That was not natural. And secondly, that the operation was a shit-storm was not our fault. Not one bit. What was unbelievable is how the Brits handled it. They'd asked for our help with the target so as not to get their own hands dirty and yet they'd also contracted some crappy private firm as well. Apparently the idea was to ensure there were enough resources on the ground! But who does a thing like that? Put two teams on the ground who aren't linked up?

We got torn a new one because we let him get away, and they knew it was the biker's fault not ours, but did they listen? No. Of course not. It was meant to be non-lethal force and then he draws a gun? In central London. Of course that was going to draw the cops. That is not how you lift someone off the street with no fuss.

But that guy, his strength, what planet was he from?

PC Janet Homes - On patrol at the time

Luckily no-one was hurt. No-one that matters anyway, the boy and girl were scared but completely untouched and their mum was a bit shell-shocked. I did my best to calm them down and they recovered ok, although I did worry about the mum.

As for the rest of them, it was all a bit fishy, if you ask me. As soon as the man, the one we never tracked down, ran away and the others saw I was there and then my other officers, they all just stopped and waited. Normally if you arrest people, and catch them red-handed you get some real issues: they're either angry or nervous, or de-fensive; but they all just kind of downed-tools and waited for what was coming. They didn't seem worried in the slightest, or sorry, just… bored. A few weeks later I did try to find out what had happened but got no an-swers. You get that a lot now though, so I presumed there must have been a terrorism connection or something like that.

Michelle Blake

Being attacked by the woman, seeing the kids so upset, it shook me to the core, but not as much as seeing him again. He was exactly the same but completely different. Before he took off I saw his face crumple after he looked at the children one more time. I knew then he'd made a decision and I felt sad for him. I didn't feel anger, I thought I would after we were attacked like that because of him, but I had no anger towards him at all. I just felt sorrow.

SUBJECT SIX'S SECRET RETREAT

Subject Six is remarkably matter-of-fact about what happened that night on Regent's Street. I know him well enough to know if he'll only give me the details and facts about something, it's because that something hurts him. When I interview him about his role in the failure of the mission he gives me what I need - as you have read previously - but he isn't prepared to give me any more, which is why I used other people's accounts as well as his to explain that evening.

What happens next that night in London is Subject Six switches to practical mode and continues with his back-up exit plan to get himself to safety. If the reunion had gone well, he had hoped Oscar and Tuppence would have left London with him. As it is, he goes solo.

After crashing through the crowds, he picks up a car he's parked nearby and leaves London behind. I say car, but it's not just any car. Subject Six has always wanted to stay as clear from fictional heroes as possible, but he's always loved cars and the ones he drives are straight out of a movie. This one is a customised, souped-up 4x4, a top-of-the-line Land Rover with a corvette engine and - because when he bought it as Enosh he was planning on driving through the Sahara Desert - some of the most advanced radar and navigation technology on the market.

Now might be a good time to explain how he has this. I've already mentioned the trust he set up for his future self and the trust for his children. What I haven't mentioned is what he sheepishly now refers to as 'the-assets-that-got-away'. You see, one thing about Enosh Blake was he'd had a serious spending problem. Not serious because it left him in debt, he had too much money for that, but serious in the fact he had so many things he didn't always remember them.

Me

Like what? What slipped your mind?

Subject Six

Nothing slipped my mind. I don't forget anything. It's more... I just didn't shine my light on a certain part of my brain.

Me

The parts of your brain that knew where all those assets where?

Subject Six

I know, I know, it sounds incredibly arrogant and gross and greedy, but by the time I sat down to go over my accounts I was so close to being frozen I hardly paid attention. They went through my receipts and I just nodded.

Me

Which is why so much stuff was forgotten?

Subject Six

Exactly, which was a nightmare for my lawyers when things I owned kept turning up which weren't properly accounted for in the will.

Me

A nightmare until you turned up again?

Subject Six

**Right, because as soon as I checked in with my lawyers
from my Airbnb they just gave me a list of things that
were mine to use as I wanted.**

It's hard to quite believe, but so nonchalant was
Enosh when he drew up his will, that it's estimated he let
over four million in assets simply slip his mind.

I'm still astounded by how blasé he must have been,
but as he keeps telling me, if you're a billionaire, then
millions do almost become lose change. The inventory of
things is mind-blowing really. Some perhaps understand-
able, because he forgot about certain trading accounts - of
which he had many - which totalled a lot of money. Others, like the customised 4x4, a yacht, an off-plan pent-
house (it was off-plan when he bought it, it was finished
when he came back), half a country pub, the leg of a race-
horse, are way more difficult to get your head around. It
kind of makes me sick that this guy had so much money
that these things didn't even register for him - but there
you go. And as it turns out, the fact these things are still
in his name and not his kids' when he reappears, helps
him out no end.

That evening, the place Subject Six is driving to was
also his when he was alive. Well, apparently, it was his in
everything but name as he'd bought it through a series of
holding companies and off-shore accounts during a time
he'd been trying to cut his taxes. What this means, or so
I'm told by Subject Six who understands the details better
than me, is that no-one can, or could ever, trace it back to
him.

When I tell Mina about this, that a house that size, and
with quite a bit of historical significance seeing it was
built during Henry VIII's time, is legally being purposefully kept empty she's outraged. Mina is very big on the

housing shortage crisis, having done a couple of documentaries about it, and the idea that someone so rich has a place with something like 18 bedrooms just sitting empty is one that antagonises her like almost nothing else. Subject Six agrees. He admits it's wrong. And when he tells me this, and I tell him my wife thinks so too, he insists that I find her and put her on the phone. Which I do, and the first time Mina and Subject Six talk is when he's apologising to her.

A couple of weeks later, I make my first trip to see him at the house. And while I do think he meant his apology to Mina for his past greed, the fact is having an empty home which is completely off radar is perfect for him. He meets me at the train station. Then he takes me on an incredibly convoluted and complicated journey to get to the mansion so I won't know exactly how to find it.

Subject Six

This isn't me hiding away. This is me getting ready to launch.

Me

But anyone would understand it, I think, after what happened.

This is from the first sit-down interview I do with him after the failed mission to see his kids. Christmas is approaching, and I want to know how he's feeling about the fact it now looks very unlikely he's going to see them during the time of year that's so family-centric.

Subject Six

Seeing them, in the flesh, and not being able to hold them, to look into their eyes, that was very hard.

Me

I bet.

Subject Six

You must know it, Benji. You'll get it tomorrow when you go home, when your kids see you, and you connect, don't you? Your eyes meet and they recognize you and throw all their love and spirit out for you to catch… you know it.

Me

I do, I do. But you'll get that at some point, won't you?

Subject Six

No.

Me

Why not?

There's a long, brooding pause. I always try to say as little as possible to people I'm interviewing. The longer you wait for them to say something, the more they tend to say. In the end, he waits me out.

Me

I mean Michelle is obviously happy for you to see them, so why not bring them up here? Even if they're followed, you do what you did with me, throw off anyone watching… it'd be perfectly safe, wouldn't it?

Subject Six

I have to leave them behind me.

Me

What? Why?

Subject Six

They can't give me what I want and I can't give them what they'll need. I thought I could, and then I saw them, and that was enough.

Me

What was enough?

Subject Six

Seeing them alive.

This is where he stops. He refuses to talk about them again during my visit. Instead, he pours himself into his training routine. Working on his martial arts mostly, honing his reflexes. To help him, he's enlisted the help of a guy called Walton Walker. He's a school friend of Subject Six who worked for Enosh Blake in security after a stint in the army.

While Subject Six constantly asserts he's not using the house as a retreat, Walton very much is. After a car crash in which his wife and twin girls died, he decided to leave his London life and on Enosh's insistence he became the custodian of the country pile Enosh had just bought.

The mansion was meant to be a break-out and team-building hub for Enosh's company, but he was diagnosed just after he bought it so no-one apart from Walton and Enosh had ever actually been in it. Four years later, when I go up, Walton is as close to a doomsday prepper as I've ever seen. He lives off the land, is a walking, talking, mass of rugged sinew and is a strange cross between the ultimate marine and the stereotypical hippy.

But I digress. More on Walton later. Let's go back to Subject Six and the fall-out of his attempt to see his children. The next time I got to speak to him about them and how he was feeling was after his Syria mission, about three months later.

Me

Oscar and Tuppence? How are you feeling about them now?

Subject Six

In what way?

Me

Well we haven't spoken about them for a while. Do you think about them? Are you in touch with them, or Michelle? Will you try to see them again?

Subject Six

Obviously. No. No. What? Why are you looking like that? That's the truth.

Me

Ok. So, you still think you can't see them and carry on doing this?

Subject Six

Doing what?

Me

Your... missions.

Subject Six

I know I can't do both. And I know you disagree about that. Why is that?

Me

I guess I think you're being a bit melodramatic about it. Maybe a bit of a martyr.

Subject Six

Wow. Say what you think, Benji.

Me

But think about it. In all the superhero movies - which I know you watch, I've seen your Netflix account - I always get annoyed by the whole 'I've found a woman, but we have to split up so I can carry on saving the world' thing... it doesn't ring true.

Subject Six

Why not?

Me

It's creating jeopardy and drama and loss and sadness when there doesn't need to be any. In real life who turns their back on what they love like that? Who sees things in black and white like that, so they deny them-selves something they want so much?

Subject Six

Well, your life of no black and white is created by your environment. Middle class comfort. It bubble-wraps you from the sharper ends of life. Now, watch someone put a gun to your child's head and in an instant things become black and white. Forget about what your kid might have done, what the motives of the person with the gun are, those things might be grey, I know that... but the act of a gun being held at your child's head... that is black and white. You understand?

Me

Sure.

Subject Six

When I think about putting my child in that situation again, I have to see it in black and white. Yes or no. And the answer, is no

Me

Right.

Subject Six

But that doesn't mean it's over for me, when it comes to the kids.

Me

How come?

Subject Six

When your kids are alive, what you want as a parent, as far as I see it, boils down to knowing they're alive and happy and then the joy and wonder at following them as they grow into the world and start to achieve things. When I was frozen, the thing that cut me up was that I'd never know what happened to them. Like watching a film and never getting to the end. Well now I get to do that, I get to watch again.

With that, Subject Six ends the interview. I still disagree with his standpoint at that stage, and I'm not convinced he'll never try and see them again, but I can also see in his mind he's squared it off. He's happy with what he's got when it comes to Oscar and Tuppence, which is more than he could have hoped for when he was diagnosed with cancer and when he was frozen.

WHAT'S IT LIKE TO RIDE SHOTGUN WITH A SUPERHERO?

I'm sitting in a helicopter. I've convinced Subject Six to let me come on one of his missions. He's beginning to get up a head of steam and with each successful mission he grows in confidence and determination. The moment he comes back from one operation, he starts on his next. Which is why I ask if I can 'ride-along'.

Mina

What annoyed me the most was being put in the role of nagging, worrying wife. Of course, if the person you love is going to be in danger, going to put themselves in danger, you're going to be nervous. Aren't you? Not just for me, but for the kids too. So I knew being nervous was normal, but what I hated was being forced into the stereotype. Woman stays at home with kids, waits on news of husband who's gone into the danger zone. Checking email, WhatsApp, every five minutes to get that message that lets you know he's come out unscathed, alive.

So the day he set off, I was doubly pissed off. One, because why did he have to put me in that boring, obvious role of fearful female? And two, did he really need to go? I didn't completely see why he needed to go with Subject Six and put himself in danger. I mean the story was about Subject Six, so why not just ask him about what it felt like on a mission, did Benji really need to see first-hand? He said it was like method acting, he wanted to feel it so he could write it... he wanted to go along so he could describe Subject Six in action first hand... but I couldn't shake the feeling it was a macho thing. Maybe Benji wanted to show Subject Six, show himself, that he too had the balls to go on a mission.

Let me just state here that Mina and me worked all this stuff through. And for the record we compromised, because isn't that always best (and yes, I know how smug and annoying she'll find me writing this)? But we worked it all out after, which put me in the position of power, slightly: because by then I had come back alive, although not totally unscathed.

The mission Subject Six allows me to join him on, on paper, isn't that exciting. On the way, after the initial buzz of getting into a helicopter, I'm feeling a bit disappointed at how low key it seems compared to some of his other trips, but once we land the adrenalin kicks in.

For my own safety, and I mean safety from the law, I can't tell you how we get to the target site but we land a mile from it. I'm not recording during the mission in case my device could be picked up, so I know I'm going to be relying on my memory when it comes to using this for the book. So I'm alert, keen to take everything in.

Walton drops Subject Six and me off and is going to meet us at the same place in 12 hours. We check our kit and set off. The target is Winona Standish. She's one of the world's richest people and we're on our way to one of her many mansions, the one she calls home in the magazine interviews she gives.

Winona Standish, Subject Six, explains to me when he first sets out the reason for the mission he's taking me on, is in the 1% club he used to want to be in. Now he despises it. The people who make up 1% of the earth's population but who own 99% of the world's wealth. Subject Six always stresses that not everyone in the 1% club is inherently evil, but the fact that the club exists is. As for those members of the club who are purposefully and actively bad, well that's who Subject Six wants to stop.

We have one mile of countryside to cover in the pitch black. For all my talk about going on a low key mission, every step taken that gets us nearer to our destination, my heart starts beating louder and faster. As I walk behind him, looking at the woods surrounding me through my night vision goggles, my skin is tingling, I jerk my head around at the slightest of noises, terrified we might have been found. It takes me back to my days when I followed the army in Iraq. Back then I was single, childless, young, so I had less to lose, but even so, I don't remember feeling quite so on edge.

Before we left I had asked Subject Six about his new role as a - because there is no better term - superhero. Syria had obviously gone down well, and as far as I knew all of his missions had pretty much gone according to plan as well. So how come? I mean before he'd been frozen he'd been a techy geek for the most part. A rich one, sure, and one who liked to spend lots of cash and trying to be the ultimate playboy to counter his nerdy side, but he did spend most of his time in front of a computer. So how did he know he was going to be a natural out in the field, on a mission? How did he know he'd have the balls do this? He said he didn't know, not until he reached Syria and set off alone for the first time. All he knew was that he was doing the right thing, what he had to do, and he hoped that would be enough to force himself to get the mission done.

After thirty minutes that seem like forever and nothing, ahead of me Subject Six crouches down and comes to a stop. Hidden behind and beneath a bunch of bushes and trees I follow his lead and take out my binoculars.

The mansion, our mission, looms into view. I immediately see a guard, can tell he's armed, and regret not listening to Mina. That's the thought swirling around my head. I shouldn't be here.

"As Walton and I thought, ten guards. We'll make our entry over the pool-house. Then we'll be able to disable the alarms in the guard-house and find her safe. Let's go."

I nod.

"You can do this, Benji, I wouldn't have brought you otherwise."

I nod again, my throat too dry to speak. I mean I know he's right. For the past week I've been training with him and Walton and as long as it's Subject Six who does the tough stuff, I'm easily in decent enough shape to climb what I need to climb and follow behind him. Every challenge they set me during training, I passed - something which boosted my confidence about my Dad-Bod no end. That was all in theory, but on the field it's proving to be far harder.

He leads me down the hill to Winona Standish's mansion so we can disarm the cameras (him) and then scale the walls (both of us). Not for the first time, and not for the last let me tell you, a mixture of marvel, disbelief and bafflement rises up as I see him walk straight up to the camera covering the wall we're going to climb over and put it out of action. He's got a piece of kit - from where I'm not sure, that's Walton's job - that overrides the system and loops the last few seconds of footage rather than recording anything new. It's not fool-proof, but while we're in the house it's unlikely anyone will notice we've hacked them.

Sure, Subject Six can't be caught on camera, but I can and the doors he opens, and the things he moves can as well.

"You first," he tells me, "Easy does it."

Subject Six gives me a leg-up and then, I'm up and over and inside the gates. I press myself against the wall. There's a warm ringing in my ears, there's a silent thudding in my chest, and yet over all this hubbub I feel like my hearing is primed and honed. If anyone or anything makes a noise near me I'm so focused I know I'll hear it. My fingers have stopped shaking. The clammy hotness that's been covering me since I left the helicopter has gone. Is this the mission headspace Subject Six has been talking about, is this how I coped in Iraq? He's told me that as soon as he knows he's in danger all the worries go and all you do is focus on the here and now. And that's how I feel. I mean, I'm aware I'm not invincible like he is, but that's just background. Front and centre is what I've got to do.

Subject Six lands silently behind me and I follow his lead. We've both memorised the floorplans which Subject Six managed to get by hacking his old contacts in the insurance and security industry who look after Winona and people like her. Whenever we know a camera is coming up, Subject Six goes ahead and fixes it with another one of Walton's bugs. The guards are all outside the house and no-one else seems to be around.

We make it to the study in good time. Subject Six is prepared for the safe and gets to work on it. I keep watch. Not that we're expecting anyone, but because it would be foolish not to take the precaution. Inside the safe Subject Six is hoping to find documents that will prove Winona Standish's illegal involvement in the trade of minerals that are being stolen from the Democratic Republic of Congo. Winona owns a company who have five employees being held hostage by rebel groups, which is how Subject Six first comes across her. He soon sees through her company as a front. As he unravels her affairs, he discovers she's a key figure in a group of people using force to illegally remove the minerals and natural resources found in the Congo that are used in smartphones and other tech.

It doesn't take Subject Six long to find this out, so why hasn't anyone else? Well, simply because the world looks away. To us, it's only a corrupt country being robbed of its natural resources, so in a way they deserve it. To us, the people who are killed, raped and tortured by the gangs who head up the extracting process of these minerals are only Africans. And on top of that, we really like our smartphones, don't we? We really need them, don't we? Which is why well respected and iconic brands who make our smartphones are also connected to this il-legal trade of the minerals, although by the time they get the minerals they need they are of course classed as legal.

Subject Six looks up at me, "These will do it," he nods, and I know he has what he needs to expose her. We get moving, going back the way we came. And I know it sounds clichéd and corny, but it's just when I start to stu-pidly wish I was on a tougher mission, that the shit hits the proverbial fan.

The first thing we hear is the helicopter. Subject Six stops in his tracks. Laughably, I bump into him.

"That's Walton," he whispers, confused.

I notice his fists clench then I hear the first shot ring out and simultaneously feel like I've been stabbed in the leg. The bullet spins me round and knocks me back. I do see Mina's face flash in front of my eyes - but it's not a romantic thing, it's a 'fuck-she-warned me' and a 'fuck-she's going to be so fucking mad' thing. My hand goes to my leg. The bullet's ripped a hole in my trousers and I can see a deep, open gash. But that's all.

Subject Six is by my side, "A graze. You'll be fine. Let's go."

From where I'm slumped against the wall, we're hidden, but whoever saw us is still shooting through the window. Subject Six is talking to Walton who's been monitoring the real CCTV feed from his helicopter which his bugs have been sending him.

While we were in the study a guard went to the toilet. He got lucky when he saw us through a window. Rather than taking us on immediately he tracked us and raised the alarm. Which means, according to what Walton can see, by the time they start firing we're pretty much surrounded. Bad news. The only bit of good news is it gives Walton time to get into the air and come and get us.

Down the corridor we can hear people running towards us. Instinct tells me that we need to run away, but Subject Six says our only choice is to head towards them. I grit my teeth against the pain, wanting to argue. Then I realise this is the way to the pool and, knowing the layout of the house, that's the only place Walton can land.

They're on us a lot quicker than I thought possible, maybe my wound is slowing me, tethering me. Four men charge around the corner, guns raised.

This time I do think we're dead. I see Mina and the boys. I really do. I'm not exaggerating, here, I'm deadly serious. Their guns rise up in unison. How can they miss? The corridor we're in is like a firing range and we're less than 10m away.

Subject Six screams like a warrior. He charges, waving his arms at them. And thankfully, because I don't decide, I just do, I follow directly in his wake. They fire. They hit. Or three of them do. But he's Subject Six. He takes the bullets and keeps on going. And that is something they've never seen before.

As he ploughs into them he moves fast and quick. A blur of martial arts. I don't see any of them go down but they all do. The more I move, and the quicker I go, the more the pain from my bullet wound rises but I push it away.

Walton's take-off is as quick as Subject Six's attack on the guards and we're away. I'm hit, but I'm ok. I'm grinning like an idiot. Laughing deliriously. I pick my phone out from where I left it and work out which emoji to send Mina.

Subject Six leaks the documents while we're still in the air. Within 48 hours Winona is arrested and on top of that the internet blows up about how western companies are pillaging minerals from Africa. Online outrage builds and builds, celebrities and governments get involved and soon tech and mobile companies are forced to re-examine how they source the things they need. As a result of our raid, it looks like there will be a real change in the lives of the people in the Democratic Republic of Congo.

It's not over, it'll still be a long time before they're fully protected from people trying to steal what their land has, but it's got better. And Subject Six did it. With me, helping... a bit.

WHERE HAS SUBJECT SIX COME FROM?

Subject Six

No-one else spends all their time wondering where they've come from, so why should I?

Me

There's only one of you. It's more important.

Subject Six

How can one be more important than everyone else? That's like a needle in the haystack, why not focus on the haystack?

Me

Well, now we're just talking in clichés.

Subject Six

Asking about why we're here, who made us, how much more clichéd can you get?

Me

Because of… because of how unique you are. How can it not affect you?

Subject Six

I think it's better asking what I should be doing with my time, rather than asking why I have it.

Once I get back from the mission to expose Winona Standish, I shift my focus back to the bigger picture.

Subject Six

I'm actually in the same situation as you are.

Me

In what way?

Subject Six

You're an atheist, right?

Me

A certain type.

Subject Six

What do you mean a 'certain type'? There's only one type. An atheist: someone who doesn't believe in god.

Me

Well, Mina and I would both say we're atheist as in we don't believe in any of the gods that organised religion talk about - but while I think there's nothing, Mina thinks there must be a higher being of some sort... we just don't have the ability to understand it.

Subject Six

Must? Define must.

Me

She says life, and earth, it's just too perfect and too unlikely to be chance... that something has to have planned it, created it.

Subject Six

And you?

Me

I think it just... happened.

Subject Six

What, big bang, evolution, here we are?

Me

I guess… well, no, it's not a guess. I think that, yes, because that's the accepted theory from the best minds in the world.

Subject Six

And before the big bang? You don't think a higher being did that, like Mina does? Or God, or Allah?

Me

No. I don't.

Subject Six

Why not?

Me

It's a feeling, I guess.

Subject Six

Blind faith?

Me

No, I have my eyes open, I think I've looked, and there's no certain answer. Which means, well, it's irrelevant in a way, isn't it? Why worry about before the big bang?

Subject Six

Benji, welcome to my world.

At the same time as I totally understand why Subject Six doesn't want to spend time wondering why, how, what and even who, I totally disagree that it's not important to try to understand how he came to be. Sure, it might be unexplainable - it might turn out to be a what-happened-before-the-big-bang question, but it's still important to investigate.

So, I'm going to set out some of the most common and likely theories that have surfaced about Subject Six, in the papers and online, and break them down to see if I think they hold any weight.

As we go through these theories, I'm aware you'll get alarm bells in your head as some of the things I write don't fit in with what we think we know about Subject Six and his arrival. For instance, some people believe he's a robot, created by the military to become a super soldier. And when I say believe, they've complied documents and even blueprints explaining how he might have been created. They're convinced they have the answer, and yet they have no comeback when you ask why this robot looks like Enosh Blake, and why does he have his memories and mannerisms?

But just because these theories have issues, I still think it's worth looking at them. Because at this stage of my investigation there's so much we don't know, I have to look at anything that has some substance. I need to stay open-minded because closing things down instantly isn't going to get me anywhere.

THE RELIGIOUS THEORY

Carly suggested I try religion, so, I do. I don't go into this line of thinking expecting to find an answer, I'm also not just doing this for the sake of it. Not quite. Sure, I don't believe in God so I don't fundamentally believe Subject Six has been created by a higher being, but I once believed that a being with superpowers didn't exist either. And look how that turned out.

That then, is where my head's at when I begin approaching religions to explore what they think about Subject Six. If millions and millions of people believe there's an almighty power who created us, then surely they'd have an opinion on who created him?

The concepts of resurrections, life-after-death, second comings, are prevalent in most major religions. It's

fascinating and eye-opening to compare the different in-
terpretations of immortality and second birth the various
dogmas have. Seeing as so many faiths have stories about
people coming from back from the dead, and all of them
say that in 2018 and 2019 their gods are watching over us,
I hope they'll engage with the idea that if Subject Six has
come back from the dead, how are they, as a religion, rec-
onciling that with their beliefs? Does Catholicism see him
as a son of God, and what would he have to do to prove
he was - in their understanding, why would God be moved
to create a second Messiah, and is there provision for this?
Do Muslims think that Subject Six could be a prophet?

The people I approach aren't your average 'Joe Public'; I take this to the top, because people on the street are
like the rest of us. They've read the stories about him,
they're gossiping about him, they have their own views
about him. No, I'm interested in those who are in charge
of the theology and the direction of each religion. I contact the Vatican in Italy, the Archbishop of Canterbury,
Sharia Law courts.

What do they say? Quite simply, none of them engage
with me once I get into the specifics of Subject Six.
They've heard the stories of him and they point-blank say
he doesn't fit into their theology. They stonewall me.
Claim he's a hoax, a government weapon, an experiment
gone wrong. Nothing to do with them.

I press them, saying religion is full of miracles, of
people taking it upon themselves to help people, but they
don't respond. I ask whether they would think differently
if he 'came out' as Jewish, or Muslim. If he started telling
the world he was Catholic, would the Pope engage with
him and bring him into the fold? It's all dismissed out of
hand, and why is this?

Jaynet Rootle

The reason I upped and left my Church was the very same reason you seem to be talking of. When I heard we had a Messiah amongst us, sent back down to be an Angel of light, me and my friends just knew this was an act of God. We knew it and yet when we brought it up with our Pastor, he said we were committing a sin. He implied we were worshipping a false idol and told us to forget it. Well, how can you forget a thing like coming back from the dead? Imagine the Lord sending someone down to save us again, only for us to ignore it, again! Don't we ever learn?

This is from an interview with Jaynet Rootle, the founder of one of the first Churches to accept Subject Six as the Third coming: aptly called, The Holiest Foundation of the Third Coming.

Jaynet Rootle

All across Virginia where I live, I found people who thought like I do. We began to meet, to ask questions, to try and make sure we could give the Lord's work the celebration it deserves, and it sure does warrant a celebration. The more we talked it through, the more we started to see it was fear that was blinding our Churches and fathers. They'd been so used to controlling everything about our religion, they didn't want to lose it. As long as they have the Bible as a foundation, they can protect and promote the same message as always, because it's done, it's in the past. So, the fact the Lord was at work again, it scared them and being so big, the Church was slow to move, scared to do so. Which is why we had to start on our own Church. And I'm mighty glad we did so.

Ever since the Syrian story broke, the rumours about Subject Six have been flying around and after each mission that the press finds out about, they ramp up further still. Not much is known about him for certain, still just the basics of his powers, but the idea that he's immortal has come out and so for some time I've been reading people online who say he's a third coming.

In America, there are now over ten movements like Jaynet's, claiming to be religions, who say Subject Six is their figurehead; and around the world I think there are probably over 100. All of these off-shoot religions I've found have links to Christianity; I haven't seen any linked to Islam, Judaism or Sikhism yet. Subject Six grimaces whenever I bring them up, or whenever he sees a member on TV, or in the papers, but isn't it inevitable that people would see him as a miracle? And haven't miracles always been worshipped?

Jaynet Rootle

But that's what he has done. Subject Six coming down, that's God saying hello, that's his way of telling us he's still here, he still cares, and he's someone for us to follow.

To an extent I understand Jaynet's viewpoint. He is godlike, in many ways, there's no denying that and I admire her conviction. What? He's come back from the dead and he's immortal? Well, there's only one way that could happen in this world: God.

But on the flip-side, no. Just no. If none of the major religions are allying themselves to him and laying out a strong, theological argument that links him to their faith, texts and dogma, then I'm not going to truly be able to entertain the fact that he's the product of a higher being.

Until a god, any god, comes down and tells us he exists, I'm going to be looking for a more finite explanation.

THE ROBOT THEORY

There have been arms races since, well, probably since people started fighting over food when they were hunting. In the modern world, it's kind of written in our DNA, isn't it, the knowledge that the armed forces everywhere are constantly seeking the next breakthrough that will give them the edge? So what about Subject Six? Some people online believe he's a synthetic robot who's been created as a new breed of soldier - is this plausible?

Nav Hamed

Ok, so think about the private companies and how much they've invested in robotics in the last few years. Google, Amazon, have put billions into research... not to mention all of the Chinese and Japanese tech companies that are going for this. It's huge, a massive growth industry.

Me

And have they got far enough to do something like this? To create a cyborg like Subject Six?

Nav Hamed is a robotics expert. He's a consultant who's worked for private companies and for the military in the US. Suffice to say, this guy knows his stuff.

Nav Hamed

No way. Not yet.

Me

Are you 100% on that?

Nav Hamed

From the notes you've sent me about him, there's no way any company, any armed force has made anything so advanced that it could do what he does.

Me

What about any crackpot inventors, you know, like Doc Brown in *Back To The Future*? Could anyone have done this... like, on their own, off the radar?

Nav Hamed

A Citizen Scientist? No way.

Me

I like that term. I haven't heard that.

Nav Hamed

There are lots of them out there, especially in robotics, but to get to anywhere decent you need money, you need resources. For a while my job, a bit like what you're trying to do I guess, was to try and find out if anyone was making progress, off radar...

Me

Like who?

Nav Hamed

Everyone, unfriendly governments, friendly ones, big companies setting up robotics divisions, specialist companies. I had to know everything, and like I mean, everything... especially the breakthrough stuff that people wanted to keep to themselves...

Me

And did you manage? Can you really be sure you found out what everyone else was doing? That sounds like a huge job.

Nav Hamed

Can I be 100%, no. 99% certain, yes. Let's say, corporate espionage is growing as fast as robotics and leave it at that.

Me

You're 99% certain no-one can have made him, that's pretty…

Nav Hamed

Listen, there are loads of ways I know this guy isn't a robot someone has managed to create, I could list them all but let's focus on one; in the end it comes down to this guy's skin.

Me

His skin?

Nav Hamed

His regeneration, as your doctor calls it. We can make robotics do some great stuff and, to put it in simple terms, if we were to put out the best soldier robot it would be pretty kick-ass. But one thing it would not have, and not have anything anywhere near it, is skin, flesh, that feel like skin and flesh. And then, on top of that, this skin and flesh regenerates. That type of technology, to make something that can do that, it's just not there yet, anywhere… it's not even close.

Nav, without directly breaking any secrets acts or agreements, sends me some details on what types of robots are out there. He's right, they are kick-ass, I mean these things they're making are awesome and I'd love to include them in here, but I promised Nav I wouldn't, but the thing is - they are not Subject Six.

Nav Hamed

After the Syrian mission, the world I work in went ballistic. At first everyone presumed it was a Special Ops team, of course we did, but when the stories came out it was one guy, then of course, the rumour mill went into overdrive.

Me

Saying what?

Nav Hamed

Well, exactly what you're saying. Who in the hell has created something that could do this? The closest we thought was maybe some kind of drone-soldier, we know that's getting closer...

Me

A drone soldier? Is that what I'm thinking it is.

Nav Hamed

Yup, and they'll be here soon. But once we found it was some kind of... man, some guy, then we knew this wasn't military tech, or any tech. And that's why your man is such hot property... and still is, right?

Me

Oh, yeah.

Nav Hamed

Well, take it from me, that won't change. People I've worked for, and people like that all around the world, will not stop trying to find him and get him. And I mean it. Will. Not. Stop.

Me

Why? Why does he mean so much? What would you do to him if you found him?

Nav Hamed

If I found him? Me?

Me

Yes.

Let me point out here that while Subject Six was happy(ish) to meet with Carly, he refuses point blank to meet Nav the moment I even suggest it. He suffered at the hands of the government scientists too much to want to meet with anyone remotely connected to their industry.

Nav Hamed

Well, from what you told me about how he was treated last time by the Brits, I would not do that. But, hypothetically, if you could understand what it is that allows him to regenerate, to be invincible, then you're probably saving billions of dollars and years and years of research. He's like the missing link to an evolutionary state that we can't even contemplate yet.

Me

Hence why the governments and those like them will keep on trying to find him?

Nav Hamed

Oh, they will find him. I can't believe they haven't yet. Seeing as you know him, I can't believe they haven't done more to you... not wanting to sound too dark... but you know what I mean? It must be because you're a journalist, and all this new transparency and human rights stuff. 10 years ago, you would have been hauled in and...

Me

Ok, Nav, I get the picture.

After our chat Nav sends me some more articles, puts me in touch with some other people in the industry. Everything he says, people agree with. There's no-one in the military tech or robotics industry who's close to being able to create Subject Six and the chances of there being someone unknown who could do it are next to zero. It just can't be done. Yet.

Now that 'yet', has - and I'm sure some of you might have been thinking this, especially the sci-fi lovers amongst you - time-travel connotations. Of course, it does. Because when I asked Nav whether Subject Six could be built in the future, he said of course, simply because anything is possible in the future.

THE GENIX THEORY

So, it doesn't seem like it's divine intervention, and neither is Subject Six some sort of government weapon, a soldier robot. Which leaves us where? Well, one theory that has been put to me is that while he's not the result of any robotics or technological intervention, what if something or someone has enhanced what he was? Either intentionally or accidentally?

Just as the many news journalists did when they first got the details of how Subject Six came down to the earth from his Cryopod, I spend a lot of time trying to go straight to the source for answers: Genix and Fabian Tree. Because they are in many ways the root of all this - sorry, not sorry, for the pun. They're the company that froze him, they're the ones who sent him into space, they're the ones who didn't seem to know he'd fallen out of orbit and they're the ones who've remained totally silent since his arrival. Why is that? Apart from the leak of the client list, nothing apart from rebuttals citing client confidentiality has come from them. Have they got something to hide? Could Subject Six be a result of something they've done?

After months of asking for an interview with Fabian Tree, or simply whether they could give me any information about what happened rather than a flat denial to discuss it, I decide to take things in my own hands and head down to a place I know Fabian Tree will be. A TV awards show where he's up for an award as best reality host. I badger some people I know to swing a press pass and manage to get close to him on the red carpet:

Me

Fabian, Fabian, fantastic series once again.

Fabian Tree

Very kind, we try our best, we really do.

Me

I can tell. Now, one moment of your time, please

Fabian Tree

What publication are you from?

Me

It's about Subject Six…

Fabian Tree

No, no, I won't be talking about that…

Me

…and the accusation I've heard from sources that Genix carried out an experiment on him that changed him.

Here Fabian pauses. He sizes me up. I feel like his prey.

Fabian Tree

We can only talk about this when the time is appropriate. Nice to meet you, keep watching the show.

Now, that's not much. Is it? But reading between the lines, or to be precise, the one line, it does tell me something. That there will be something from Genix at some point. Why they need to wait, I have no idea, but Fabian does give me just enough to believe that there is a narrative to do with Subject Six and Genix worth telling.

Fabian and Genix might be a brick wall for the time being, but remember the guys and the girl from DEBRIS? The group who spotted his Cryopod coming down from orbit? They are the people making the accusations that Subject Six is a result of experiments by Genix. Fuelled by their vendetta against Fabian Tree and Genix, they've been carrying out their own investigations.

Eileen

We've found the guy we were talking about. He's agreed to meet us. You too. Has to be tomorrow - it's father's day, but I think you'll want to be there!

As you can tell from this WhatsApp message, Eileen and Dan and Nicholas summon me to a meeting at the very last minute. Sorry again to Mina and the kids who'd planned something special for me, although I don't know what it was because as a punishment they've never told me. I say that's childish, they say it's deserved. Who knows, perhaps they'd forgotten it was my special day and it's all a ruse?

Anyway, Father's Day 2020, I find myself back in Swindon at DEBRIS HQ. As ever they're keeping a beady eye on Genix and have a huge amount of stories to tell me and gripes to get off their chests. It doesn't take long, though, before we're joined by the 'guy' Eileen messaged me about. His name's Micky Chang and his claim to fame? He's one of the people who created the Cryopod for Fabian Tree. Specifically, Micky was in charge of a chemical compound that people have to drink before being frozen - without getting too technical, it acts like a preservative from the inside, allowing you to be frozen without your body breaking down. How it works I have no idea, but work it does. This is the thing that sets Genix apart from all other cryogenic companies.

Micky's work is well known. As one of Fabian and Genix's star scientists he received a lot of press when Genix launched. Times, though, have changed. It becomes obvious as we go along that Micky is now very much on the side of DEBRIS when it comes to Fabian - although I don't find out immediately what's happened to make him leave the company and make him so angry. His falling out with Genix is why he's come to this meeting, and DEBRIS are keen to grill him on what Fabian's next area of research is. Once we sit down, I start recording.

Micky

Well, stage one of my brief was the pods, stage two was refining the process so that we could be sure the freezing would work in space, with all the challenges involved in sending something into orbit and bringing it down.

Me

Which must have been no easy feat. You must be proud.

Micky

Of course, we broke boundaries. My team and I.

Eileen Raymond

But were you trying to break the laws of nature, that's what we want to know?

Dan Raymond

Absolutely.

Nicholas Singh

What was stage 3, Micky? We have our suspicions. That's how we found you.

Micky

What are your suspicions? Have there been leaks? Genix was always very keen to stop that. Any employee guilty of that... well, let's just say I'm no longer an employee but they conditioned me against speaking to anyone so much, I have to say, it still feels strange. I've been looking over my shoulder all week.

Dan Raymond

Well, don't worry, the only thing over your shoulder right now is a picture of Saturn that Nicholas's little girl painted.

Eileen Raymond

She's quite the artist.

Nicholas Singh

Thanks, guys, I'll tell her. She'll be made up.

Me

So, what, guys, is your theory? Exactly.

Micky

You said over the phone it was to do with this Subject Six fellow?

Eileen Raymond

It's everything to do with him.

Dan Raymond

Look, he went into one of the pods and when he came out he'd changed.

Micky

I've heard about that, but I've seen nothing I'd ever class as evidence. It's all gossip in the papers isn't it?

I jump into a quick - well, five minutes - summary about Subject Six. I must quickly say here how amazed and shocked Micky is. As a self-confessed sceptic, he tells us he's been leaning towards the idea that the whole superhero thing is a hoax and that all the headlines are tittle-tattle and hyperbole. After what I tell him and the proof I give, his mind is changed.

To be honest, after so many months working with Subject Six I have to admit I've become a bit inured to how incredible the facts are - so to see someone like Micky react so openly, and to be so astonished, it reminds me all over again how I felt when I first found out about him. It tells me how important it is that I nail this book; because this truly is a story like no other. I promise to put Micky in touch with Carly - and he has since been helping her analyse her findings - and then push the conversation back to DEBRIS and their theory.

DEBRIS's theory starts with Subject Six and works backwards to Fabian Tree. No surprise there. They think that Fabian Tree is determined to turn Genix into a global superpower and have found lots of direct, and indirect quotes from him that point to the fact he wants to diversify the company's expertise - DEBRIS have looked at the fact he has departments working on rocketry, on human chemistry, on space travel and think he wants to be part of the weapons industry in the future.

With this in mind, DEBRIS believe Fabian Tree is developing a way of turning humans into super soldiers, and Subject Six is either a prototype or an experiment gone wrong. They think Enosh Blake drank different chemicals to every other client and was put into a new type of pod - which is why when he came out he'd changed.

Now obviously, I've had similar thoughts. Of course, I have. Fabian Tree is a shady individual to say the least, Genix is a powerful, hungry company and Subject Six has undergone a life-altering procedure under their watch. So, it's not hard to connect those dots, is it? But the thing that DEBRIS have done, as they proudly show Micky and I, is to start to add some proof to the idea and turn the dots into actual pictures. Or so they say.

One of their biggest bits of evidence is the materials being used in the research labs. Somehow, and they won't reveal how, they've got copies of the lists of supplies of chemicals and equipment Genix have been buying for the past five years. It's slightly beyond me, but they say they've done the research and after Genix launched their Cryopods, the chemicals being brought in changed slightly.

Me

Well, what does that mean?

Nicholas Singh

We're convinced this change in order is the beginning of stage 3?

Eileen Raymond

And having spoken to a couple of scientists, our understanding is that these extra chemicals could be to make changes in the compound they've got that allows freezing.

Dan Raymond

So, we believe that this is when Fabian decided to try and create a chemical that could alter the human form, to freeze it in a way that Subject Six has been

frozen... and whether they meant to do what they did to him, or not, he was the result.

Nicholas Singh

Then when we saw that Micky, a known pacifist I might add, left in acrimony around the same time as the chemical order change we... well, we just thought we were onto something.

Me

Well, Micky, is this the case? Was Genix trialling something?

We all turn to Micky. He takes a deep breath. Winces.

Micky

I'm allergic to dogs.

Nicholas Singh

Pardon?

Micky

And cats.

Dan Raymond

I despise cats. The devil's animal if ever there was one.

Me

Oh, dear.

Nicholas Singh

What Benji?

Me

I think I know what Micky is getting at.

Micky

Stage 3 was pets. People who want to be frozen with their animals. But I can't be near them, which meant as soon as Fabian announced the next stage I told him I couldn't work on them... I left, in acrimony, because

even though I'd done so much for Genix, been at the forefront of their research, they just said well if you can't be in the lab with animals we don't need you. We own all your breakthroughs, see you later.

And just in the way Micky's job goes in a second, so does DEBRIS's theory.

Micky goes on to say he never discussed, or heard anyone talking about, using the tech they use to preserve the bodies to create some kind of invincible soldier. Like he says, when he first hears about Subject Six he doesn't think 'oh stage 3 is working, they've made a superhero', he thinks the press is lying.

THE HOAX THEORY

Shortly after I get home from the Winona Standish mission the Hoaxgate story breaks. In fact, it's the day that I go into the hospital for a check-up to see if I can take the dressing off. I'm sat, waiting to be officially discharged when I get a call from Laura. I record it, because even though I think she's off the Subject Six story it was her who put me onto it and it's better safe than sorry.

Laura Freeman

Before you read it, I want you to know that this is one of those pieces I'm doing as a job, rather than as part of my vocation.

Me

What do you mean?

Laura Freeman

It's just gone up online, on the Post. They'd written most of it but when they found out that I was the one who pitched the Subject Six story out to begin with, they offered me a lot of money to be able to attach my

name to it and run it as an exclusive from the first person on the scene. You see where I'm coming from?

Me

Kind of yes, kind of no.

Laura Freeman

The editorial I wrote, I sound very black and white about it, because being grey doesn't sell...

Me

Unless it's cheap erotic literature...

Laura Freeman

Well, quite. Just remember, I'm not sold on this theory in real-life, but I do think they make some interesting points. Call me after, if you want. I don't think it will affect what you're doing... but I didn't want you to read it out of the blue, ok?

What Laura's talking about is the first allusion in the mainstream press to the theory that Subject Six is, in fact, nothing more than a hoax. It's a line of thinking that picks up quite a lot of traction.

Subject Six

I was wondering when you'd call. Hoaxgate is on your mind, is it?

Me

So, you've seen it?

Subject Six

Yup.

Me

Anything else? I mean, how do you feel about it?

Subject Six

I'm seriously not that bothered as long as they stay away from my family.

Me

You're not bothered because as long as your message is getting out there, you don't care how?

Subject Six

Pretty much.

Me

But what if people who think you're hoaxing decide what you're doing is fake too?

Subject Six

There's not much I can do about haters, Benji, I've just got to hope enough of us humans have enough humanity...

Me

And do they?

Subject Six

I used to be certain they did.

Me

And now?

Subject Six

And now I'm dealing with the worst of it every day.

The hoax theory is founded on the idea that Subject Six isn't possible, and therefore he doesn't exist. As in he doesn't exist as he wants us to believe. In the article Laura put her name to, and the editorial she wrote to accompany it, the mantra is Subject Six is the legend somebody has created in order to try to bring about change.

This theory has done the rounds online for a few weeks, without much traction, until journalists and experts begin to hone in on the fact that Subject Six is most probably Enosh Blake.

No-one knows for sure, and until this book he's never officially confirmed it, but after Syria the identity of who this person is goes under intense scrutiny. They know Genix is involved and as Subject Six carries out more missions, a few eye witnesses come forward with vague descriptions. On top of that, speculators, profilers and psychologists of every description turn up on news programmes and in articles saying we're looking for someone with narcissistic tendencies who loves risks and knows how to lead.

Eventually, they get what they're after - the list of Genix clients is leaked. About 80% of people who've used the company are over 60, 10% are children frozen by their parents, which leaves a very small number of possibilities. Based on the physical descriptions and mental profiles, the article claims that realistically, Enosh Blake is the only person who could be Subject Six. Out of respect his family are left alone, mostly, and neither Michelle nor anyone else ever confirms anything but, as you can tell, they have got their guy. They have got it right.

With the idea that Enosh is Subject Six, The Post and Laura put bones to the hoax theory and make it stand-up. Because, with Enosh centre-stage you have someone with the ability, power, money and, frankly, balls, to try and pull off a hoax like this.

The story goes that Enosh Blake has achieved everything he wants in business. Like many ridiculously rich entrepreneurs he starts to look into humanitarian causes he can help - perhaps born from the idea of getting better PR for himself, for his business, perhaps born out of an egotistical desire to be seen as a leader of people, a solver of problems; perhaps simply because he wants to use his money to help people without it. But as he looks into the charities he could help, or foundations he could start, he sees stagnancy. The world of philanthropy is full of grand gestures but not great results. He sees money going nowhere and not making any difference.

Laura, being the great journo that she is, digs out an interview that Enosh once gave to a journalist at a music festival just after it was announced that the G12 had failed to get a huge climate change initiative off the ground. In the footage, he rails against the people in power - essentially he says that politics is too short-term for anyone currently in charge to really try to make long-lasting change because all they want is quick wins that generate good headlines.

Laura's article proposes that because he's fed-up with the powers that be and the humanitarian avenues on offer, Enosh begins to plot how he might inspire people to act differently. To be precise, he comes up with the idea of Subject Six. To help back-up their point, Laura's team dig out a seemingly endless number of photos of Enosh attending superhero film premieres and professing his love of all things comic-book.

So how does he do it? Well, they say, he fakes an illness, he fakes being frozen, he fakes his landing, he fakes being picked up by the government and then he starts going on missions. It's the oldest trick in the book - and by book we're talking the Bible - to inspire people to follow you, become more than a man. Then lead by example and try to make the world a better place by stopping corruption and the bad guys.

Ok, you're asking, that's fine in theory, but how does he fake all this? And would he really go to such lengths to do it? First, the hoax theory starts with the how. The article points to Enosh Blake's technical capabilities - he would be more than capable of faking doctor's notes (especially as he's a private patient, having not been with Michelle anymore by the time he becomes ill) and colluding with Genix he could fake his freezing and landing too - to clarify, at this stage Genix have never commented publicly on anything to do with Enosh or Subject Six.

I guess those bits are plausible, but surely being picked up by an armed team, that's harder to fake? And being held by the government in a detention centre. And going through the courts. Surely, I tell myself as I read Laura's article, surely he couldn't have faked that?

Well, this is when Laura comes into her own. One of the biggest questions I've had about Subject Six, that's been there since the start, is how is he arrested so quickly? Think back to what happened that day. The pod comes down and lands in the sea - and DEBRIS, remember, say they're pretty sure that no-one else notices it apart from them. Then the pod drifts to the shore and Subject Six swims to the beach - again, while some people do spot the pod, no-one spots him coming ashore. He just looks like someone who's been for a swim. So, no-one's noticed the pod coming down to earth, no-one thinks there's anything strange about Subject Six on the beach, then he orders a drink. Then he's surrounded by armed police and led away. How does that happen? Who calls them?

Laura, and the article, suggest this is a set-up and have some evidence that they say backs this up. Knowing Enosh has links in the insurance and security industry, Laura finds out that one of the private companies that provide security personnel for the government are TDB. Following the rise of terrorist threats, they're one of the companies who provide armed cops on the streets - and, guess who's one of the main shareholders? That's right, Enosh Blake. No-one has confirmed for sure, but having looked at rotas and squads it's highly likely it was a TDB squad who swooped on Brighton Beach that Saturday evening and picked up Subject Six. And the detention centre he was taken too? Well, after Laura's article I did some digging and remember the guard who talks to me about Subject Six escape? Issy? Well, turns out she's only ever been an employee of TBD - who look after the contract for the centre.

So, the believers in the hoax argue, Enosh engineers his capture, ensures his own people are the ones who look after him in the centre and then gets out. Why does he do all this? Why not just come land back on earth and get to work? Well, couldn't it all be about his legend, about creating hype? And it could also, Laura suggests, help him keep the government off his back. Because having been released by them, something he knew he could take an educated gamble on, he protects himself from undue attention in the future. Something he wants to avoid, aware that some might see his actions as vigilantism.

But what, I guess you're asking, about the physical side of things? How does he fake that? According to the article, it's all fake prosthetics, misdirection and the only TDB employees, his employees, and other allies of Subject Six have been able to examine him. Being invisible they put down to some secret tech and being an amazing fighter they put down to body armour, training and him generally being really tough. They even try to suggest that Subject Six has always been immune to pain, like the girl Carly speaks about. They bring out some people who used to know him who say they've never seen him get hurt even when he should have, so perhaps he's simply using the powers he already had?

Now obviously, Laura and the writer of the article aren't privy to the knowledge I have about Subject Six. Which is why I don't buy into the hoax. When, I speak to Laura, and tell her that I've seen him being opened up with my own eyes, she suggests that Carly could be in on the secret too and could have helped him fake it. When I tell her I saw him run at the guards with guns, she puts it down to him relying on his legend to mess with the guards' heads and the convenient fact he could be wearing a suit he knows will protect him

I've spent some time going over this theory, because it's a strong one and I think it's worth examining but it's also time to leave it. To finish, though, it's worth bearing in mind how Laura ends her editorial. She says Enosh was always brilliant. Always known for thinking like no-one else and being able to surprise people with strategies and plans. And she thinks this, the Subject Six hoax, is his defining moment. Far more important than anything he's done before. You see, Laura doesn't end the article criticizing him for this apparent hoax. She praises him for it.

THE SUBJECT SIX MONTAGE

I should probably point out that the next time I see Subject Six, when we talk about Laura's article again, he's not entirely 'not that bothered' about the Hoaxgate article as he said to me on the phone. In fact, he's pretty pleased. There's still a huge ego in there, and her article validates him, pushing him onwards. The only downside would have been if Michelle and his kids had been hounded once his name was out in the public domain, but he's got security looking after them and after an initial swarm around the house, it seems that the press pretty quickly realise he isn't hanging out with them at their home and go away.

Instead, spurred on by successful missions and endorsements like Laura's, Subject Six and Walton power on. Now, there's no way I can cover every one of Subject Six's missions in detail. Which is why, in time-honoured tradition, it's time for a montage. Of sorts.

I imagine many people will have followed the stories in the papers and online at the time. Someone set up a fake twitter account for him, on Reddit people were predicting where he was going to strike next, Buzzfeed got millions of views with a very funny list of people pretending to take selfies with him (essentially just people with their arm around thin air). There's another list of best things to say to Subject Six if you ever bump into him in a supermarket.

There's a genuine sense of excitement about what he's doing, a real feel-good factor exists as he goes about his work. I mean, he's this real superhero! And it's helped by the way he goes about it.

From the start he always asserts he's not simply a vigilante, which he says implies violence. Subject Six admits he has to use violence at times, but not always. He's not just hurting people because they're hurting others. He's not randomly patrolling the streets on the look-out for trouble. He sees himself more as a surgeon, having to make small incisions, cuts, in order to root out the illnesses. The cancers.

For the first time, someone is going out there and making a difference. Obviously, the police take down bad guys, but they're the police, they're tainted. Subject Six on the other hand is new and fresh and… well, incredible. People embrace what he's trying to do. For a few months, we all get caught up in a groundswell of optimism and energy. After so many bad stories of bombings and wars and corruption, there's now a way to make things right.

It even filters down to my kids. They become obsessed by Subject Six. They want to be him when they play, renaming their action figures after him and talking about what he's going to do next.

As a slight aside, one night at dinner they start comparing me to Subject Six and obviously, I come off pretty badly. Apparently, all I do is sit at my computer and write boring books. I'm not a hero, they tell me. Which of course I'm not, but I do get the urge that night to tell them my secret. That I might not be Subject Six, but I do know him. During this time, as a cover to protect me, my family and Subject Six, I've officially just signed a deal with my publishers to write a book about corruption amongst the richest 1% of the population. For the moment, I have to go about my investigations into Subject Six as quietly as possible. I can't tell my kids the truth even though I want to, so they'll love me more and respect me more - because that would compromise everything.

Right, enough about me lying to my children, back to the montage. Taken from sources I've found through websites, newspapers and emails and interviews I've carried out in the lead-up to this book, here are some pieces of eye-witness testimony that show the growing impact of Subject Six and highlight some of the missions he called out.

Holden Mensah - witness in Paris

I know it sounds geeky, but the moment I knew it was him I got out my phone and started filming - you know to see if it was true, about him not being visible on camera?

So, there were these bank robbers, wearing the Usain Bolt masks, and apparently Subject Six had been waiting for them when they came out of the bank and he just set about them while he waited for the Police to arrive.

By the time I got there two were down, not dead, injured and he was dealing with the rest of them. I could see him fighting this guy who had a knife and then when I looked down at my phone through the viewfinder, all I saw was this Usain Bolt lookalike slashing at thin air with a machete. It was a total mindbender.

The Police came soon, and he'd managed to keep eight of the robbers by the bank, and everything they'd stolen. Two robbers had managed to get away, but apparently, they got picked up later that day, all because of Subject Six, and man were his moves good, I wish I had been able to film him! But anyway, I still get to say I saw Subject Six take down the Bolt Brigade.

Nev Hitchens - witness in London

I'd been campaigning for the STAND 35 group since the beginning. All of them were single mums and when I heard that they were losing their homes, so even more posh twats or bloody foreign owners could knock down their building and put up yet another block of flats none us locals wanted, then I knew I had to help.

We got a lot of press at the time and we even got some famous comedians and actors to come and join us, but in the end what does that do apart from create headlines. Does it actually do anything? Most of them are luvvie duvvies who go back to their mansions at the end of the day, not like my 35 mums and their kids.

Anyway, one thing the press did get us, I have to say, is in touch with Subject Six. I was cycling to work one day, and there he was, cycling beside me. Along the bloody road. I almost fell off when he said who he was! He knew everything about us, he even knew the names of some of the mums and he had a proposition - did I want him to help? Was he joking? Of course I did! Yes please, he'd been exposing cheats left, right and centre and at STAND 35 we knew our case was as dirty as it gets. So yes please, Mr Six, hack away, break and enter away, whatever it is, do it!

One morning, I see in the news there's been a break-in in the City, at the offices of the bastards trying to sell the property. Seems like a roof-top entry and no-one's quite sure how the robbers have made it in - hence the article, everyone loves a bit of whodunit, don't they? But I know and let me tell you, invincible or not, climbing up that building is about the craziest thing I've ever heard.

Anyway, sure enough, that day Subject Six asks me to convene a meeting with all the mums. What strikes me, as soon as I see him is he doesn't exactly look happy. When I ask him why, he says because he hasn't found any corruption, anywhere, the deal is clean, legal, eve-ryone's paying their tax and obeying the rules and what-not. They're being greedy, sure, but no-one's doing an-ything illegal.

So some of the mothers say why call us here? Which is when he gets out this folder and tells us that he was so angry at not being able to help, that these ladies were going to lose their homes and that it was going to be ok with the law, that he decided to overstep his normal boundaries. You see he went into the personal folders of the head guys and on three of them, he found some, well, shall we say compromising info, photos and the like, of them getting up to no-good on a few work trips, prossies, brothels, you get the picture. He asked us what we wanted to do? Did we want to try and stamp out the deal using these photos as blackmail? He said he wasn't proud, but thought that if it saved the homes of 35 fam-ilies, it might be worth it. Without going into things too much, well, we won didn't we?

The De Muniot Twins - witnesses in international air-space

Tyler

It was without doubt the most awesome thing I've ever seen. We were right next to the wing of the plane, so quite far back from the terrorist fuckhead who'd hi-jacked us.

Casey

I didn't see who was flying the other plane. All I saw was that someone was standing on the wing and coming near us. The hijackers hadn't seen it so I nudged Tyler, making sure no-one could see.

Tyler

I knew, instantly, who it was. Who else could do something like that? At first I was sure he was going to jump from the wing onto our plane and then do something awesome to get inside, but he did something even cooler.

Casey

You think it's cool? I think it's kind of sad.

Tyler

Sad? Why? Because he used a kid? No freaking way! He saved over 200 people in that plane, and who knows about on the ground? So one kid is traumatised for a bit. A kid whose Dad is a jihadi fuck, big deal.

Casey

Well I guess I just found it sad it had to happen at all.

Tyler

Jeez. I hope you never come back as a hero... that's the thing about Subject Six though, he thinks outside the box, he's got his own goddamn box. He finds out about a plane hi-jacking, finds who the terrorist is, gets the police to find the fuckhead's family and puts a gun to the son's head then goes and flies his own plane up and gets so close to the plane he can show the terrorist what's going on back home. Crash this plane and say goodbye to your first-born, jack-ass, or land and give yourself up! Genius!

Lyndi Patel - witness in Amsterdam

She was a pick-up I'd had a lot. Apparently, she often asked dispatch for me by name and most often I'd drive her to the red-light zone and to a place she liked. A classy one, but a cat-house all the same.

She always invited me up, said I could pick any man or any woman I wanted to join us, could help myself to champagne, and that I could keep the metre running and she'd pay the fare in the morning.

I'd always said no before, cab-driving isn't much, but it is honest. That week though, I was having money troubles and I did find her sexy and I was about to say yes when the top floor windows of the place blew out and a body landed on my bonnet.

Then the building erupted with gun-fire, it seemed like from every floor. It was mayhem, I tried to drive away but the body had hit hard and I couldn't get the engine started.

I saw one of the girls in the windows grab a fire extinguisher, smash the remaining shards of glass and then run away to escape. She was being chased by this big skinhead guy who was waving a knife at her. She tripped and then he was on her, dragging her up by the hair. I was about to get out when I saw this guy jump out from a window above and with one punch he had the skinhead down and was calming the girl.

It was Subject Six and in the next five minutes I watched him save all these girls who'd been illegally trafficked into the country and drag out all the guys who'd been keeping them there. He was incredible.

When the Police arrived though, he disappeared instantly. Didn't even wait around to talk. He saw the sirens, the flashing lights, jumped on a motorbike and drove away.

Johnny Malcolm - witness in Birmingham

I'd seen the march a few times. It made my skin crawl, really, to see the skinheads and racists legitimised by being able to walk through the streets. It overlooks my flat, one of the roads they finish up on and as I sat in my living room I heard them chanting, shouting. Horrid stuff. Then I heard a scream and I stood up and saw that there was a group of them chasing four, well I could only assume Muslims. Two were women, wearing Burkhas and two young looking guys.

I got my phone out and called the police, I mean there were coppers around but this did not look good. They were being chased down the street, coming towards me. The skinheads were throwing stuff, bottles, cans, anything they find on the street.

My flatmate was with me and saw that the four of them were heading straight for another group of the racists. She tried to shout out to them, to get them to go down a side-street, but when they looked up they suddenly ducked. I thought at first it was because someone had thrown something at them, but it wasn't, it was fucking incredible, Subject Six on a zipline. He went right past the window, so freaking fast, down to where he'd shot this hook into the wall. In one motion he rolled onto the floor and called the four Muslims to him and then stood there, looking hard as nails.

Man, it makes me laugh just thinking about it! The skinhead twats kept coming forward, mouthing off and then as soon as he turned to them, or stepped forwards they'd run back. One guy, holding off about 100 drunks, it was immense.

Sallie Armeson - witness in Calais

It was only my first week as a volunteer in the camp and I have to say it was more distressing than I thought possible. On my first day I'd been about 40m from a young Iraqi man who set himself on fire to highlight how young men like him were being lost in the camps. You see only women, children and families were being moved on - you haven't heard about that? No, well that's the point he was trying to make with his death, but not even that worked.

Anyway, back to Subject Six. You see, within days of arriving I was shocked to see how much and how bad the crime was. I don't know why I was so surprised, I mean what else is there, these people are living in absolute squalor, desperate and mostly only have people like me to turn to if anything goes wrong. The most terrible crime, the one that really got me, was that every day young children were snatched from their families and would be gone forever. I mean can you imagine? Getting all the way here, risking your life, seeing other children die along the way, only to lose them once you arrived?

There were rumours about who was helping the child abuser gangs but the local police didn't have the resources. Neither did we. One day I was helping a family with their papers when a cry went up, a 3-year old was missing. The camp, which had been quite calm (for the camp) suddenly reared up into madness.

The first thing I saw of it was after a scream. I was near the edge of the camp and ran towards the gate and there he was, Subject Six, just like I'd read about. There was one guy down on the ground near him and he had six more backed against the fence. I could see a gun, some had knives. Two were volunteers and one holding a baby and at first I didn't quite know what I was looking at - but then a woman, the mother, started shouting; the volunteers were the ones who had stolen the baby.

Subject Six was telling them to give the girl back and to stand down, but one man with a gun aimed it at him, another aimed his at the girl. Her mother screamed and then, without me even having time to understand it Subject Six went from being completely still to a blur. It sounds silly, but that's what it was like. He threw two knives in a flash, hitting the two gunmen in the shoulder and then launched himself into them as they dropped their arms.

The mother screamed, but Subject Six had the girl in his arms almost straight away and then rolled her, and I mean rolled her, away from the fight before he leapt up and took the rest of them out. He just walloped them.

HOW SUBJECT SIX STARTS WORKING WITH OTHER PEOPLE

It's pretty obvious that Subject Six's arrival and what he sets out to do begins well and continues well for a long time. The number on his wrist keeps counting but it doesn't bother him because for now he's making the most of his second chance. But as with everything, it doesn't last. Bubbles always pop.

The initial burst of optimism can't carry on forever. Subject Six is no longer something new and novel and having amazed the world with his arrival and smashed all expectations, he now has to start matching them. Which is easier said than done, especially when you've been put on a pedestal.

It's in May 2020 that the first real issue occurs. He learns that in the Philippines there's a village that's being terrorised by a drugs gang. He's on his way back from Australia where he's helped the police uncover the evidence they need to bring down a neo-Nazi group and decides to step in and help the village instead of flying directly home. He manages to recover two teenage girls who the gang have kidnapped and have been doing unimaginably horrible things too and then leads the police to the cartel's HQ where they're busted for having large amounts of heroin.

The problem is, this gang aren't just any old gang. In a bid to return order to the streets of some parts of the

Philippines the President has allowed vigilantism. If ordinary citizens see someone breaking the law - drug-dealing, prostitution - then they can step in. And stepping in means that people are shooting these criminals before calling the Police and telling them what crime they saw the now dead person committing. As long as they have evidence, or enough witnesses, they're good to go and it's signed off as a lawful killing of a criminal.

It doesn't take a genius to guess that this legal lynching is being corrupted, even the President admits it is, but he also says that on the most part this way is better than what he could achieve just using the Police. So it goes on. The gang Subject Six takes down has been using the cover of vigilantism to wipe out all of their direct rivals. They've killed hundreds, maybe thousands of criminals in the past year, making them one of the President's most useful, or successful, squads. And by cleaning the streets of rivals, they've taken control of them.

Subject Six knows the background before he goes into the village. Walton and him carry out as much due diligence as possible before they act on every mission. He knows the gang have been killing in the name of the state and is aware that they'll claim they've taken over this village because it's full of criminals. But that doesn't stop him going in. In fact, it makes him want to do the mission even more.

The President, on hearing this leading squad has been stopped by Subject Six, reacts in anger (to be clear, Subject Six doesn't kill any of them, he disarms them, locks them up for the Police and then leaves, but before the cops arrive, a mob of angry locals who've fallen prey to this gang turn up and kill all of them). The President says Subject Six is a war criminal, he says he's a foreign power who's forced his way into the country and interfered in matters that don't concern him. Supporters of Subject Six fight back, saying the mission exposes how corrupt the Philippines has become under this legal vigilantism.

The row escalates and won't stop. For the first time, Subject Six starts getting a concentrated amount of bad press. The President is a powerful man; millions of people support him and are swept up in a tide of nationalism as they put the issue of the state-backed civilian killers out of their minds and take to the streets to march against Subject Six. Within days he's officially banned from the country, outlawed from setting foot in the Philippines and soon, across the world, more people jump on the bandwagon.

Now this may seem like a classic superhero turn of events - superhero is misunderstood and soon becomes hated, before he convinces the world he is actually a good guy. But, it's really not. That's not the point I'm trying to make. He doesn't give a damn about the President using rhetoric to badmouth him (because it's the President's corruption he wants to expose, he expects the guy to fight back) and there's not a moment later where he convinces the world he's a hero after all. The crux of this, is that it gets Subject Six thinking about how picks his missions. The fall-out from the Philippines made him reconsider whether only focusing on his own targets was the best way to go - perhaps having some partners and support might help, even though creating relationships was bound to bring its own complexities.

Subject Six

The first time they got in touch I ignored it. Without knowing Walton, though...

Me

Sorry, hang on, why did you ignore it? Were you scared?

Subject Six

Scared?

Me

That they were trying to capture you again?

This is from a conversation we have at the mansion, when Subject Six tells me the British government have been trying to recruit him.

Subject Six

No, we knew they were doing that. We were monitoring the people who were trying to do that.

Me

Monitoring how?

Subject Six

Technical ability. I said a long time ago that we're now in a world where private companies and individuals will always know more than governments when it comes to tech.

Me

Ok, so part of the intelligence services are looking for you. What did these other people want?

Subject Six

She called herself Cynthia Barkley and for a couple of weeks I had no idea what she wanted. I cut her off.

Me

Until Walton...?

Subject Six

Until Walton came to me, said he'd been doing some digging into her.

It's about time to say that at this time Walton refuses to talk to sit down and talk to me on the record. When I'm with Subject Six and him at the house he's perfectly civil, and when he relaxes we get along great, but, for reasons he never even gets close to explaining, he won't talk to me directly on microphone. If Subject Six tells him, he'll let me record their conversations, but nothing one-on-one. Not at this stage. It's always frustrating when you miss out on a valuable source, but I completely respect his choice and that's why we don't have Walton's voice during these parts of the story.

Me

And what did he say?

Subject Six

That she was someone we should listen to.

Me

Are you glad you did? Given what's happened?

Subject Six

Yes, no. Look, I couldn't just shut myself off, I knew that. I wanted to help the world, the whole world, and to do that you can't act like an island. Especially not now I was beginning to rack up enemies.

In his initial assessment of Cynthia Barkley - not her real name, an alias - Walton gets it spot on. She's an incredible woman in every respect. Born in Hong Kong to a pair of British bankers, schooled in a private co-ed in a sleepy English town, she graduates from Cambridge and goes straight into a career in war journalism before she's approached by the government and becomes an intelligence agent for the secret services. Her proposal for Subject Six is a simple one. Although why and how she's making it isn't.

Me

So, I know we haven't got long so I'll cut to the chase. The idea to use Subject Six, that was yours?

Cynthia, or the woman who calls herself that, gives me ten minutes on the phone. Why such a short time? I don't think it's a risk thing, if she's truly worried talking to me could land her in trouble then she wouldn't talk to me at all. I think it's because everything she ever does is focused, efficient and to the point. She says something once; she's not going to waste time saying it again. In the emails we exchange setting up the call she uses Textspeak. Not one message is more than five, abbreviated, words long.

Cynthia

Not entirely. Someone made the quip we should enlist him the moment the story broke after Syria.

Me

And this someone was…

Cynthia

Of no interest to you.

Me

OK, so this person, they make a joke and then…

Cynthia

Trying to turn him into an asset was a logical thought. But not one anyone would seriously contemplate.

Me

How come?

Cynthia

At the time, with all the rumours flying around that we'd had him and then been forced to let him go, no-

one wanted to go anywhere near him. It was too political, too steeped in fuck-ups and pressure.

I should point out here that Cynthia thinks Subject Six is handed his freedom by the courts after he wins his case, not that he escapes and then has it ratified later.

Me

Yet you did?

Cynthia

My role included running assets around the world to help us. It's not a transparent thing, it's murky and secretive, because it needs to be to protect lives. Every time I saw the news of what he was doing, it made me jealous. Eventually I figured that if I could enlist Subject Six's help, no matter how difficult handling him might be, it would be worth it.

Me

So, no-one else knew you'd reached out to him?

Cynthia

Not at first. It was my operation. I spent a long time working on how to get a message to him and once I did I set out my proposition.

Me

Which, as I understand it, was to use him to assassinate someone?

Cynthia

Essentially that's correct, yes.

Me

Is that something you did a lot on the government's behalf. Try to get people to kill for you?

Cynthia

Of course. Don't be so naïve.

The way she spits that last sentence out at me reminds me completely of Subject Six.

Me

That first target, how much did you plan who you put on his radar? Did you have one name to give, or a list of potential people you selected from?

Cynthia

I'd profiled the things he'd been doing. There was a clear pattern of the type of people he was trying to stop, or get at, and so yes, I made sure I gave him someone he couldn't resist.

And she gets it bang on. After the Philippines, Subject Six is determined not to veer from the path he's chosen, but now he's looking at his next mission through a new, more critical lens.

Me

So, who were you thinking of next?

Subject Six

I was going to go to America for the first time. A risk, but one I was prepared to take as long as I could get it right.

Me

What would it have been?

Subject Six

Well, I guess the guy's dead now so there's no harm in saying.

Me

Dead?

Subject Six

Thankfully.

Me

Killed?

Subject Six

Yes, no, probably. The guy was an evil fucker in every way so he deserved it. In fact, he wasn't evil in every way…because in his mind he was pure as the driven snow.

Me

So, who was he?

Subject Six

Derren Defey.

Me

The gun guy? He's dead?

Subject Six

Heart attack. Yesterday, as it happens. I'm surprised you know him, he tended to hide in the shadows.

Me

I once did a long-form story on the gun lobby in America after the Kindergarten Massacre. In between my other books. That guy's the worst. He stopped gun law after gun law from being passed. I spoke to so many people who said, without him laws in the States would have stopped 100s of killings by now, and he led the campaign to stop every piece of legislation. I mean he's an utter, utter cunt.

Subject Six

Language!

Me

He was though. You're right, I am glad he's dead.

Subject Six

You are? 100%?

Me

Damn right, what type of mission were you planning?

Subject Six

Ultimately I wanted to stop him, but I knew I would have to tread carefully. It was a polarising mission if ever I saw one and I was trying to avoid any flak… at the same time the more I found out about him the more I knew he had to be taken down.

Me

You were going to kill him?

Subject Six

Not necessarily, that would have got the Americans right after me… not exactly wise.

Me

Ok, so you were going to look into his accounts? His lobbying records, try to expose him as dirty?

Subject Six

I would have done… hang on, why are you looking at me like that?

Me

Because when I'd done that piece, I'd tried that angle.

Subject Six

And?

Me

I suspect that you and Walton have more skills in hacking and digging like that than me, but I got nowhere. The scary thing about that guy was even though he was doing the work of the gun companies who funded his operation, I could not get anything dirty on him. He wasn't that rich. He didn't do it for the money, he did it for some twisted belief that gun laws would impact on his supposed freedom, his rights as an American. Kids are getting shot by kids who can easily get hold of assault rifles and every time he's militant about not trying to stop it. No compromise, no nothing. Jeez, did you see the speech after the Kindergarten shooting? Guy was an evangelical manic and the scariest thing was he was working for belief, not money. I think you might have had to kill him.

Subject Six

Really? You think that? Do you think I'd have been justified to?

Me

From what I could see, his lobby would have relented and compromised if he hadn't been there. Many others were in it for the money and under pressure to allow some gun control... he was the one who vowed never to give in to the government. Without him, they wouldn't have been so powerful or so hard line.

Subject Six

So, you're saying if there's total proof a death will make things better, pre-medicated killing, assassination is ok?

Me

I think I am.

What to do with Derren Defey is on Subject Six's mind when Cynthia makes contact. Once Subject Six and Walton engage with her, she makes it clear that she thinks his next target should be a guy called Ronnie Osman. He's a British-Turkish guy who's making loads of money helping young guys get from Europe to training camps in Syria and Iraq. She presents them with a document about his network, shows the projections that without him recruiting and then helping people cross borders, the flow from the West to the terrorist camps will fall as much as 60%.

As I'm sure you can tell, that is a target right up Subject Six's street. You can see how tantalising taking this guy out must be. So, he thinks about it seriously. The sticking points being one, exactly what 'taking him out' means; two, will Subject Six's involvement with the government be kept secret; and, three, why are they passing him a mission and why do they need him in the first place? If they're so sure he should be a target, why don't they do their own work?

You decide. What involvement? Resources.

That's the message that comes back from Cynthia. And it's enough.

Subject Six puts Derren Defey on the backburner and starts to prep for a mission in Istanbul, fully aware that he doesn't want a repeat of his last mission in the Philippines. Well, let me correct that. In terms of his mission going according to plan he wants exactly the same result. What he's desperate to avoid is a backlash. But, he figures, what is more clear-cut at the moment than taking out someone who's making money from terrorism?

SUBJECT SIX'S MISSION ISTANBUL

Subject Six

As I write this, we're on a boat. Ridiculously it's called the Wet Dream. Walton rented it under a false name from someone who obviously doesn't speak English very well. We're looking to dock in Volos, Greece. From there we'll make our way back to England but before we get there, while everything is still fresh in my mind I want to record exactly what's just been done. And why. And by who.

If I was a bald-headed American character actor playing a General in a movie I'd call the Ronnie Osman mission a cluster fuck. That's why Subject Six is so quick to get down on record a debriefing for Cynthia. He guesses the aftermath of the mission could easily get messy and he wants to get his version of why he had to do what he did, down on the table instantly.

Subject Six

I arrived in Istanbul eight days ago and immediately began watching Ronnie Osman at the address I'd been given. During his stays in the city he always rents big houses under false names and this one was a walled mansion by the Bosporus, close to the city centre.

One of the members of his entourage was the person Cynthia had put me in touch with, a Turkish woman, in her 40s, who'd been working with the US and UK for

*some time helping them monitor Ronnie Osman's oper-
ation. Her name was Jade Yakin, she travelled with him
as a doctor and according to my information had started
to leak news on Ronnie Osman after one of the wannabe
terrorists he'd helped pass from Turkey to Syria had
killed three members of her family in a suicide-bombing
attack at an airport.*

Subject Six's account of Istanbul isn't the only one
that exists. I've been able to track down some other ver-
sions of what happened which corroborate what Subject
Six says. The only main angle that I don't have is the government's - they supposedly don't want to give any details
in case it jeopardises national security. All Cynthia tells
me is that it's a success because Ronnie Osman is taken
out of the picture. But there's no way you can class the
mission as purely a success.

It's important to hear these different POVs because it
puts Subject Six's role in perspective and, for me, shows
that despite the criticisms, his actions are justified. Doing
what he's doing, as in being on the frontline and putting
himself in dangerous situations, is not always going to be
easy. Not every mission can be as well executed as when
he freed the Syrian Four - and sometimes things go
wrong. But that doesn't make him bad. In fact, how he
acts when he's in the worst situations can be a better sign
of who he is and what he's trying to achieve, than when
things are going smoothly.

Subject Six

*From what I was told she was trusted by Ronnie. He was
a man in his 50s with many illnesses and complaints due
to his increasing reliance on prescription drugs and
heavy drinking, which made her crucial to him.*

Having used the messaging system Cynthia had given me, I met Jade on my first morning at the local coffee shop.

We had a brief conversation in which I outlined my plans. I was impressed with her, she was direct, forthright and in control. It was me, actually, who was thrown, when she told me that recently Ronnie had held a security meeting in which I had come up - a paranoid guy, he'd asked his head bodyguard to try and find as much about 'Subject Six' as possible and draw up a contingency plan as to how to stop me should I try to infiltrate them.

Bella Yakin - Istanbul resident

My mother never had to tell me anything, I always just knew what was going on. From when I was a child, to when I went to university we had this other-world connection. So, when she took me to the café that morning and I saw her chat to the pale, wiry guy I knew something was going on and I knew it was something to do with Ronnie.

This, obviously, made me worry. Now my mother had always, always been able to look after herself. She'd had me very young and had then brought me up alone while still studying to be a doctor, but I also knew about Ronnie. I'd never seen him act badly, he was a very charming man, but I'd heard things and you could tell underneath his smiles there was steel. As we left the café I asked mother about what she was doing.

She didn't tell me anything. She said she'd be fine, to forget about it.

Subject Six

Ronnie's paranoia about me was, technically, not paranoia. How could it be? He was right, I was after him. One of the reasons he'd been known about for so long, but had still been able to operate, was how seriously he took his security to protect himself and his whole operation - having local police, politicians and even some members of the military on his payroll.

He was so well protected the Western allies couldn't take him down without a huge amount of resources and probably without creating a very messy diplomatic incident. Which is why, of course, Cynthia handed the file on him to me.

The fortunate thing was that even though he was worried about me, Jade didn't think he'd worked out how to defend himself from me yet, they'd been too busy. Ronnie and his team were apparently working on getting high numbers of people to the camps because the recent bombing by French and US military on their territory had resulted in a large-scale recruitment drive that had left 100s of potential Jihadists trying to get through Turkey. So, as long as I acted quickly, as intended, I should still have the advantage.

Yasmat Tuncay - Istanbul Police Department

I can admit it now because it is out in the open. The first day of my training to join the Police was the first day I was contacted. That day, as I was getting ready for the bus home he put an envelope of money in my pocket and said I'd get the same every month. The money was four times the amount I was being paid as a trainee. When I asked him what it was for he told me not to worry, and said I should use it to help pay for my wedding and for things for the baby when it came.

How did he know that? At the time, I had no idea, now I know. The money arrived on time, every month and it was too much to say no to. When you live in a world like I do, you don't refuse money for nothing. I didn't know who was paying me and I tried not to think about it.

That was five years ago, it began. Then, last year the man caught me on the way to work. He'd never done that before so I knew my time had come. He said I had to call in sick for the next week and that instead of my commander telling me what to do, he was going to. He gave me a photo of a man, British, and said they needed me to patrol an area of the city and to look-out for him. I was to act just as I would do normally when working as a Policeman but my only job was to watch for this man.

Karim Tuschal - Terrorist recruit

We arrived in a truck, well late at night. So late I had no idea what time it was but I knew we'd got to Turkey 'cause of all the flags, I'd seen, you get me?

As I told the Feds, I was on edge the whole time. Yeah I'd signed up and I knew what it meant, but I wasn't sure about it, not by a long shot, not like the others. Those lazy boys slept like the whole way from Birmingham to France to Germany to Turkey. Like they ate, prayed, read and slept, that's all they did and they were happy with it because they were sure of it, you get me? It was their idea and they were like, at peace or something.

Me? Not me? Why was I there? The Feds have been on at me about this the whole time, the head doctors too, and I saw your face hanging around the court where they did the trial so I know you know all this already, innit, but it was everything in my life, that's why I went along.

My mum and the cancer, my dad's new wife, my brother being attacked at the mosque by the Nazis and the Feds doing nothing. All of that was in me, you get me? I had a lot of anger and rage and, well, I guess that's why I was heading to Syria and when we got to Turkey, and we met Ronnie and he said everything was ready, everything was sweet and I was doing the right thing, I guess, in a way, it really felt like I was.

Subject Six

For the next few days, backed up by Walton and a small-team of techies he'd brought on board for this job, we watched Ronnie's house constantly. We were checking he hadn't put any new measures in place and also waiting for this next group of Jihadists to arrive. The idea of this was to get him caught in the act of trafficking. We didn't want to disrupt what he was doing, we wanted to destroy it.

The way we figured we'd do that was once they were set to move the Jihadists out of the city, I'd get in, disarm them and then call in the cavalry... the local police and Interpol.

We wanted there to be no wriggle room for Ronnie, he had to be caught red-handed along with his team - then they'd be found guilty and go to jail. Short of killing them, and I'm not an executioner, that was the most efficient way of bringing them all down at once.

Bella Yakin - Istanbul resident

I saw the guy from the café again four days later. I'd been out at work and then gone to a party, so I came back to our apartment later than usual. I climbed up the fire escape stairs and came in through the back way. I'm 19, and couldn't hide anything from my mother if I wanted to, so I wasn't trying to sneak in, I just didn't want to wake her.

But as I was about to climb in I saw her on the balcony talking to him. They were looking at an iPad, pointing at it. My mother was explaining something, I could tell she was concentrating, that this was serious. Then, all of a sudden he thanked her and jumped.

My heart leapt, because we're four levels up, I thought he was going to be dead when I looked down, but he landed safely, like a cat, and then jumped on a motorbike and disappeared. When I looked up I saw my mother was staring at me. We both knew we wanted to ask each other questions.

I still remember my mother telling me what she was doing and why. I've gone back to that moment a lot. Do I wish I'd tried to talk her out of it? I didn't know much about Ronnie, but I knew enough to know you didn't go against him.

But it didn't seem crazy, what my mother said she was doing. Once she told me why she'd started to work against Ronnie, once she told me how my cousins and Auntie had really died, and once she'd told me why she'd decided not to stop working for him but to stay close to him and try to bring him down, it all made sense. And because it made sense, because I was proud of my mother for being so brave, I didn't try to change her mind. I think I'm glad I didn't.

Karim Tuschal - Terrorist recruit

When we first got there, we were allowed to wash and sleep in a bed for the first time since we left England and it was, hands-down, the best shower I've ever had. My bones felt raw and they were aching something chronic, over a week on the road getting bashed and knocked, it was like a life-saver once we got there. And the place was amazing, all 5-star pimp stuff. I felt like royalty, you get me?

The next morning the chat was all about when we'd be going, how would they get us over the border, would we all be training together or would they split us up? Then this guy Ronnie came in, and you could tell he was the man. Even though he looked proper fat he had this air about him, like he could do damage, innit. He said we'd be heading out at some point during the evening and that we should rest up and enjoy ourselves. He said we could treat the place like a hotel, his gift to us because of what we were sacrificing for the cause, and said anything we wanted, food, drinks, whatever, we could order and his people would get.

So, we had a whole day to fill, and I was just expecting to have to let the boredom eat away at me, like it had on the journey, you get me? But actually we had the best time. I was kind of surprised, but they had an Xbox VR system and we went to town on it, shooting each other to kingdom come and then the Turkish boys came in and we kept swapping up the head-sets and going at it and in a way, it felt like we all really bonded.

Even though we couldn't talk the same language we were all getting proper excited whenever someone got a headshot on anybody or took them out without them expecting it. I was having a great day, I really was, until, you know, it happened. You get me?

Subject Six

It was imperative we struck at the right time to catch Ronnie and all the key players together. We'd seen the truck arrive the previous night and five people get off. Walton had used some of the clearances Cynthia had given us and traced the truck back to Belgium, so we were confident that the five people we'd see were the Jihadists, the cargo we needed to catch with Ronnie.

Just after ten we watched Jade enter the compound and at 10.21 I received an encrypted message from her confirming everyone we needed was there. It was time to go. Walton double-checked the hack he'd created that was going to take down their perimeter alarms so I could get in without being detected and we were all set.

Yasmat Tuncay - Istanbul Police Department

It was on the second day of my search for this man that I saw him. Only briefly, but it was him. He went past me on a scooter. As I'd been ordered, I let my contact know, who told me not to tell anyone else and to continue doing what I was doing and to try and find where the man was staying, or, if I could, find out what he was doing.

For the next three days, I didn't see any sign of him. Then, on the morning of the fourth day, just after ten thirty I was buying some cigarettes when I saw him come out of a block of flats. He was moving fast and I lost him in the crowds. When I messaged my contacts, they congratulated me and then told me to find out who was in the flat he'd left.

Further up the same street was an almost identical mansion to the one that Ronnie was in. For the past few days I'd been practising scaling the wall without any equipment, with minimal noise and without drawing attention to myself. It was 6m tall but I knew that as long as I got enough speed up before I jumped and managed to get a decent enough grip between the stones, I could get over in less than 10 seconds.

Ronnie had cameras and alarms on his wall, but they weren't going to trouble me. The only risk was if one of the guards saw me directly. To help with that I had one of the guys Walton had brought in. From our flat, he'd climbed out onto the roof and taken up a vantage point so he could scope out where the guards were on the side of the compound I was going to be entering. I marked out my run-up to the wall, which took me off the pavement and between two parked cars and crouched down… hoping I wouldn't have to wait long for the signal to come. We still had no idea when Ronnie would be on the move and I wanted to get going as quickly as possible.

I have to admit, I was wound up tight. Not stressed, just ready to move. My eyes locked on the phone in my palm, waiting for the message to come in. Which is why I didn't see the policeman at first.

The moment I did see him, I got an all clear message to go. What to do? I needed to get over but if he saw me it would be game over.

I held my ground. Sure, I was against the clock but I couldn't risk it. I knew my spotter would soon realise I hadn't made my move, that we could try again the next time the wall was clear.

Luckily the policeman hadn't noticed me. I felt reasonably certain of that because he wasn't focusing on me, or even looking my way. He was on my side of the street but not facing towards me, in fact he was scoping out the block of flats Walton was in. I watched him for about 10 minutes. He seemed unsure what he was doing, more intent on smoking his way through his pack of cigarettes than being vigilant. I decided to take the risk that he had no idea who I was and neither would he notice me scaling the wall - he was facing the other way and as he'd been staring dead ahead for the whole time I'd been watching him, I figured I'd have to be very unlucky for him to turn around while I climbed.

When the message next came that I had the all-clear, I went. Using Walton's gadget, I disarmed the alarms and then ran for it. My spring took me almost 2m up. I made my mark and stuck my toes into the cracks in the wall I'd picked out as being the best footholds and then started hauling my way up.

Bella Yakin - Istanbul resident

I think I first realized I was being followed when I left the café and went for my lunch-break. I walked through the mall and stopped to check out a bike I've been thinking about buying forever. It's right in the middle of the shop window, so I looked at it for a bit, counting up how much money I had, then left, then I decided I wanted one last look and went back.

That was when I saw him. In the window's reflection, on the other side of the mall, a guy almost fell over doing a U-turn, trying to spin around. He had a big, bushy beard and I realized he'd been in the café earlier which sent a chill down my spine. Then, once he'd got back on his feet, I saw him look at me, with a bit of anger. Then he just hovered behind me and I got this sense he was waiting for me.

When I got back to the café to start my shift again, I asked my friend Sanli to have a look around for me. Sanli's a really kind guy, and he hates it when his women friends get hassle from guys, so when I told him I thought someone was stalking me he went and checked and the guy was there.

Sanli wanted to confront him but I told him not to, said I didn't want a scene and I was sure by the end of my shift he'd be gone.

I don't know why I did that, apart from I just thought, knowing what my mother was doing, I didn't want to upset anyone. I wonder now if I had got Sanli to get him to go away what might have happened.

Karim Tuschal - Terrorist recruit

Things changed up properly quickly, you get me? Before, with all the games and the chilling, I guess I was a bit surprised that these guys were who they were meant to be, you know, running a gang to get us across the border. It seemed too chilled to be serious. But then, that guy Ronnie came in and started ordering everyone about and it all changed.

He was shouting in a different language, Turkish or something, but these guys who'd been all relaxed, suddenly became soldiers. No panic, but on it, and I mean on it.

One moment we were gaming, the next everyone but us had guns out and we were being pushed out of the room and down into the basement. We had no idea what was happening.

Subject Six

I'd been studying the schematics of the compound, and with Walton's surveillance team's help we'd picked out where it was most likely I'd find Ronnie and the wannabe Jihadists.

On my way into the house, there was only one unexpected moment. I got into the kitchen through the window and as I jumped down I found one of the guard dogs staring directly at me. It was drinking water so I leapt, wrapping my arm around its neck and legs around its body - sacrificing my left hand which I shoved into its mouth to keep it quiet. I held it hard for what must have been thirty seconds, one of the toughest tests I've faced, until it passed out.

My hand was mangled, and while I wanted to carry on into the house I knew it would be wiser to wait for it to regenerate a moment. If only I'd had the chance. I'd say bone was still showing on at least three fingers when I heard footsteps. I knew intuitively it would be the dog's handler.

I positioned myself by the door, waited for him to enter the kitchen, see the dog, and then before he could grab his walkie-talkie I was on him, grabbing him by the neck and ramming his head down hard onto the marble kitchen counter. One blow, out cold. I dragged him into the bathroom, tied his legs up and put him in the recovery position then moved on.

Bella Yakin - Istanbul resident

At first I thought he had gone. Sanli had waited behind for an hour to help out and walked with me through the mall together. Both of us were looking but we did not see him anywhere, or anyone else. Until it was too late.

As we were leaving the mall, two men on a scooter swerved off the road and onto the pavement. I saw one on the back had a hammer in his hand. I ducked, just in time, but Sanli didn't see it until the hammer was coming for him. I screamed as Sanli was hit, right on his cheek.

The man who'd been following me wrapped his arms around me from behind. Another ran forwards and picked me up by my feet, I struggled, kicked, but couldn't stop them pushing me into the car.

The drive was very frightening. I was crying, I don't remember much, I was panicking a lot. All I knew was that this had to be about my mother. I hoped she was all right. That soon everything would be all right.

Yasmat Tuncay - Istanbul Police Department

I've had a lot of training sweeping blocks of flats. Since all the terror bombings it was something we'd done a lot and it's actually quite simple to tell a family flat from one that a group of men are using - sometimes it's just sad men without wives, but often they are making drugs or worse, bombs.

In ten minutes, I had checked the block and two flats were suspicious to me. I called a friend at the police station and asked him to check out the block. One of the flats was suspected of being a place local drug dealers used, so I knew that the foreign man I was watching for hadn't come from there. Which meant it was the other one, a flat looking out onto the street on the top floor of the block. I let my contact know and waited for instructions.

Subject Six

As I walked through the house and found it all empty, with signs that people had left in a hurry, I knew something was wrong. It didn't take a genius to work that out, did it?

Worst case scenario, they'd already left. Next worst case, they'd found out about me, probably through Jade, and were lying in wait for me.

Did I think about aborting? Honestly, no. I know what I'm capable of. I knew at most they had just over ten guys. Ten guys with guns versus me? It wasn't anything to worry about on a personal level. When bullets don't hurt, you can back yourself, can't you? And I figured that if they had got wise to our plan, this would be the last time in a while we'd get this close to Ronnie.

If he was to get away now, he'd go into hiding, massively ramp up his security. Even if it wasn't quite a case of now or never, it was certainly a case of now being much easier than at any other time in the future. So, I pressed on.

Having swept the ground floor and upstairs I found the basement steps. It was cold, dark. Some kind of old underground system, like caves, with old sandstone walls.

The first bullet hit me. A good shot, square in the chest. Unluckily for them, the other shooters were a few seconds behind. If they'd all hit at once they could have stopped me in my tracks. But the split second I got before the next shot, was all I needed.

Karim Tuschal - Terrorist Recruit

They'd led us into this underground hall, which looked like a church or something. They divided the five of us up, one of us with each of them. I was with Ronnie as he led me to a place and told me to watch the door. His eyes were on fire, massive pupils, like he was blazed, you get me?

'Take this', he said, handing me a piece, 'I hear you can use it. As soon as you see him shoot.'

I took it. It weighed nice, a proper shooter, not one of the home-mades you get back home. I have to admit it felt good to know he'd heard about me and what I could do. Like, in a way, it validated all those hours I'd spent with Dad at the shooting club and in a way, that I'd made the right choice coming here. They'd promised they'd teach us how to be men, and here I was, being given a piece and treated like a man, you get me?

It sounds crazy now, but we literally never saw him coming. The room was silent as we waited, so we should have heard something. But we never did. One second the door was empty, the next he was there.

My finger hit the trigger sweet, my shot was sweeter and I knew in an instant I'd hit him right in the chest. I was buzzing, I was going to be the man, the one who'd taken him down first, Ronnie was going to love me. All of this was running through my head at double-time, but then, in front of my eyes, he didn't go down. The guy didn't go down after I'd hit him square and centre. It was freaky. It hit, he jerked back, then sprang forward. Like he'd burst into life, you get me?

He was like a blur. Everyone else was unloading now, me too, but we couldn't stop him. Even when we did hit it made no difference.

Ronnie was going crazy next to me. Shouting into a walkie-talkie, unloading his piece, pushing me away from the guy. He was hunting us out, pair by pair. Taking people out like they were nothing. Proper kung fu shit, all out cold, broken bones, this guy was lethal.

In the end, there was Ronnie and me and two others left. We backed away from him, all of us out of bullets. I was sure he was going to do us, I braced, ready. Then I heard a woman scream.

From the door, the woman doctor who'd checked me out when we got there was dragged in and Ronnie put a gun to her head.

Yasmat Tuncay - Istanbul Police Department

I felt nervous when my contact turned up with some other men because it made it very real to me. I know I had been taking money, but without doing anything it was easy to ignore. Now, as they joined me, obvious criminals, it made things feel very real.

Inside the flat, however, things went smoothly. There was one man, English, who we caught packing up lots of computers and laptops. We grabbed him and secured the room then I was told to take the Englishman and follow them.

Out on the street was the most nervous time. If I had met any of my fellow officers and had to explain what I was doing, I don't know how I would have got away with it.

Subject Six

I'd known Ronnie was a ruthless, clever guy and as he pushed the gun into Jade's temple I knew one wrong move could be very bad.

'We can't hurt you, but we can hurt her', Ronnie said, flashing a grin.

Jade, and respect to her, was holding it together really well. She tried to argue with him, her voice balanced and calm as she said he'd got it wrong. He spat at her, slapped her, told her he'd been following everyone since they'd come back to Istanbul and told her to stop lying.

I needed to buy time. Walton was waiting, ready to move in if I was out of contact for too long, ready to call in the police.

Ronnie knew he couldn't kill me. If he'd known about me coming, why had he stayed? Maybe he hadn't had time, maybe he wanted to face me down? Maybe he hadn't been sure about Jade until now and needed to see it play out. Either way, I was sure that now his angle would be to get out, quickly, and escape.

'Stop him,' Jade told me, 'He'll kill me anyway.'

My fists clenched.

Bella Yakin - Istanbul resident

They pushed me along a corridor and out into a large, underground room. I heard a scream. My mother. A gun to her head. The man she'd met in the cafe and at our flat was 2m away. Angry.

Then I felt a huge pain and fell to the ground. My head was ringing, shaking and then one of the men stood in front of me and shoved a gun into my forehead too.

I couldn't hear properly, but I heard my mother wailing, crying and Ronnie shouting and ordering people about. It's embarrassing to say but I wet myself and I heard someone laugh. I could hardly breathe. I thought I was going to die.

Karim Tuschal - Terrorist recruit

That was the moment that changed it for me, do you understand? Seeing this young girl, as young as me, crying, soaking wet, a guy's gun to her head. I suddenly felt wrong and dirty and sick, you get me?

I'd left England to become a man, thinking going to Syria was the only way I'd get that. Killing an unarmed girl, or doing what these guys were doing, that wasn't being a man.

Instinct was telling me the only thing I should be doing was aiming my gun at Ronnie and shooting him dead straight.

Subject Six

For the first time being Subject Six, I felt like a busted flush. I'd have bet on myself to save Jade. But to save both of them? Impossible. I've always worked on trying to do everything without using lethal force. During all of my missions before, only a few people had died and none were by my hand.

Faced with the fact two people who'd been helping me with guns to their heads, I knew things might be about to change for the worse.

Yasmat Tuncay - Istanbul Police Department

They led me and this Englishman us into a big house and down into the cellar. What I saw down there was chaos, a nightmare... or would soon be. Two women were being held at gun-point and a man in the middle had guns pointed at him.

I wanted to turn and run but I knew that would be the worst thing I could do, so I pushed the Englishman forward and then stood back.

'Walton' the man in the middle said, 'Glad you could join us.'

Subject Six

The way Walton nodded I knew he still had the knife he kept hidden by his ankle. Ronnie began bragging, laughing at how he'd got the better of the famous Subject Six. As we spoke, my eyes were drawn to the boy to his side. One of the Jihadists. I could tell by the way he was looking at Ronnie that he was unhappy with what he was saying.

'You don't have to join them', I whispered, staring at him, 'You haven't done anything yet.'

He stared back at me as Ronnie roared with laughter. But I knew the boy was on-board.

Looking back, I'd make the same choice again.

Karim Tuschal - Terrorist recruit

The moment Subject Six dived I shot. I hit Ronnie in the face, Subject Six grabbed the woman, reaching out for Ronnie's gun at the same time. Ronnie got a shot off, which smacked into Subject Six's hand I thought he'd done it, I thought he'd saved her.

Bella Yakin - Istanbul resident

I heard a gun-shot and then saw the man they'd just brought in, squat down, grab a knife from his boot and throw it in one motion. Faster than I would have thought anyone could ever have done. I screamed, the man holding the gun to my head fell back. The knife in his neck.

I jumped away. The guy who'd saved me had a gun now and someone else was on the floor. The shooting stopped. I was choking, sobbing.

Yasmat Tuncay - Istanbul Police Department

I couldn't believe what I was seeing and at the same time I could hear behind me police sirens. Who had called them in? I had to get away and it looked like now was the time to do it.

The guys I was with were down or at gun-point, there was nothing but trouble for me now so I turned and ran.

Subject Six

For a split second I thought I'd started to bleed again, but then I realised the bullet had gone through my hand and hit Jade.

She was hit in the cheek. I tried to stop the bleeding but it was too deep, too hard. Her daughter ran over. I could hear the police coming.

Walton and I needed to go. Ronnie was dead, the boy who'd shot him was trembling. Perhaps, this once, I should have waited to help the clear up but I couldn't risk it.

My conscience was clear, but I had blood on my hands and I had to go.

HOW SUBJECT SIX IS FOUND FOR THE FIRST TIME

The first time I see Subject Six after the Istanbul is a trip that's full of surprises. Surprise number one is walking into the gym where Subject Six is kung fu training and finding Carly there. Post-workout, she's grinning like a Cheshire cat and devouring some freshly-chopped melon. She clocks my surprise and immediately tells me to start recording, knowing that I'm going to want to hear this.

When Subject Six invited me to his house I thought he'd want to debrief me about Istanbul. The press have got hold of the fact someone helping Subject Six has died in the mission and he's taking flak. For being reckless, dangerous. But it turns out, there's something else on his mind.

Carly

You pleased to see me?

Me

Always? When did you arrive?

Carly

Bland politeness doesn't suit you Benji, go on, admit it you're a bit annoyed you didn't know I was here?

Me

I wouldn't say…

Carly

It's classic rejection anxiety. You introduced us and now you're wound up because we've...

Subject Six

Ignore her, Benji, she's winding you up. She's in a weird mood. Has been all day.

Carly

I am, I am, I'm sorry... I'm just excited. You're not annoyed, are you?

Let me assure you, seeing as you only have the audio transcript, I'm not annoyed in the slightest at this. Confused, maybe, as I struggle to catch-up, but not irritated at Carly. As I'm about to find out, she'd been giddy all day because of a new development.

Carly

He called me over because of the number.

Me

On his wrist? I thought he didn't care about it?

Just to clarify, by now Subject Six has moved outside to continue training; judging from the sounds coming from the yard he's practising his driving skills - so we're not talking about him in front of him.

Carly

I think you'll find a few things about him have changed. Like his attitude to what he is, or how he is.

Me

How come?

Carly

It seems Istanbul put some things in perspective.

Me

I haven't heard too much about it yet, but it must be bad if he's finally trying to work out where he's come from?

Carly

Well, I…

Me

I guess he must be to get you all the way over here.

Carly

True, but it's not the only thing he's wanted to see me for.

Me

I do not want to know about that. So, have you found anything out about the tattoo?

Carly

Well that' what he wanted to see me about, but after this morning that's on hold.

Me

Why? What is it? I can see in your eyes you've got something to say. So, tell me.

Carly

Ok, ready, certain you're recording? Right then, this morning Fabian Tree got in touch.

Me

Fabian?

Carly

He says he created Subject Six. He's demanding to see him.

At this point, my mouth naturally drops open. Then I unload a torrent of questions. None of which get answered, none of which you can really hear on the recording because at that moment an alarm goes off. And not just any alarm. We're talking sirens, lights. I feel like I'm in disaster movie. Carly jumps up tells me to follow her.

As she leads me upstairs it feels like she knows what she's doing. We're in the kitchen, then the hallway, up the staircase. From the landing, I hear the door open and Walton runs in. My heart jumps when I see he's got a rifle over his shoulder.

Walton

Intruders!

Carly

I can't believe he called it right.

Walton

He has his ways.

Carly

Let's find out if he's right about who.

I'm lost, feeling out-of-the-loop. But I know this is no time for personal insecurities. Someone uninvited has obviously found Subject Six and is incoming. This could be very serious.

Walton takes the lead and we hurry into the main bedroom and then through, further into the east wing. The second master suite has been kitted into a panic room since I was last at the house. Inside, staring at a bank of screens and in front of a system of computers, Subject Six is controlling the CCTV.

Walton

Any idea who it is?

Subject Six

Nothing obvious.

I lean forward. In one of the monitors I can make out two people. They're in the forest which I know is to the north east of the estate. The area nearest the road I came in on. They're dressed like soldiers, moving through the undergrowth like soldiers. It's not possible to know if they have weapons or not but no-one thinks it's wise to act as if they don't. Who could they be?

Walton

Just these two?

Subject Six

Yes.

Carly

Phew, that's…

Subject Six

Two is enough.

My first thought is that they might be government. Not simply based on appearance. Let me go backwards to go forwards. When I first talk to Subject Six on the phone after Istanbul, the same call in which he asks me to come and see him, he says the government are threatening to bring him in again. Not because of Istanbul, but because he's turned down the next operation they want him to do.

He doesn't go into too much detail, apart from the fact the target is a nuclear scientist who they think is selling secrets to rogue states, or terrorists, or both. Cynthia says they want him exposed so they can lock him up for whistleblowing, or what they class as treason. Even though

Subject Six is prepared to work with Cynthia again, he refuses to help with this one. Having looked at the scientist he thinks they want him taken out because he exposed some malpractice in the government, not because he's a real threat to humanity. He doesn't want to be the government's enforcer, taking out anyone they don't like.

When he turns the government down, they're angry. Cynthia's boss takes the news personally and according to her, orders Cynthia to bring Subject Six in. When Subject Six refuses, threats follow and they say they're going to find him and get him. Which is why, I'm sure you can guess, I think the two people who've entered Subject Six's grounds could be from the government.

Walton

They're not government.

Walton says as if he's been listening to my thoughts. I see him notice I'm recording. For the first time ever, he doesn't ask me to stop, perhaps because he thinks this could be key and knows Subject Six will want it on record. From them on he doesn't object to me taping him.

Subject Six

Agreed, too sloppy.

Carly

So who are they?

Me

How worried should we be? Could these guys be... I mean, could they be connected to Istanbul?

Subject Six and Walton turn to each other

Walton

We need to act like they could be.

By now the two intruders are about five minutes' walk from the house. Walton is sent around to the back of the house and is aiming to outflank them by walking around the converted barns before doubling back behind them. Subject Six, Carly and I take up positions in the main house around the courtyard. The idea is to wait for them to come into the courtyard before we show ourselves once Walton seals off their escape route.

I'm given a gun. But before you start worrying, it's for show, it's not loaded. Same as Carly. Although she argues for bullets much harder than I do. Her family got her shooting when she was a kid. Subject Six refuses. Saying that if it gets so bad that Walton and him can't fight back then the best thing for everyone would be to surrender.

Wiping the sweat from my forehead, temples, the gun feels clunky and heavy in my hand. The extent of my shooting experience extends to one afternoon when I was about 12 shooting chickens up the bum with an air rifle to make them jump. Which to me, and my mate who lived on the farm we were at, was the funniest thing in the world until I accidentally hit a chicken square in the eye and killed it in the spot. The blood, the frantic clean-up, the dead body, put me off shooting forever. In Iraq I always steered well clear, helped by the fact protocol banned me from as much as touching a weapon.

I know the gun I'm holding isn't loaded, but it still feels alien. I raise it in front of me. If I'm going to face down the two intruders and look like I know what I'm doing, I need to look like I know what I'm doing. I'm still grappling with how to look tough and natural while holding the gun, when I become aware of a smothering silence. I slow my breathing, crouch down and I can't hear a sound. Can't see anyone else. I have no idea who's hunting who.

There's a shot. Another. Instinctively I'm on the floor, ducking for cover. Then a cry rings out. It can't be Subject Six, it's not a woman and it doesn't sound like Walton. I wait, though, needing to be sure before I move. Just because one intruder is down, doesn't mean the other is too. I only get up when I hear Subject Six call for Carly.

Carly

Walton was a good shot, I knew that from spending time at the house, and when Subject Six called me out to see to the injuries of the intruder. I could see how exact he'd been. The wound was just above the knee; the bullet had grazed him rather than going in. In other words Walton had winged him, nothing more.

I stopped the bleeding, gave him some quick stitches and knew that as long as I got him antibiotics he'd be fine pretty much straightaway.

By the time I arrive the scene is calm, but Subject Six isn't. Walton explains he shot because he thought one of them was reaching into his jacket for his gun. In fact, he was reaching for a white flag to show they came in peace. These two guys aren't armed; they're desperately trying to explain they've come to help Subject Six on his mission.

SUBJECT SIX MEETS HIS BIGGEST FANS

Subject Six is pacing back and forth. Agitated. Angry. He tells Walton to inspect the rest of the estate in case there are others - completely ignoring the two intruders who promise they've come alone.

Once Carly has bandaged up the wound of the guy who's down, Subject Six orders us all inside the house, his face bitter, serious.

Subject Six

What are you doing here? What are your names?

Niall

I'm Niall, this is Rueben, we're here to help. We love what…

Subject Six

How did you find me?

Both are in army fatigues, but up close they seem too thin, too ratty, too old, to be serving soldiers. I'm about a metre away from them, trying to size them up as I record the conversation. Although, as I'm sure you can tell from this transcript, it's essentially an interrogation.

Rueben

We're ex-military.

Subject Six

I didn't ask that, by getting here you've proved your worth... what I need to know is how you found us.

Later I ask Subject Six why he was so worked up. To me, it feels bad there's been a breach in security, but why is he not at least a little bit relieved these guys are friendly? Pretty soon it becomes apparent they're both Subject Six fanatics who love him and unless they're very convincing liars, their devotion is clear as day. Yet he's acting like it's the government who've come storming in to bring him down.

He tells me that the reason he's so worked up is that he's been worried for a while he'd be found. He's been expecting it, which is why when the alarm goes off Carly says he 'called it', and he's been dreading it. People finding him for the first time, fans or foe, is a watershed moment. It takes his life as Subject Six into a new phase, a more vulnerable one, and not one he's looking forward to.

For the next fifteen minutes or so Rueben and Niall explain, in precise detail because that's what Subject Six keeps demanding, how they managed to track him down. I'm going to gloss over the details partly because there's a lot of pedantic back-and-forth, partly because I don't want to leave any clues in here as to how to find Subject Six's estate. Suffice to say that it involved satellite imagery, searches on the land registry and following people: including Carly and me. Having spent so long trying to remain hidden, Subject Six is furious.

Niall

I wouldn't worry, not many people are as devoted to the cause as we are.

Rueben

Damn straight, we've got the skills and the belief… there's a lot of chatter online about people wanting to join you, but how many people are actually doing it?

Subject Six

Two too many… but if you found me, others will follow! Goddamn it.

Niall

Then we wait for them and we stop them!

Subject Six

We? What we?

Rueben

That's why we're here. To join you.

Subject Six

Are you going to get down on one knee and swear your allegiance?

Rueben

If that's what it takes. If that's what you want.

Subject Six

Of course, I don't fucking…

Me

Ok, ok… let's calm down. How about we all…

Subject Six

Don't you dare suggest a fucking cup of tea!

Me

It's a beer I want, or something stronger. Why don't you take a minute?

In the end Subject Six takes about five hours. Why? Because Walton comes back and the two of them carry out extensive background checks on Rueben and Niall. Finally, Subject Six is satisfied. He still briefs Walton, Carly and I to look out for signs that these two could be moles and isn't really anywhere near to trusting to them, but he's calmer and knows it's time to give them time to talk.

Niall

You're the only one who gets it.

Rueben

For years, the world has been at war, and you're the first person to acknowledge it and start fighting the right people.

Subject Six

'Fighting the right people'?

Niall

The 1 percenters. The people who take and take and kill the rest of us… Rueb and I have long tried to work out how we can act against them and now you are.

Rueben

You see when you're trying to redress society so it's fairer you can't have the rich in charge and hope to change things, can you? But when we try anything we get crushed. We've tried politics, we've tried marches, anarchist groups, everything… and the rich, they brainwash and lie and cheat to keep themselves on top.

Niall

It's the greatest con ever. Convincing billions of people to support a system that is weighted against them. The world has always been divided by money and it gets worse and worse every year…

Rueben

Until you.

Niall

Rueb's right, you change everything. Because you've started to bring them down and you are something they can't have, they can't buy. For the first time ever we've got something to fight them with that they can't own.

By this stage I'm focusing more on Subject Six than Niall and Rueben. I know this will not sit well. While what they're saying is based in a truth, and one that he thinks needs addressing, everything about these guys tells me they're too militant, too close-minded for Subject Six's tastes.

Subject Six

And war? You say you're at war?

Rueben

Of course.

Subject Six

And I am too?

Rueben

What? Of course!

For a moment, I meet eyes with Carly. Something unnerving, intense is coming out of Rueben and Niall. I have the impulse to join in, tell them the calm down, to warn them that whatever mission they're on and whatever beliefs they've assigned to Subject Six, he doesn't share them. But I'm the reporter. I'm not here to intervene.

Niall

I define war as conflict between two sides. Since the 1990s two sides have risen, the richest 1% of people in the world have more wealth than the rest of the world combined…

Subject Six

So, it's us versus them?

Rueben

Yes, you know that.

Subject Six

And war is the only way?

Rueben

Why are you talking like this? I thought…

Niall

Do you know the two most equal countries are one's who lost the war? Japan, Germany, they lost a war… which means they were stripped of their assets and everyone had to start again. Now they have rich and poor, of course they do, but the gap is far smaller than in the West and so…

Subject Six

Stop it, just stop it.

Rueben

What do you mean?

Subject Six

You sound like first year university students, not Iraq War veterans.

I can see Niall's fingers trembling. Rueben looks crestfallen. Confused. Vulnerable.

Subject Six

You're right, I am trying to correct some injustices, but I don't want to start a war and I don't think we need one and I…

Niall

It's too late. We're in a war, you just don't know it yet.

Rueben

You can't do this to us.

Subject Six

Do what to you?

Rueben

Cast us aside like this! We've spent months finding you and now you stand there and…

Subject Six

I didn't ask to be found!

Niall

Now who's sounding like a kid? You can't start changing the world and then get upset when people try and help you!

The conversation carries on, oscillating between re-crimination, misunderstanding and frustration. I think this is the first time Subject Six is confronted with the reality of what it means to inspire people - you can't control exactly how that inspiration will manifest. I know he enjoys the fact people are thankful for the crimes he's exposed and that he's got people thinking more about evils that were previously hidden. He's also been aware of what he calls the crazy fringes of his fan-club, those that see him as a God - but they've been easy to dismiss and laugh at.

Now, though, he's face-to-face with a different type of devotee.

Subject Six

How have they got it so wrong? I could never stand for what they think I stand for.

Me

They were extremists before, you just gave them something to hang that too.

Subject Six

But I don't want them. And how many others are there?

Walton

You can't just throw them out though. It would be a massive security breach.

Subject Six

Thank fuck they were so scared of moles and spies they worked as a pair and didn't let anyone else join them. Imagine if I had ten of the fuckers here.

Carly

Do you completely buy the fact they're working on their own?

Subject Six

Yeah, I do. Walton?

Walton

I'm about 95% sure they're not plants, but we should still lock down the estate in case they were either followed or are part of something else.

Subject Six

Agreed. Now, what do we do with them? Outside of here, pissed off with me, disappointed I'm not Hitler in disguise, they're too dangerous. They could flip and give me up, or they could get so riled up that I've failed

them they could turn on me… but keep them here, they'll drive me mad.

Eventually the plan is to appease them and keep watch on them for the time being. Subject Six tells them that even though he's not completely aligned with them in terms of ideology and methodology, the fact is they want the same thing: a fairer world. He thanks them for offering to help, tells them the government have threatened to take him in and asks them to help him guard the estate.

They agree willingly. Walton gives them a location tag so he knows where they are at all times and sets them to work. Subject Six finds himself with the start of an army he doesn't want.

SUBJECT SIX ASKS ME FOR A FAVOUR

The following day Subject Six decides that he's going to keep on the move in between missions until Walton, Niall and Rueben can finalise changes to the security to combat the government, or any other fans, finding him. If numerous entities are after him he figures he needs to stay on the run so he can't get trapped. Seeing as Niall and Rueben used Carly and me to track him down, he's also decided to break off contact with us for a while. To protect him, and us; because if it gets out we're in close contact with him, he doesn't want us to become targets for those who want to find him. He says he'll be in touch when he needs us, and it doesn't seem final, but there does feel like something has changed between us as he rides away on his motorbike.

The last thing he does, is ask us to do something for him. After Fabian Tree's incredible claim about making Subject Six, Carly and I are about to head to Genix HQ. Now the dust has settled after Niall and Rueben's arrival, what he's saying is huge and we're both keen to get there as soon as possible. But when Subject Six tells us the place he wants us to go, and who he wants us to see, I agree immediately because I know how important it could be to my investigation and book. What is it? It's to see Michelle.

Michelle

You say you're working with Enosh?

Me

Yes, I have been for a while.

Michelle

But you're a reporter?

Me

I am. I'm…

Michelle

Isn't his whole thing to keep a low profile?

Over the phone, as Carly drives like a Formula One driver around the M25, I explain how I'm helping Enosh investigate what's happened to him in exchange for being able to write about him, once he thinks the time is right to make sure the truth of who, what and how he is ready to be made public.

I also tell her that just as Enosh has been outed as Subject Six it's now possible my cover has been blown. That two people used me to track Enosh down, so there's now no longer a need for me to pretend I'm not on the story.

Me

So now I don't have to hide away, he's asked me to come and see you.

Michelle

Why?

Me

I can't say on the phone, just in case, but it's important.

Michelle

**And if I say no? If I say I think spending time with a
known associate of his could put me at and the children at risk, what then?**

Me

**I'd say you're already at risk, that's what I'm coming
to talk to you about.**

When we get near the house Carly drops me off and I
walk the last five minutes. It's unlikely Michelle would
work out Carly and Subject Six are having a fling - if
that's what it is, neither will confirm - but we figure why
risk it? And anyway, Carly's got some research to finish
off before we go to Genix.

Inside the house, which is warm and inviting, I find
myself immediately at ease. Michelle may have sounded
guarded on the phone, but from the moment she opens the
door she's smiley and open. I can instantly see what
Enosh saw in her, just as much as I can see why she was
a good match for him. She's as sharp as he is, easily.

One of the things I've not been sure about is whether
she'll introduce me to the kids. I want to meet them, because even if they're not a big part of Subject Six's story,
they're a big part of Subject Six. But I can't force a meeting and the task Subject Six has given me doesn't rely on
it. It surprises me, then, and pleases me, when the first
thing she does is lead me upstairs to meet them.

Tuppence is polite, poised but wants to get back to
talking to her friends on a group call. Oscar is the one that
gets me. He's nine remember. Nine. And when I go into
his bedroom I find myself in a room from Oxford or Cambridge. There are piles of books, whiteboards with formu-
las on, about five computer screens displaying graphs and
charts.

Mozart is playing. Oscar is in a pose I recognise from Mina's yoga DVDs. Michelle rolls her eyes, goes straight to the speakers and wakes him out of his trance by suddenly turning the volume up to full blast. He doesn't jump, like I expect, but slowly opens his eyes and wags his finger at her in a mocking, playful way before he stands up and shakes his legs.

When I ask him what he's doing he speaks with the same energy, same tone, same determination as his Dad. And even though what he's telling me seems preposterous, his charisma and his certainty give it more steel, more depth. What he's doing is inventing a time machine. He began when we heard his Dad was being frozen and that he might not be unfrozen for 100s of years and he hasn't stopped. He says he won't stop.

As Oscar tells me about the troubles he's having, but also the successes he thinks he's getting, I wonder what his Dad will think when he finds out the lengths his son is going to. I also can't quite work out if he knows that Subject Six is his Dad. He must know about Subject Six, he's all over the news, but the allegations that he's Enosh Blake haven't made such a splash. It hit the headlines for a few days then disappeared because it seems people care more about what Subject Six is doing now and the fall-out from each mission, than what he once was. So has Michelle been able to keep Subject Six's identity from Tuppence and Oscar? That's one of the things that sits in the forefront of my mind while Oscar talks on and on about his project.

Once we've left his room, Michelle leads me out to the decking in their back garden. She pours wine, we sit in deep, comfortable wicker garden chairs, and she shrugs when I ask if I can record our conversation.

Michelle

They're not entirely normal kids, but they're close, considering what's happened to them. I don't want to subject them to anything else they don't need, so whatever it is you've come for, be aware of that.

Me

Do they know about the Subject Six and Enosh Blake stories in the papers?

Michelle

They do.

Me

How did they…

Michelle

The journalist called before the story went up.

Me

Someone called Laura?

Michelle

Yes, how did you know…

Me

We're old friends and, in fact, she's the one who told me about Subject Six. What did she say to you?

Michelle

She just wanted to warn me, it was decent of her. It gave me a chance to tell Tuppence and Oscar.

Me

And how did they react to that?

Michelle

I couched it in the same way as I couched the birds and bees talk with them. This is a thing, you're going to come across it in your life, be aware... but I didn't tell them it was certain. I said a paper was saying Subject Six could be your Dad, but we don't know and neither do they... and then asked if they wanted to ask anything.

Me

And did they?

Michelle

Tuppence said it wasn't their Daddy, because if it was he would have come to say hello.

Me

And Oscar?

Michelle

Who knows about him? But he seemed to accept what she said. They haven't mentioned it since and the school and their friends, they're very good, very sensitive about it. But what is it you've come to say?

The job Subject Six has asked me to do is two-fold - he wants me to give Michelle a burner mobile phone that Walton has encrypted and convince her to call him so he can tell her what's happening and stay in touch.

Michelle

He could have sent me a phone. What else is there?

Me

Now he's been found by two people, and, well, he's had a falling out with the government...

Michelle

Over that thing in Istanbul?

Me

Yup, and it's got him worried about you three.

Michelle

He's been worried about us since he came back.

Me

True, but he thinks, well he gave me this USB key, it's got information about a bank account and some people, a security company, he wants you to get them to help look after you. Just for the time being. That's what he said.

Michelle

I told you, I'm not going to become…oh why am I bothering, you're just the messenger. Ok, hand it over, I'll talk to him.

Me

He wanted me to get you to call them while I was here.

Michelle

Fucking hell.

Me

I know.

Michelle

And what about you? About your family? It seems to me you're in more danger than us, you're the one running around with him… are you having to live in fear as well?

Me

Erm… he's offered to help, yes, but it's not fear… it's just being practical.

Michelle

I hope your wife feels like that.

Michelle sees my face drop after this and she eases up. She even makes the call to the security company so I can feel like I did what he asked me. But she's curt after that, and I don't hang around.

Carly

How did she take it?

Me

Not thrilled.

Carly

But did she take the phone and agree to the extra security?

Me

Yes.

Carly

Good. He feels the walls are closing in on him; it'll do him good to hear from her.

Me

I wish I could record what you two talk about.

Carly

Pervert.

Me

Talk about, Carly, not what you get up to.

Carly's about to give me some chat back when we both stop. Our phones are going off. Walton's sent us both a link to a news report. There's been a terrorist shooting in Wolverhampton and this is the transcript from the link he sends:

Imam Omar Yusuf - press conference speech

I have today witnessed what no father, husband, friend, man, person or human should have to witness. I have suffered what no Muslim, Christian, Jew, Hindu, Sikh or any other believer or non-believer should have to suffer.

My wife, my loyal, generous wife, was celebrating her birthday. Surrounded by our family, friends and colleagues from the local school she worked at for over 15 years. We were eating at a restaurant near her school that we often go to when she finishes work. They know us well, and often, when we're there, pupils will stop in to say hello to my wife or children who also attended the school.

Normally these meals, these meeting, are full of joy and laughter. Not today. At around 5.30pm as our group had just sat down to eat, and tragically a group of pupils approached us to give my wife a birthday card they'd made, all of us were attacked.

Three men, fanatics, with knives and guns entered the Queen's Road shopping centre by the south entrance, opposite the restaurant we were in. They began shouting 'Allah Akbar' although they have no understanding of what that means. 15 minutes later all three were dead as were 34 others. Including my beloved wife, my two twin 14 year old daughters, my brother, his wife and their newborn son and eight pupils my wife taught, all aged between 11 and 12.

These murderers were young. They killed in the name of a religion we share, yet not in any beliefs we share. I am known in this community, the community they came from and that formed them. I've been an Imam for 11 years, I have met all three killers, helped their families, and yet they attacked blindly. Shooting at my table, calling us infidels, killing everyone they could see. They were not thinking, they were not acting for a cause, with any higher motive in their hearts, they were acting only to kill.

Forgiveness is a beautiful, wonderful thing. It is something I teach, something I strive to learn from others and it is the one thing a civilised, harmonious society needs to flourish. I have seen many, too many, fathers, mothers, husbands, wives, speaking after atrocities like this one and have always found solace that their words at press events like this are full of forgiveness and togetherness. They say they won't hate, they'll love and they'll pass on love.

But today, as I held the bloody bodies of my wife and children in my arms I knew one thing and one thing only. Gone is the time of forgiveness. We are no longer dealing with people capable of being loved, deserving of forgiveness. We are facing monsters who hate us and who we need to hate in kind.

We need to stop trying to understand, to excuse, to blame economic or political factors. These killers aren't thinking about that when they stick a knife into the heart of an 11 year old girl or aim a gun at a six week old boy's head and pull the trigger. They're thinking only of death and hate and so must we.

It is time to stamp them out. To kill them as they want to kill us. Their hate has caused this and once we have succeeded in wiping them out then, and only then, can we return to love.

To beat them we have to act and act now. Years of war have failed, but now finally we have a weapon that cannot be beaten. In the name of my daughters, and all those who have died in attacks from these terrorists, I call on Subject Six to use his power and his skills to lead us to victory and rid the world of this terrible blight.

WHAT ROLE HAVE GENIX REALLY PLAYED IN SUBJECT SIX?

Arriving at Genix HQ, having spent the journey from Michelle's talking about the repercussions of Subject Six being called out in that way, Carly and I see just how big this statement from Imam Yusuf might be.

In the Genix reception, the TV screens are showing lots of channels and all of them are focusing on the attack. The headlines, the reporters, the members of the public being interviewed are all emotional and seem to be on edge - an uneasy mix of fear and defiance which Subject Six is being thrust into. With his position as superhero in the spotlight, it seems especially pertinent that we're at Genix meeting Fabian Tree. His message from the other day now looking increasingly important.

Subject Six, I am Fabian Tree. Greetings. We could say that we met in another life. I know you're wondering how I managed to contact you, but don't worry. It's perfectly natural. And why do I say that? Well, because I created you. I made you who you are and now it's time to talk, don't you think?

If you've ever seen Fabian Tree on TV you probably won't be surprised at the slightly obnoxious, trumped-up tone of this note. I don't think I know of anyone else who would announce such a big thing in quite the same way.

Waiting in reception I think back to what Subject Six wants us to do.

Subject Six

This guy has an angle, find out what it is.

Me

Of course. But tell me, what's your gut?

Subject Six

My gut?

Me

On whether he did it. You met him, you did your research on the company before you signed up to be frozen by them. Could they have made you, did this guy Fabian strike you as the kind of guy who could do that without people knowing?

Subject Six

I thought your DEBRIS people and the ex-staff say there's no way he did it.

Me

They do. But someone did, and I want to know what you think. Well, more what you feel.

Carly

Every time I've seen him on TV, and read about him, he's struck me as a slippery fucker.

Walton

But that doesn't make him the man in charge of the most important, and secret, scientific breakthroughs ever.

Me

No, so what do you think?

Subject Six

He's a man who won't stop to get what he wants. Ever. And the way he's demanding I have to go and see him, that doesn't sit well. Not one bit.

As well as thinking over Subject Six and Walton's words to make sure I tackle Fabian Tree in the right way, I have to admit I haven't been able to resist sending DEBRIS a message to let them know I'm meeting him. I am fully aware their responses are going to be entirely one-sided, and as they pop into my inbox it's good to know they don't disappoint.

Eileen Raymond

Watch out for him. Most despicable man, but can be likable. Remember what we've said about his capabilities. If he has made SS then he's done it with no leaks and that is unlikely considering how much surveillance we have him under.

Dan Raymond

Just heard you're meeting ft. Carefully does it.

Nicholas Singh

Tell him he's a prick. From me. Actually, tell him everyone thinks he's a prick and they always will

Nicholas Singh

And tell him we're coming for him.

I like DEBRIS. From everything I've seen and from the one time I've met him, I don't like Fabian. But Subject Six has sent me to talk to Fabian and I have to take an objective view otherwise what's the point?

We don't get off to a great start, because as soon as Fabian greets us he tells me I can't record anything and he doesn't leave any room for negotiation. This disappointment is countered almost immediately though, when Fabian excitedly tells us he wants to show us something. As he leads us into a warren of corridors, he makes a bee-line for Carly and isn't afraid to hide it. He's got a reputation, that he loves to foster, as a lady's man and while it's way too full-on for my liking, he's certainly a funny guy and a fast talker. Carly, for her part doesn't seem perturbed.

He leads us to a large room, a hi-tech aircraft hangar. Wheeling around to bring me into the picture and really playing the showman he reveals what he wants to show us: a Cryopod. Subject Six's Cryopod. Fabian promised us a jaw-dropper and he hasn't let us down.

Carly

I'll never fail to be amused by how easy it is to distract someone who wants to fuck you. I mean Fabian was such an obvious letch about it, I guess he uses his power and money to surround himself with girls who'll do anything for him, so he's just lost all sense of not being a dog about it! Anyway, at least it made it easy for me to help you out, didn't it Benji?

What Carly's referring to is our plan, instigated by Subject Six, to try and collect any evidence we can from Genix that we might be able to look into ourselves. So, as soon as I get over the shock of seeing the pod - trying to work out how Genix have it when it was last seen being taken away by the police - we spring into action.

Carly

We were like clockwork, just as Walton and Six had told us to be. Locate the cameras, block the view, distract your host, grab the evidence. While he was trying to make out just a hint of nipple down the front of my low-cut top you were in and out of the Cryopod like a… well, not like a geeky reporter. Joke. Like a man with a mission.

I don't exactly get a haul from the pod, but I get a couple of things which we then send to a forensics lab for testing. The results of which we'll come to soon. Once I have them, I turn my attention to why the Cryopod is with Fabian. When I ask him about it, he simply smiles and says Genix made it so it belongs with them, but when I push for more details on how he got back to their HQ, he smiles and doesn't answer, returning his gaze back to Carly. Which doesn't sit right with me. Why not? Well, I'm not saying necessarily that there's a big conspiracy here, the pod is after all Genix's property. But if you're the government and you have the pod that came down with Subject Six in, and you're trying to find out what made Subject Six, wouldn't you want to keep the pod? Sure, you might not have found any answers, but as far as I can see you'd keep it just in case.

Anyway, back to our time in Genix. Fabian whisks us out of the pod and through the shiny glass and metal interior of the Genix lab and into his office. It's as plush and as hi-tech as you'd imagine. It's like the ultimate swank-fest except for one thing - on one wall he has a framed photo of every single person who's currently cryogenically frozen by Genix which, to me, is just so utterly creepy I can hardly focus. A wall of blank faces, some of who are lying in the basement facility beneath us, some of who are orbiting the planet high above us.

There's one gap in the wall of photos. The missing frame is on his desk and it is, of course, of Enosh. Carly and I sit, and Fabian begins talking to us about Subject Six. In fact, it's more of a pitch.

He references the bad press in the Philippines, he brings up his computer screen and shows the reaction to the Imam calling out Subject Six earlier. Some of the tweets, messages, vlogs are harsh. It seems in the wake of the attack people are desperate for an answer; for someone to blame and for someone to act as a saviour. The spotlight falls on Subject Six and a growing number of people seem to go from viewing him as a kind of lucky break for the world, to someone who owes the world:

Fuck Subject Six. Staying silent while our streets bleed! Fuck that guy.

If Subject Six doesn't help this poor man who lost his family, Subject Six is as bad as the attackers. If you can help, but choose not to, you're as bad as they are.

Subject Six is a terrorist plant. To make us feel safe while they go about killing.

Anyone else think SS might be in this for financial gain? He's bringing down the rich. Why? To make more money for himself? If he was a hero he'd help everyone not just take down his rivals.

If Subject Six can stop people in Syria, why can't he stop people here? What's going on? Why doesn't he care?

The guy was shooting for over 20 minutes, if Subject Six was in UK, which I think he was, he could have got there. Why not?

(Real posts from time we were in Genix office)

I wonder how Subject Six is taking the news, and this reaction to it, wherever he is. I know he wants to avoid the hysteria of the online crowd, but the negative headlines are hitting the mainstream news. I start to see that if Genix have created Subject Six then maybe that's a good thing. He could do with all the support he can get and these guys are known for good PR. Fabian is slippery, but doesn't slippery work?

Fabian stares at Carly and me as he turns his screen away. He's standing now. Feet wide apart. He says that now that the bubble of Subject Six has burst, it's time to reconcile the maker with his creation.

'The maker with his creation', that's how he puts it. It's time for the prodigal son to come in from the cold and together they can make things right. I can feel Subject Six pushing back from this but there is something about Fabian that convinces. He seems to believe it and, for the most part, the questions Carly and I throw at him are dealt with.

Carly

I think I, like you, could certainly see the sense in what Fabian was saying. He seemed to have the process of how they made him mapped out, he had details, he had plans. If he was making a fake claim that he'd made Six, he'd put a lot of effort into making it look credible.

That's why I asked him about the tattoo. How did he make the changing tattoo and why? Biologically speaking, the idea of a self-changing skin would surely be the toughest thing to synthesise or make. His answer? A dodge, I know that, you know that, and yet also explainable.

What Carly is referring to, is that instead of telling her how he'd created Subject Six's tattoo, he simply hands over an encrypted USB and tells her all the details are on there for her to look at later. On the same drive, he says there's proof that he set up and is still running the Cryoman (his name for Subject Six) programme. He says there's everything from the design of the lab, to the hiring of the staff, the signed NDA forms which are so iron tight that no-one working on the project has ever leaked a thing.

To Carly and me Fabian's story is looking more and more likely. He began the Cryoman project after seeing some test results during cryogenic freezing trials that pointed Genix towards the theory that they could create self-regeneration. Having already acquired some companies into the corporation making money from military sales, Fabian came up with the idea of a super-soldier - and not just that, a super-cop, super-fireman - and decided to plough millions into it. The result. Subject Six.

Although not the intended result. Subject Six was a test they didn't think would succeed which was why they weren't ready when the pod came down early and why the police beat them to it.

Carly

The next dodge, I thought, was when you were questioning him on the exact malfunction with Subject Six's test and also I think he looked uncomfortable when you pressed him on how the police, the armed police, were able to capture Six the moment he came to shore.

He claimed ignorance, but for someone so secretive about his programme, who was able to keep the whole thing under wraps for years, wouldn't you have made the effort to find out how the government had tracked the first Cryoman's pod? I know I would have... because to me that sounds like Genix had a government mole in there. You know?

But when you pressed him on it, all he did was deflect attention onto the growing outrage online.

A few dodges aside, Genix's Cryoman programme seems to be the best explanation I've seen yet about how

Subject Six came to be. We've grilled him, but he'd expect that because what he's claiming is so important. He's tried to charm us and get us onside, but he's done so with enough proof and enough credibility that we don't feel that he's being too slippery or coercive.

Which is why, when Fabian asks us to help him contact Subject Six, I agree. He's prepared another message for Subject Six and wants us to get it to him.

Subject Six, or as I want to call you, Cryoman. You have by now heard from your associates, who will also be able to furnish you with all of the evidence of what I went through to produce something as marvellous as you are. Now that you know the truth, I want you to be aware that I know not everything is going to be smooth-sailing. You were after all, a paying customer, sent up into space to come back down, fixed. And yet while you are now cancer-free you are also, undeniably changed, and for that, perhaps, you are angry with me. Why didn't I ask you? Why did I pick you? You may feel angry or confused at not being able to assent to this huge change before it happened and I acknowledge that and I will tackle it head on with you.

To do that we need to meet. The reason I am getting in touch now is for matters of security. For you, and me. Since you arrived the government have been tracking you. Now, though, since your trip to Turkey things have changed. You have angered them by turning them down and in doing so, you have distracted them. Whereas one branch of the services was tracking you, now there are more stakeholders which has led to infighting and will lead to our advantage. While their sights are compromised, we will be able to arrange a meeting... and then we will be able to discuss our purpose.

And what is that purpose? Well, I think you know. The world is spiralling out of control. Western countries are fighting a war at home against an enemy that doesn't need to invade. Middle Eastern countries are sniping and bombing and getting closer to all-out conflict. In Asia the growing economies are trying to suffocate and subsume each other. Not since WW2 have so many wars been on the brink and the world needs a saviour. Together, we can act. Together we can change things. When we meet, I will show you how to use your invincibility to balance the world and get the conflict under control. It must be soon. The world needs us. Join me now, it is the only thing you can do.

HOW CAN YOU TELL IF FABIAN TREE IS LYING?

Me

So, what did you think?

Carly

You recording, is this on?

This is from the moment we get in the car, the moment in the Genix car park.

Me

Er, yes. So what do you think, do you believe him?

Carly

Do you?

Me

Erm…

Carly

Let's say at the same time. Yes or no. Three, two one…

Carly and Me

No idea.

Both saying the same thing, both coming down from the intensity of our time with Fabian Tree, we burst out laughing. I drop Carly off at Heathrow because she's heading home and then call in to a forensics lab that I know to hand over the things I got from the Cryopod. All this time, my head is blank. Or, in fact it's probably more accurate to say, it's whirring so much it feels like it's blank.

Part of me wonders should I feel happy, relief, satisfaction, euphoria? I've been chasing down a mystery for over a year and now it seems I might be very close to having the solution. As I've said before, most people I've spoken to think it's unlikely Genix could have made Subject Six. Yet would he make this up? Does even Fabian have the balls to do that and if he does have the audacity to try and lie about this, why would he? That seems unlikely.

Almost as unlikely as Subject Six existing. Yet he exists. And having heard Fabian, I do now think that while Subject Six's creation is still irrational, the most rational explanation is that Genix did it.

They had the access to Enosh, they're the closest to having the technology, they have a boss who's undoubtedly a bit of a megalomaniac with a chip on his shoulder. Exactly the profile of the type of person who could make Subject Six. Unscrupulous, intelligent, secretive, rich, greedy, driven.

So, how will we be sure? Well, Carly has the USB and is going to see if what's on it backs Fabian up. We've also got the things I took from the Cryopod too. Jumping ahead in time slightly, I think it's now the best time to show the findings from those objects. We don't learn a lot, but the clearest thing we learn does back up Fabian's timeline on how his Cryoman was made.

***FROM WRJ FORENSICS** - a private forensics company (co-owned by an old school friend, the Jack in Walter Roger and Jack)*
Re: Pod Finds

Benj,

Hey, thanks for asking us to do this for you! Always glad to take on new clients.

When you asked me whether I could do this for you, you said you hadn't had much time to collect this evidence and were worried about whether you'd a) contaminated it b) had enough for us to test. Well, the answer is yes and no.

Sadly, the piece of plastic that the label said you'd found in the foot-well of the pod is inconclusive. The only prints I can find on it are yours. Same goes for the piece of card.

I did have some fun with it though in terms of the seatbelt material - there was nothing that I could use to identify anyone but I ran some tests and it does seem to have gone through a level of disintegration that is certainly consistent - from what I've been researching - with a launch into space and time in space. Roger keeps telling me the wear and tear on the belt piece could be from other things, which are true, but if you want my opinion on whether this pod experienced space flight... then yes. This pod went into space and came back which puts aside that theory you told me about that Genix didn't even send it into space.

Finally, the hair. Ok, a complicated one. I tested it against Subject Six's DNA sample you gave me. So, it seems we have a conundrum... the DNA of the hair is related to him. It's very similar, so same family and a male. Possibly a child, or his father? But then, when I thought about it more, knowing what you told me about the pod and that no-one from his family went near it when he was frozen, I've started to wonder whether the hair you found is from the old him, 'Enosh' and the Subject Six sample you gave me is the 'new' him. So, in becoming this 'new' being, his DNA altered. Does that make sense? Somehow Enosh's DNA changed and now he's Subject Six. You said you had a doctor looking at DNA and genetics on him, has she found any shift like this?

Call me, I'm curious,

Jack

When I get home, the kids are already asleep. The moment I walk back through the door late that night, Mina reads me. She can see it's been a big few days. I realise I haven't even told her about Niall, Rueben and the shooting yet and that makes me feel guilty as I normally tell her everything.

Mina

To be honest I was pretty angry with him. I was aware it wasn't completely fair of me to be annoyed - he was away with work, not on a stag do or anything - but when you're looking after two kids on your own in a house that's undergoing a renovation, you kind of reserve the right to be pissed off at the guy who's left you holding the fort.

He'd told us he was going away for one night. It had been three. I bit my tongue. Deciding it would be fairer to let him settle. Hoping he'd see what the past few days had taken out of me and ask me about it himself, rather than me having to tell him about it. And I don't just mean a cursory 'Are you ok', I mean him properly asking about me as if he cares and wants to give me time to answer.

But then, as I watched him take off his shoes and give the whisky decanter on the spirits table a long and thoughtful look, I could tell the last few days had taken its toll. He was safe, he wasn't limping like that awful time after he'd called me from hospital, but he hadn't just been out interviewing either.

I realised this wasn't a guy I entirely recognised. I mean it was Benji, but it was Benji doing a new type of job, going into dangerous and unchartered territory. Which made me feel angry, admiration and fear all at once. As I looked at him I saw a gleam in his eye that he wanted to tell me something. I'd seen that look before, when he's got a new idea for a book, when he's excited.

I told him I'd get ice and two glasses.

As Mina leaves me, I know I need her input, her instinct. I feel weary, like I want a whisky, to watch a film or a couple of episodes of a box-set and go to bed, but I know I can't. I have to hear her reaction to what Fabian is claiming and I need it on tape.

Mina

I said I'd bring them, you sit down, sweetness.

Me

It's crazy in here, how is it so messy? Isn't it a nightmare for you with the kids?

In case you're wondering this conversation is happening in the shell of our kitchen. Literally. We're having a side-return extension done and we don't have a wall at the back of our house. Just a hole where's they've knocked out the wall. Piles of cement, pallets of breeze blocks and brick, a cement mixer, our fridge freezer covered in dirt but still plugged in. The ground is full of holes and is more dust than floorboard. The apple tree and rose brushes in our garden seem to be encroaching, like the whole place will soon be overgrown and abandoned.

Mina

We've kind of spent the last three days between the library and Becky's house.

Me

I think we should move out for a bit. It's not right you being here on your own.

Mina

That's not necessary.

Me

I don't like the idea you guys being here, with me or without, when there's only a screw and some chipboard at the back of the house. It's not safe. And the dust, the noise, how can you stand it?

Mina

Because I have to.

Me

Maybe you don't. Let's go somewhere.

Mina

Where to?

Me

A hotel?

Mina

We can't afford it.

Me

I think we will be able to actually.

Mina

What do you mean?

Me

This story. It keeps getting bigger and it also, might be winding up.

Mina

Really? I saw what the father of those two girls said on the news. How did he react to that?

Me

I don't know. I haven't seen or spoken to him since. But get this, are you ready?

By the time we have our whiskies and we're sat on the sofa in the living room, the only room in the downstairs dust hasn't invaded, I'm anxious to hear what she has to say.

Me

Ok, get this, are you ready?

I tell her about the trip to Genix. What Fabian is claiming.

Mina

Bullshit. I don't buy it.

Me

Why not?

Mina

You're going to tell me that in the flesh, he was believable, right?

Me

Right. I still didn't like him, don't like him, DEBRIS have told me too much about him to get past it, but he was… well, he seemed, credible.

Mina

And what did Carly think? The same?

Me

Yeah, but we were both aware he was trying to charm us. It's just the most rational explanation. Don't you think?

Mina

No, I don't.

Me

You don't?

Mina

Ok, let me explain, I mean I think you've told me enough about what's going on to have a decent overview of the story.

Me

100% agreed.

Mina

From what I've seen the most rational explanation is he's lying. That's much more likely than him doing it.

Me

Is it?

Mina

Of course. Subject Six is a miracle and I'm not using that word flippantly. Could they have made him? Without anyone knowing? You've got that guy from

Genix, you've spoken to a bunch of stalkers who monitor everything he does and no-one thinks he's working on a secret soldier man, and then one just turns up?

Me

He'd say that's hearsay.

Mina

Fine, but does he really have the tech or the skills? Subject Six isn't just the next step on from a robot, or cryogenic freezing… he's like 100 steps on. It's like going from having a wheel to inventing a formula one car in a day. And that's not rational, it's not rational that today, or back in 2018 he could produce what Subject Six is. I find it too far-fetched.

Me

He's given Carly all the details. He says…

Mina

Well, let's see what they're like, but if we go back to logic, the fact he's lying is more likely. Isn't it?

Me

Go on, work it through for me. I'm recording, I want to get your thoughts down.

Mina

Ok, so what's more likely, Genix has made one of the biggest scientific breakthroughs ever or it's lying and being opportunistic?

Me

How would Fabian benefit from claiming he made Subject Six?

Mina

You don't need me to answer that. No-one else has come forward to claim the triumph, have they? There's a vacuum around him, and Fabian, knowing he's got links to Subject Six because of the freezing, has decided the time is right to try and fill that space.

Me

All for publicity?

Mina

All for profit. Imagine the boost it will give Genix.

Me

But it'll also kill the company if it's proved he's lying.

Mina

Who's going to do that? No-one has so far. And in the meantime, Fabian presents himself as the builder of this saviour, this super-soldier. He's going to be hot property, hotter than Subject Six himself.

Me

Mmm... I guess. I don't know.

Mina

The theory has its flaws, but less than the one that Fabian made him... in my view.

WHERE HAS SUBJECT SIX GONE?

The following morning, well it feels way too early to be morning, Mina and I are woken by a loud banging on the door. At first we leave it, putting it down to the builders. When it continues, I have no choice but to drag myself out of bed. I look through the shutters and see a police car. Mina is trying to get back to sleep, I think about letting her, but as a lurching sense of dread starts building up I realise that this could be bad - and that it'd be better to have Mina with me.

We grab our dressing gowns - matching, which is cute and embarrassing in equal measure - and go to the door. Ignoring the sounds of the kids calling for us in semi-asleep voices.

Mina
Seeing the police at the door, hearing them tell Benji they needed to speak to him, that was perhaps a threshold moment for me. Obviously, when he'd come back injured from that damn mission, the reality of what he was doing hit me, but I hadn't seen the danger myself. He'd promised joining Subject Six on a mission was a one-off, so it didn't feel like there was any long-term danger or damage - apart from the scarring of course.
But being present, seeing cops walk into the living room, treating Benji with suspicion and caution, that made me worry. Here was a situation that could have a lasting impact on us as a family.

It was very formal, very stifling, and when the children started to shout louder I was grateful to get away, just for a second to clear my head. Remarkably, seeing as I felt panic coursing through me as I went to them, I suddenly decided that even though it was the fucking story that had got us into this mess, the story needed me to record what was going on.
They'd said they wanted an informal chat to begin with, and didn't think Benji needed to come to the station yet. With the emphasis on the 'yet'. So, when I came back in to the room to ask if anyone wanted a drink, I dropped my phone behind a cushion on the sofa with the camera on.

At the time, I have no idea that Mina's got my back and has hidden a camera. All I know is that when she comes back in, she's got a false mask of politeness on and I get a sudden, shock of fear that she might leave me. That if this goes wrong, and I'm into something too deep, then she'll have no choice but to leave me for the sake of the children. Here I am, being questioned by the Police, have I already gone too far?

Now all along, I've been aware that Subject Six is operating in a grey area legally. Vigilantism is not legal, many of the things he does to find a target and expose them are not legal. And in a court of law the argument for it being for the greater good cannot be relied on. As a journalist, reporting on events rather than causing them, you're afforded a certain amount of leeway and it's unlikely you'll be in trouble with the law if all you've done is witness. But I've always known I have to be careful.

I know what you're thinking, you're saying, Benji you went along on a mission. You broke into a house, stole something. And of course I did. The whole of my career that's the only time I've been active in a crime. But it was a calculated risk. I knew that by the time I published this book, the crime would be at least two years old, I knew I could write about it without giving details which would make it hard to prove. Which is why, as I sit down and get ready to answer the policeman's questions, the possibility they're here to question me about the mission isn't preying on my mind. These are British cops and there's no way they'd want an informal chat about something in another country.

So why are they here and what do I need to be aware of? The dread I have, as far as Mina and the kids are concerned, is the recent mob mentality that's been building up around Subject Six. People trying to own him, people telling him what he should be doing, people denouncing him. He's become such a big issue, he no longer has full control of what he stands for and that, I'm seeing firsthand, is dangerous. And if it's dangerous for him, it could be for me. If the authorities think he's a risk to the public, they might want to bring him in. To stop him. And I could get lumped in as an accomplice.

I might be waffling, I might not be as concise as I want, but as I sit opposite these policemen, the fact is my thoughts are jumbled. What happens if the knives are falsely out for Subject Six and I get thrown to the wolves alongside him?

DC Hesketh

You're a journalist, we understand?

Me

I try to be.

DC Capes

I listened to your podcast. It was good.

Despite the situation, or probably because of it, I find myself wanting to laugh. Are they really using the good cop, bad cop routine so quickly? I've never really met a cop who I think is super smart, but surely they're better than this?

Me

Thanks. That was a fun project.

DC Hesketh

And is it fun, your job?

Me

It certainly can be.

DC Capes

What are you working on now?

Officially my publishers and agent have me working on a ghost-writing project. My cover while I follow Subject Six, but after my visit to Genix and Michelle that cover isn't worth keeping.

Me

Officially? I'm ghost-writing for a retired sport-star, a footballer called Brian Parr.

DC Hesketh

And unofficially?

Me

I've been following someone. You probably know him as Subject Six.

DC Hesketh

Why the cloak and dagger? Is that how you normally work?

Me

Erm, no. Not normally. But it's not the first time I've pretended to be working on a project while actually looking at something else. You know, so no-one else starts sniffing around, so I can keep the story and revelations under wraps until I publish.

DC Capes

So, what have you been following? You must have seen some exciting stuff.

Me

Well, not really. It's mostly been interviews, rather than me following him... you know, in the field.

From upstairs I hear one and then two kids throw themselves into a tantrum. Mina tries to stop it at source, but I get the feeling this one could build. Perhaps the kids can sense the atmosphere in the house? Stamping and sobbing comes through the floorboards directly above.

Me

Look, if you'd like to tell me what this is about, what you need, perhaps I could help you quicker?

DC Hesketh

I think I'd like you to carry on doing the telling if that's ok.

Me

Fine. Sure.

DC Capes

Is it true, what they say, about what he can do?

Me

I'd say there's a lot of nonsense written about him, but yes, some of it is true.

DC Hesketh

What kind of nonsense?

Me

Well, he has some capabilities, but he's not... he's not god or anything like that.

DC Hesketh

Where is he?

Me

I don't know.

DC Hesketh

How do you get hold of him?

Me

He gets hold of me.

DC Hesketh

Where does he live?

Me

I don't know.

DC Hesketh

You don't know?

Me

I've been blindfolded every time I've visited.

DC Hesketh laughs at this. I sense he's getting into his stride.

DC Hesketh

You can't hazard a guess?

Me

The Midlands.

DC Hesketh

You won't tell me more?

Me

I wouldn't be comfortable in doing so, no.

DC Hesketh

DC Capes, do we often care about comfort in a counter-terrorist investigation?

DC Capes

Not that I can remember.

DC Hesketh

No, nor me. Care to elaborate?

Me

No. I don't think I do.

Now, in this recording I have to say my voice is remarkably stable and calm. Let me tell you that's not how I'm feeling.

DC Hesketh

Why is he so insecure? What's he hiding?

Me

He's not hiding anything.

DC Hesketh

What's he hiding from then?

Me

I think you know that.

DC Hesketh

Do I?

Me

I imagine so.

DC Hesketh

I can see you're a clever man, but don't get too clever.

Me

When he arrived, he was wanted. He was arrested without cause, he's had death threats against him, so he feels the need to be watchful.

DC Hesketh

Hence the blindfolding.

Me

Yes.

DC Hesketh

When will he contact you again?

Me

That's up to him.

DC Hesketh

If I asked you to tell me when he does, would you?

Me

I could.

DC Hesketh

I know you could. I asked whether you would.

Me

I know. Can I just ask, is this about yesterday? About what the Imam said about Subject Six leading a war?

DC Hesketh

I think it's fair to say it's made the matter more urgent. No matter how emotional the terrorist atrocities make us, we still have to abide by the law at all times, don't you think?

After this, the conversation doesn't cover any new ground. I'm relieved that this is more a visit asking for/threatening me into giving help rather than something more direct, but I'm still glad when they go. As is Mina. Afterwards, we don't make a definitive decision about what I'll do next time Subject Six gets in touch - whether I'll tell them or not. I don't want to, because it would ruin my story. Mina gets that, but also doesn't want me disobeying what is effectively an order from them; she thinks when he is in contact I could let them know, but not give any real details. Keeping in with Subject Six and also them.

In the end though, our conversation is academic. Because he doesn't get in touch. With me, with anyone.

He disappears. No missions, no sightings. And he doesn't just disappear from public, he vanishes from everywhere.

WHERE IS SUBJECT SIX?

The legend of Subject Six has always been one of mystery but now there seems to be a twist that nobody saw coming. Just when Imam Omar Yusuf has asked personally for help from Subject Six, it seems that the man himself has disappeared. Although the official figure is disputed, some say 21 days, some say 23, the fact remains that there have been no official sightings of Subject Six for almost three weeks.

SUPERZERO

Subject Six has gone from superhero to super-zero and now his critics have said they always thought he'd do something like this - disappear and leave others to clean up his mess. For all the hype around him, the alleged superhuman vigilante has always been controversial and now he's dropped off the face of the earth many people are saying they're glad he's gone, "What kind of person dodges their responsibilities when they're needed the most? I ask you... "

SUBJECT TRICKS!

The scariest thing about this whole issue is how un-accountable Subject Six has been. With no-one to keep him in check, with no-one to answer to he's always played by his own tune and now we're paying for it. This vanishing trick has got us all guessing and to what end? What right has he to deceive us and leads us on a wild goose chase? Promising us help then taking it away without reason. We've been conned by him and the sooner we forget about him the better.

NO SURPRISE HE'S GONE SAYS SOURCE

A source close to Subject Six has told this reporter that before his disappearance he had spoken about wanting to leave. Apparently, the erstwhile saviour had long been battling with the pressure that his fast-found fame had brought to him, "Subject Six had wanted to be a force for good and to show others how to make a difference, but he had begun to question his role, especially once people began to criticise what he was doing or tried to tell him what to do next. He felt he couldn't please everybody and that he'd found himself in an impossible situation".

Ok, let me just interject here, I'm that source. But not once did I give any quotes to a journalist. After the mystery of where Subject Six is begins to build, Laura gets in touch. Having written the piece about him being Enosh she's been asked to do a piece on where he might be and wants to see if I have any idea. I don't. I tell her a couple of things off-record. Stuff I know I'm going to be using in my book so don't want her to print, which, in her very good piece about where he might have gone and why, she doesn't. However, while she's in the office of the paper she's writing that piece for, another reporter steals her notebook and steals my quotes. Just steals them.

I'm not going to go into what happened to this reporter, but that they would go so far as to rob a fellow journalist just shows how frantic the rush for stories on Subject Six is at that time. I've never heard of any reporters doing that to someone else, ever. It's just not done. And yet the story of Subject Six is so powerful, so potent that they commit this shocking breach of ethics just so they could go to print with something new.

One of the first questions Mina asks me after it becomes apparent that something is happening with Subject Six, and he's not just on a mission, is whether I could have predicted this: his disappearance. The answer is yes - since the beginning of my work with Subject Six I've thought about three scenarios which could see him vanish.

First up is the most complicated, and most simple, and that's him dying. Is he dead? And I mean actually dead? He's always in danger and we still don't know the full extent of his regeneration powers - what would happen if he's blown up? And secondly, if the number of his tattoo is somehow counting to a date and it's an end-date, what happens when the number is reached? Both of these questions are too complex to answer, which is conversely what makes it so simple - I literally don't have the capability to respond, so I can't.

What I do know, once I speak to Walton, is that as far as he knows Subject Six wasn't on a mission when he disappeared. After leaving the estate, when Carly and I went to Michelle and Genix, he wasn't heading off to the front-line immediately. So, unless for the first time he's gone on a mission without telling Walton, the theory he's been killed in the line of duty isn't likely.

So, after his death comes the second situation, the one the papers and media are seizing on the most - the idea that he's run away. We all know the British papers love to knock famous people off their perch and having built up Subject Six as a modern day saviour, they're very quick to jump on the bandwagon and start branding him a coward, a traitor, a liar once it appears he's gone. So, has he? Many times I've spoken to him about the Catch 22 he finds himself in as the publicity around him grows. We have chats about him abdicating his position. Not many, but enough.

He tells me he's starting to believe that one person can't save the world even if they hang around forever. The longer you're on a pedestal the more time people have to take aim at you; by making yourself a target by making a stand you're inevitably going to start taking hits. So, he wonders, would it be best to bow out, to retreat and hope that the good he has done and the legacy of the exposures he's made are enough to justify his existence?

During these chats, I think all he's doing, is exploring. I never get the sense he's going to leave. Once it becomes apparent he's gone somewhere I check in with the only other people who could know how he's feeling.

Carly
I bet the Fabian Tree thing pissed him off and increased the pressure, but the way he was the last time I saw him I think it's more likely he'd take action than walk away, I really do.

Walton

The last time I saw him he was the same as ever - telling me what to do with Niall and Rueben, coming up with plans for our next excursions, getting me to work-up new tech ideas that would help him. He was ramping up if anything, and I should know, I was building the bloody ramp.

As you can see neither of them set too much store in the idea he's had enough and packed it in. Which brings us to the third principle possibility - that he's vanished against his will. As a quick caveat, Walton thinks there's no chance of that either:

Walton

Captured? No way. We were tracking everyone, I still am, and no-one could have got to him. Not on my watch.

But for all Walton's certainty, I still explore the idea that Subject Six is MIA because of forces against his will. Well, when I say explore, I try. But it's not easy. If the UK, the US, Russia, anyone has captured him they're not going to shout about it, are they? So instead I look every-where I can think of to see if there are any clues.

Remember the whole world is looking for him - or at least the papers in every country are running stories on him - so how likely is it that there are no leaks, no rum-blings? If a government had got him it would be such an event, a coup, that surely there would be some reaction for myself, Walton or DEBRIS to pick up on. There isn't.

WHAT HAPPENS WHEN SOMEONE TELLS THE WORLD THEY MADE SUBJECT SIX?

One afternoon I'm transcribing one of my many recordings - the visit I made to Michelle, Tuppence and Oscar - when Mina bursts in. She turns the TV on.

A huge headline reads **'SUBJECT SIX: BREAKTHROUGH'**. Fabian Tree is standing in the press conference room at Genix.

I feel a lurching in my stomach. This is not a move I've seen coming.

Fabian Tree - press conference transcript

As a country, as a global community, we find ourselves at a crossroads. And sadly, as we look down we see the roads are paved with blood. I'm sure, like me and Genix the company I speak for today, you've been recently affected by the words of Imam Omar Yusuf and his passionate plea for action against the war the terrorists are bringing to our shores. I certainly have which is why, in a change of strategy, I've asked you all here to make this announcement.

Omar Yusuf called for Subject Six to help protect this country and our way of life. To do this, and to help our country and our Western world, I want to confirm the rumours that so many people have heard: it's true, that here, in the Genix labs, Subject Six was made. Yes, yes I know and please, please, questions later and we have a hand-out to explain how we achieved this miraculous breakthrough which you'll all receive after this briefing. Genix owns many companies that assist our governments with military technology and has done for years. Some years back, I began to wonder whether we could combine our world-leading cryogenic freezing techniques with our military research in order to create a soldier, a weapon, that would be able to keep us safe from our enemies. Subject Six is the result of these experiments.

Due to the potential of Subject Six, who is the first Cryoman we have successfully created, we have until recently kept everything top secret. We have liaised with the correct authorities of course, but we kept everything under wraps while we carried out the proper tests necessary. Unfortunately, there were some unforeseen complications which led to Subject Six starting life in a way we didn't plan.

Now, though, we can announce we have Subject Six under full operation control. The reason he has not been seen recently is that we have been carrying out tests and ensuring that everything is as it should be. While we were planning on launching him properly in a few months time, we've decided to bring it forward. Why? Because like Omar Yusuf said a few weeks ago, we can no longer sit back and wait for more bloodshed. We must fight back and seeing as Genix have developed a new form of military power, I believe it's our duty to share it. From now on we'll be working with the authorities to do everything in our power to end this war against the West as soon as possible. And when we do, and when my creation Subject Six leads us to peace, we here at Genix will be privileged and grateful to have helped save the world as we know it.

I mute the screen as Fabian leaves, lapping up the attention really but pretending he needs to get away as soon as possible. Mina and I try to work out the implications of Fabian's speech. DEBRIS bombard my phone with WhatsApp messages. Laura Burrows leaves me a message. As does Larry from AllFree. But the only person I want to hear from is Subject Six.

No prizes for guessing that I don't. In the days after Fabian's speech, lots of people are demanding evidence from Genix, but Subject Six is under the microscope just as much. Why? Well, mostly because he's still not around. There's been no big reappearance to silence the rumours.

GENIX - TRUTH OR LIES?

Genix have been actively knocking down rumours circulating online that Subject Six was not their creation. In light of his apparent disappearance many bloggers and critics are claiming that the company known for bringing cryogenic freezing onto the mass market have very little proof they actually made him. Many people are focusing on the fact that Subject Six has yet to comment and that he's never been seen with anyone from Genix.

So many people are talking about him, speculating, arguing. In his stark absence, the void he leaves just keeps getting filled with noise. Most of it harmless nonsense, some of it malicious, some of it dangerous.

At one point, I think about stepping into the ring and speaking for him. To put his point forward, to explain that Fabian's word shouldn't be taken as gospel. But I don't think about it for that long. I don't want to make myself a target and put Mina and the kids at risk of being in the spotlight and I don't want to interfere with the story. Not actively.

As the rumours pile up it's fascinating to watch and document. If I'd been capable of being objective I would have found it utterly compelling to see how modern media and people can twist and turn truth and untruth over and over in a 24/7 news hurricane. Until everyone's in a perpetual frenzy. But by now, there's no way I can be objective.

With no Subject Six to come forward and try to explain who and what he is, it falls to Fabian to set the agenda. The evidence he puts out to show the world how he created Subject Six is highly redacted because he says he doesn't want the technology to fall into the wrong hands. Instead he spends his time talking about Subject Six in a more practical way. What he's for, what he can do. Everything he says makes sense and stands-up, mostly. Just as Carly and I began to lean towards believing him in the office, it feels like gradually the groundswell of public opinion does too.

So, where am I on Fabian at this stage? Wary, very wary that he's lying, but not sold either way. Yet. During that time, the one lie I am certain that Fabian tells is when he claims that Enosh signed up for the Cryoman program when he chose to be frozen, which is why they used him for the experiments.

I know this isn't true, because I've asked Subject Six about it directly. He tells me a few times, categorically that he didn't opt into any programmes. Mina says this is proof Fabian is lying about the whole thing. And I can't deny it stinks, yet it could also be that due to the intense scrutiny from the media, Fabian white-lies his way out of a hole. He doesn't want to be questioned over his ethics - which are terrible if he transformed Enosh Blake without asking - and so he lies. But does one deception mean everything he's saying about Genix is untrue? I still can't quite believe he'll go to such lengths to convince the world, if it's a lie. Even if he is an arrogant, power-grabbing ass.

FABIAN SPEAKS

Fabian Tree came out fighting today, claiming the rumours about Subject Six vanishing are unfounded, "Subject Six, as we have made clear in our hand-out, is not a robot or a drone. To make him the most powerful he could be, and to reach his potential, we had to give him the power of free-will. We are currently in contact with him on a daily basis. We are working actively with him but he does not want to take part in this media frenzy at the moment and we cannot coerce him into it. But rest assured, we are working with him to help secure our country and the future of the free world."

The moment this article and statement comes out, DEBRIS get in touch with me. Once Fabian announces that Subject Six is his, they've been going over the documents he gave out and have put all their surveillance techniques, all of their sources, into overdrive. They still want to nail him over the Cryopods, they're still watching what's in orbit, but now they think they might have a new rod to beat Fabian with - so they set to work.

Obviously, DEBRIS want to ruin Fabian. Which means, of course, that I take what they send me with a pinch of salt, but I have had a number of interactions with them in the weeks after Fabian's press conference.

Eileen Raymond

Heard from a source we have on the security team at GENIX. No-one and I mean no-one has heard any-

thing or seen anything about Subject Six. Are you beginning to think Fabian is bullshitting? Is that another GENIX stink I can smell?

***

Dan Raymond

Have you seen the news?

Me

Where?

Dan Raymond

The Financial Times?

Me

No, what?

Dan Raymond

Weapons companies owned by GENIX have seen stock prices go way up - seems like speculation that action will happen to stop terrorists is good for business.

***

Nicholas Singh

Sending you a link now, lots of chatter that GENIX are making more *Cryo-Soldiers*.

Me

Wow, Ok

Nicholas Singh

Been digging, looks like GENIX have been leaking that info from what I can tell. I wonder why #priceofsharesup

***

Nicholas Singh

Heard the rumour that Subject Six is called that because he's the sixth one they made?

Me

Seen a bit on that. What do you think?

Nicholas Singh

Bullshit again. Shares still going up, Fabian happy as a pig in shit fanning the flames

***

Eileen Raymond

Fabian met with ministry of defence today. Not reported on news but no surprise there.

Me

How do you know that? You stalking him?

Me

Are you?

Eileen Raymond

Everything we do is justified.

HOW DANGEROUS IS KNOWING SUBJECT SIX?

As most of the mainstream media seem to gradually buy into Fabian's announcement, believing that Subject Six is working with Genix on some sort of sustained attack on the terrorist cells targeting the UK and the rest of the Western world, I find out that not everything is going Genix's way.

In my search for the truth, I'm often in contact with Laura and Cynthia, both of whom say they've heard that Genix has had to deal with cyber and physical attacks. While some people say this is Subject Six, apparently the more likely explanation is other companies or even governments are trying to get hold of the Cryoman technology. Whoever is attacking Genix, it's apparent that being allied with Subject Six is putting them at risk. And they're not the only ones.

Walton

One of the things Enosh had tasked me with, as soon as we'd set-up shop in the estate, was monitoring his ex-wife and the kids. I did so. We had cameras on the house and over the months I kind of got to enjoy checking in on them, they seemed like a pretty happy couple of kids, you know? And I know Enosh liked to watch the feeds too, it calmed him to see them, I think.

Once Enosh had gone, I spent extra time watching the

family. I didn't want anything to happen on my watch while he was away. Which is why, as soon as I noticed they were gone, I got onto Benji. Before grabbing Rueben and Niall and heading down there myself.

The moment Walton calls me and tells me he thinks Michelle and the kids are missing I jump on it. When I go through to get the car keys Mina is the kitchen hanging shelves. She sees me, sees the stress on my face and seeing as the kids are at the childminders, tells me she'll come too. We're in the car within minutes.

Mina drives so I can stay in touch with Walton. Part of the surveillance he's been running on Michelle and the kids is monitoring online chatter about Subject Six, and Enosh Blake, from terrorists and groups they've identified as threats - government bodies included. After the Yusuf Omar speech and Fabian's announcement, there's a huge spike in traffic between the terrorist cells and Jihadi hate speech against Subject Six. Threats. Abuse. Plots. Most of it just talk and the kind of online mouthing off security services dismiss almost instantly.

Walton though, finds a credible threat. There's a group who say they're targeting Subject Six and apparently focusing on hitting his family. Or Enosh's family. These threats, coming within hours of Walton realizing Michelle and the kids seem to be missing, are why he gets me involved. He sends me the messages he's intercepted and keeps sending me information on the group.

Walton

Why didn't I call the police? Because it wasn't what we needed at that point. They're not an efficient force and with Benji and me on the way as well I knew we had what we needed.

On top of that I guess there was the security risk of bringing them into the situation. I didn't want them sniffing around and asking about how I knew they were gone, trying to find out more about Enosh and where we were based. The police are not an organisation where confidential information stays secret and I didn't want them to be in possession of any more knowledge about us than absolutely necessary.
I knew I could call on them as a resource if I needed - one thing they do have that can be helpful in a missing persons case is a great reach - but it has to be carefully managed.

Sitting in the car outside Michelle's house, I attach my Go Pro to my chest and start recording. I figure we need to capture as much evidence as possible to help our search, and since the police paid me that visit I think it's more important than ever that I can properly account for everything I'm doing as part of the story.

Mina
Do you really think you should be filming this?
Me
Absolutely. It's what the police do now, wear Go Pros on their chests... we're going into their house, this can protect us more than anything else.
Mina
How are we going to get in?
Me
Walton said check to see if anything is open first. Then, if we have too, break in. He's got keys apparently but won't be here for another couple of hours at least.
Mina
There's a window, open, up there.

Me

I see. Can we make that?

Mina

I can.

What follows is Mina being incredibly impressive. She's calm, collected and climbs up the garage and then uses a drainpipe to swing herself onto a window ledge and in through a bathroom window. For all her insistence that I'm not to get involved in anything risky, she's not batting an eyelid at what we have to do here. I think it's his kids. Their lives are at stake and she's going to do everything she can to help them.

Moments later she opens the back door.

Mina

This is a bit CSI, but it doesn't look like they left in a hurry.

Me

Show me.

We go inside and she's right. There's nothing out of place, no signs of a struggle or blood, the things I was dreading to find. Mina sets to, looking in bins, opening drawers. I follow behind, sending a message to Walton telling him we're in.

Mina

I can't think of a more immaculate house, and look, the one cup of tea in the sink. See this receipt in the bin, sun tan lotion, mosquito repellent, Zika pills. It looks like they've gone on holiday, doesn't it?

Me

It looks exactly like it.

Mina

You think someone's made it look like this?

Me

Could be. Let me call Walton.

I don't get through to Walton, which makes sense, he's driving. Mina and I don't feel comfortable sitting in the house so we wait in a swing-chair on the decking in the back garden. To pass the time we talk through the list of things that we still have to do to finish the kitchen.

Halfway through Mina brings her head up off my shoulder and says we're going through the wrong list. She wants to know what needs to be unravelled for me to understand the Subject Six story. It's got long, complicated. If I want to turn it into a book, which I need to because that's my job, how am I going to be able to process everything?

Mina

He looked at me for a while. Then came out with it all quite quickly. In a nutshell, Benji reckoned he'd have a book if he could find Subject Six, make sure Michelle and the kids were ok and then get to the bottom of whether Genix were lying or not. I was about to laugh and tell him how simple that sounded when he got another call from Walton and everything went wrong.

What Walton tells me is a nightmare scenario. No, the nightmare scenario. As I've done before, I'm going to use a few different people to help me get down what happens next.

Kylie

If I'm honest I find it incredibly hard to go back to that moment. I've run it over in my head so many times, and

I've been told by lots of people it wasn't my fault, and all of that, but I still can't pull my thoughts away from what happened. And every time I do I feel sick, physically sick.

Kylie our childminder. She's helped us for almost four years and she looks after the kids three days a week. They love her. We love her. The moment she's talking about happens while Mina and I are racing to get home.

Kylie

I go back and back, wishing I'd had my bloody phone on loud, or vibrate at least, but I'd turned it to silent during naptime. I think again about how many times I've acted in the same way, was I negligent just that day? Or did I do it every day? Were they always at risk under me? I can't get it clear in my head. I think the problem was, I was just comfortable with them, the kids, Mina, Benji, it was so easy and normal that I… well, that I just wasn't on alert.

Mina and I drive home as fast as we can. We keep calling Kylie. Mina makes 87 calls. We don't get through. We do speak to Walton who confirms what he's just told me - that Michelle has called to tell him she's safe, and that now he thinks the threat to the family could be a threat against me.

Us. The kids.

Mina

It won't ever be possible, thankfully, for me to accurately describe what it was like trying to get home. The closest thing I can think of in my life that was like it, was both births. They were too awful for words, painful beyond comprehension, just like being in the car trying to get home, they were moments of real, actual torture. But now that they're done, over, I can't, probably won't let myself get back there properly. I can see myself screaming on the hospital bed, picture myself wringing my hands in the passenger seat, but I can't feel it or remember it properly. It's like I see it in slow-motion, or through a lens. And in a way, I'm glad about that because it was monstrous, it was horrific.

As soon as Benji pulled up, essentially parking on the curb, we both ran to the house as fast as we could. An insane fumble for the keys, my heart pounding in my ribcage, and then in. To silence. No babies. Benji spun and ran out, I knew he was going to Kylie's. I knelt down and screamed. Where were my babies?

With Mina's scream ringing in my ears, I sprint as fast as I can to Kylie's house. You can see where she lives from ours, which is how she became our childminder because when we looked at the list of people in our area she was the closest to us. I see the TV's on. I can hear her voice. The hope that there's been some problem at our house so she's got the kids with her at her place, pops into my head. When she opens the door, on the phone, that positivity bursts.

Kylie

I literally just hung up on my boyfriend when I saw Benji, he looked wild, angry, scared. He asked me where the kids were and I said I'd dropped them off with Mina at home, twenty minutes or so ago. When he told me I hadn't, that that was impossible, I didn't understand him. Because I had, I was 100% certain I had.

Then I heard footsteps and saw Mina running down the street towards my house.

Walton

By the time I called Benji and had my fears confirmed I'd already switched routes and we were on our way to his and Mina's house. I guessed we were about 15 minutes away. In the background I could hear voices, his wife and another woman who I found out was their childminder.

Benji said he was going to call the police - instinct made me want him to wait, until I got there, but these were his kids and I knew we might need all the help we could get. I told him to start trying to find out if any neighbours had seen anything and promised I'd be with him soon.

Mina

How could it have happened? How could it have happened? That's all I wanted to know and now that I've heard Kylie's story I understand, but at the time, I didn't. All I saw when I saw Kylie was the woman who should have been looking after my babies and who now wasn't. I'm not proud of how I spoke to her, how I reacted, but... but it's not exactly easy to control yourself in that kind of situation, is it?

I know I have to call the police. 999 and the detectives who came to see me. They wanted to know about Subject Six and terrorism and now Walton's telling me about threats and the kids are gone. But it's not easy to keep it together. Mina is screaming at Kylie, demanding to know what happened. I find myself buckling over, vomiting into the bushes outside Kylie's house.

Spitting, shaking, I try to grab hold of reality. We need to know what did happen. I ask Mina to be quiet, implore her to let Kylie speak.

Kylie

I was trembling now, stuttering, but I managed to force it out. We came back from the park, the plan as ever was to watch a Netflix cartoon and have a snack before Mina came home and I could leave. But when we came home, the windows in the front room were open, the TV was on and I heard Mina's voice talking on the phone. I mean I heard it, so I opened the door, said goodbye to the kids and left. Exactly the type of thing that happens all the time when Mina's between contracts. I didn't look back, I didn't think anything of it. To me, for the day, my work was done.

A chill runs through me. I think I might be sick again. It's hard to get my head around this. I keep seeing their faces, their vulnerable bodies. I don't have time to go into the details of how these people got Mina's voice, what must have been a recording, but the one thing it tells me is that they're organised. This is planned.

'What are they doing? Why are they doing this?' Mina sobs, turning towards me.

I try to tell her I don't know, that it will be alright. She's beginning to hyperventilate, I feel like there's an incessant whirring building in my head, "My babies, my babies… this is all because of…"

Mina doesn't finish her sentence. Across the street a car door slams shut. I hear Bonnie say 'bye' to someone. There they both are.

We both start running. The car drives off, I half realise I need to remember it's a blue Nissan Almera, I half just throw myself and all my relief into picking up both kids and hugging them for dear life.

They're fine, absolutely fine, if a little confused. And Bonnie is holding a mobile phone. It rings less than a minute after I'm given it. I answer without thinking, Mina

and the kids still around me. Only after I hear his voice
do I snap into focus and reach for my own phone so I can
start recording. It's hastily done, so I don't catch everything we say but you get the idea.

Me

... going on?

Him

... warning.

Me

You ever come near us again, I...

Him

**Quiet. Do not anger us. This was a statement, to show
you what we can do. If you don't listen to me now,
we'll do it again and this time...**

Me

I'm going straight to the police.

Him

A bad idea. We'll know and we'll take action.

Me

My kids are not...

Him

Your children, yes, they are yours, for the time being.

Me

You motherfucker...

At this point I lose it. I've turned away from Mina,
Kylie and the kids and walked a few paces down the
street. So, I really do let rip. Then I catch sight of the car,
parked up in the street. The same Nissan the kids got out
of. I stop speaking.

Him

You can see us?

Me

You...

The car pulls out of the space it's parked in. I think I make out four people in there.

Him

You have one week to bring Subject Six to us.

Me

That's what you want?

Him

That's what we need to happen. If you don't, we'll come for you.

Me

This is insane, you're...

Him

You'll be hearing from us.

Now, in films, TV shows, whenever someone doesn't call the police I get angry. It just never seems to work out. The police always turn up at some point anyway and, rightly, are pretty pissed off that you haven't told them about the murder-kidnapping-whatever-crime-it-is until now. All you do by not informing the authorities is put a fraught situation in more jeopardy.

So, as I hang up my first thought is to call 999. I know Walton is protective of Subject Six, as I am too, but with my kids involved, it's just not a risk I want to take. I have their make of car, a voice recording, I imagine the kids can describe the people who took them pretty well. With any luck, we can get whoever this is picked up quickly. So I dial 999.

Mina

I guess I kind of surprised myself, but when Benji told me he was calling 999, my immediate reaction was to grab his phone and stop the call.

Why? Well, I'd been close enough to hear the man tell Benji not to inform the police. Not to tell them anything. And I thought, with the kids being safe, we needed to discuss things properly. Benji was adamant though, I could see it in his eyes, whether it was because he blamed himself for taking us all down this route and now he wanted to make amends and play things by the book, I don't know.

Luckily, Walton arrived shortly after. And he agreed with me and I still think we made the right decision.

For the rest of the day, I feel like I'm walking with ski boots on. As if I'm off-balance, off-kilter. I try to focus, to correct myself, but it's tough. I feel like I've come so close to something so catastrophically bad that I've looked down at hell and I can't stop seeing it. And why is that? Well mostly because this isn't the end. The threats are still there, ringing in my ears, smothering me.

Walton is a blessing. He comes in, he acts like he knows what to do, even though later he admits he was winging it.

Walton

I tell you, they teach you in the army how to lead and the most important skill in doing that is to seem like you're in complete control even when you're not. Your kids were fine, you two were a mess and I couldn't really

So, Walton begins working. Niall and Ruben are with him and they start to try and track down who the group is that are against us. Mina and I try to find out as much as we can about what happened. We don't grill the kids. We get them some popcorn, milk - I know, I know, who wants to eat popcorn with full fat milk? - and we pretend we're just shooting the breeze and we find out about what happened as softly, softly as we can.

They got home. There were two men. Younger than Daddy, lots of big hair, smiley, smaller than Daddy.
He said that he'd been asked by Mummy to give them both toys that were in the car. They walk with him to the car. The blue Nissan.
Inside is one other man. The toys are in the car, a pig and a gorilla. They work when you drive.
They get in the car. The toys move and sing when the car moves. They drive around the local streets.
They don't know for how long. They feel safe the whole time. The toys are really funny.
Then they see Mums (the name I've trained them to call Mina) and Daddy and then they're out the car.

I don't think people like me are used to feeling powerless. Helpless. We're always taught we can get what we want. That everything's in our reach. The only time we come up against something that we can't control is health.

In my time, I've had to deal with miscarriages, cancer, death. And they're devastatingly out of your control, but apart from that I've always been in charge or felt I could be. People all over the world have fights on their hand - against legal injustice, economic injustice. I've been lucky enough to not come up against anything like this.

So, now, finding myself in a situation where someone has come in and taken my children, from my home, it leaves me struggling. Desperately treading water. What was a good superhero story has now become a nightmare in reality. Once they're both in bed. We eat. We open some wine. We try to find clarity.

As Walton, Mina and I talk things through, despite the dread that I've had in me since I raced around to Kylie's, the overriding thought that keeps forcing itself to the forefront of what I want to say is straight out of Churchill's book: We need to fight them.

In an off-hand way I've often said to friends and family that if I was ever to see a terrorist attack with my own eyes, then I'd consider leaving London and moving to a place that's less of a target. But now that I have been burnt - and it does seem that it's connected to terrorism in light of Walton's research and the profiles of the people who did it - I have a growing sense that I need to stay. That I don't want to run, because what kind of life is that? Running. And what type of example of that to set the kids?

No, the more we speak, the more the reaction to my fear and lack of control is to tackle the fuckers head on.

Mina

But what does that look like?

Me

Standing up to them?

Mina

Yes, you've just quoted Churchill at us, so what would Sir Winston be saying? Because I think tomorrow morning, the best thing I can do for the kids is to get away from here.

Me

Where?

Walton

No, I don't think you should do that.

Mina

But they know where we are, I don't want to be sitting ducks…

Walton

We have to assume they'd follow you, and it's easier for us to look after each other if we're all in one place. Don't worry, the house will be watched, I've got that sorted.

Me

How?

Walton

Enosh made sure there were funds. Seriously, this house is as safe as it's ever been. The firm we're using only employ guys, ex-cops, ex-soldiers, if you stay here we have you covered.

Mina

It doesn't feel right.

Me

To me, keeping this from the police doesn't feel right.

At this point, Mina and Walton both look at me. They want this issue put to bed. Both think that at the moment we need to do what the group say. As long as we're safe, and together, what are the police going to do that Walton can't? That's what they say, I disagree.

I know Walton's been monitoring the most threatening groups for some time, and he's got leads on who we might be dealing with through the messages he intercepted about the threats to our family, but I think the more networks we can tap into the better. Why not ask the police to help us find them too? But I'm overruled.

Me

Ok, then, if we're not calling the police because that's what they've told us, then we should work on what else they've told us.

Mina

Which is?

Walton

Set up a meeting with Enosh.

Me

Precisely.

Mina

How do we do that? I thought he was missing?

Walton

He is.

Mina

Completely?

Walton

And utterly. He gave me a special signal to use if there was an emergency. I used it when I thought something had happened to Michelle and his kids, but I didn't

hear anything back. It's still going, because he needs to know about this... but so far nothing.

Mina

Where can he be then?

Walton

No idea. He's gone totally dark. He's stopped monitoring Michelle, and his other kid with that model, he's offline.

Mina

God, that sounds… bad, I mean something must have happened to him?

Walton

Not necessarily, the longer it's gone on with no sightings, no news other than this Genix stuff, my guess he's on a mission but one he needs utter secrecy for, so he's gone to ground.

Me

More like underground.

Mina

We're fucked then, aren't we? I mean they want him and we can't get him…

Me

They don't know that though, do they? That we can't. They wouldn't do what they did today if they knew he was AWOL. So, we tell them yes, we arrange a meeting, we show willing, we buy time.

Walton

That, Benji, is exactly what we should do.

So, we set about that plan, even though living normally, at home, takes its toll.

HOW DO YOU SAVE YOURSELF WITHOUT A SUPERHERO?

Mina

I don't think there's anything more emotionally exhausting than living under a constant cloud of fear, fear and love, I guess. The kids, bless them, were completely unharmed by what happened in the car and we tried to keep them oblivious to how serious that had been. They kept talking about wanting one of those bloody car toys, to the extent that after two days they did get one, each, but apart from that they didn't mention the men who'd kidnapped them.

Just thinking about it sends a chill down my spine, I hate it, I loathe it. I didn't sleep properly. I didn't dream directly about it, but every night, when I did finally manage to drop off it would only be a matter of minutes before I woke up, sweating, terror seeping through me, a feeling that I'd lost everything rooted inside me.

Benji, Walton and the other two set-up what was essentially a base in the kitchen, even though it was a building site. I didn't mind Niall, but Rueben gave me the creeps. He was too polite, too overly apologetic.

As they got ready for the meeting, I did have a few lines of enquiry I was trying out to find Subject Six, but I put most of my efforts into trying to keep the house feeling like a home.

The really sad thing, and I know it's not that sad, it's first world sad, was that finally the new kitchen would be finished. We had some fun shopping trips to do, like buying the stereo, pictures for the walls and we'd told the kids they could help us chose some beanbags for in front of the TV. And we did all that, because I wanted to carry on as normal as much as possible, but it was tainted, of course it was. Because I was looking over my shoulder the whole time and Benji was checking the burner mobile every other fucking minute in case they called.

The next call I have with them takes place in Ikea. In the canteen where I'm tucking into some meatballs. My guilt about how little the kids know about the danger they were in, and we are in as a family, has translated into a splurge of stuff for their bedrooms and for toys they can play with in the new kitchen diner. They're thrilled, their excitement rubbing off on me and wishing, perhaps, I could just spend my way out of everything.

Him

You haven't called the police, that's good. You wouldn't have liked what would have happened if you hadn't listened.

Me

I've done what you've asked. I'm putting together a meeting.

Him

You're obviously very busy.

Me

You're watching us?

Him

Who are the other men?

Me

Friends of Subject Six.

Him

From what we can tell none of them are from Genix?

Me

No.

Him

Keep it that way. We don't want them involved. Just Subject Six.

Me

Why? What's wrong with Genix...?

I'm fishing here. Walton's told me to draw them out on as much as I can. To see if we can get anything that will help us get an angle on who these people are. Anything that can give us the upper hand in the meeting we're planning.

Him

Everything's wrong with them, and we have plans for that, but not for now. Send me the details of this meeting.

Me

We're still working on them.

Him

Tomorrow then. But that only gives you three more days. Time is leaving you.

The guy's right, time is leaving us, but we're not scrambling around like headless chickens. Sometimes I feel like one, but we're really not. We have the basic plan of what we're going to do, and Walton's already bringing in some of the guys from Istanbul to help. We know that the more prepared we can be the better and all four of us, and Mina, have been working hard. Anything that can give us an idea who we're up against is going to help because, as we all know, at some point in the meeting they're going to realise Subject Six isn't with us and, well, it's going to kick-off.

Kick-off? That sounds flippant, doesn't it? I don't mean it to (or maybe I do, because perhaps making it seem less threatening is allowing me to carry on functioning without freaking out about the impending D-Day I have to face). What I mean, is that at some point they'll realise that they're not getting what they want. Subject Six will not be there.

We can plead ignorance, say we thought he was coming, appeal for a stay of execution and try to re-arrange. But in the end, they'll decide what happens next. Will they go crazy and get angry at us, putting us in danger? Will they have people near Mina and the kids and order them to move in and take the kids again? Or, as Walton hopes, will they let their guard down so we can counter-attack first and take them out?

The stakes are obviously high. Which is why we pore over the recording of each phone-call. The one I took in Ikea tells us a few things we need to take action on. One, they're monitoring us? How? Walton has swept for bugs, for a cyber-attack, for people watching the house. So far, Walton's found nothing. But from hearing his voice we all agree he's not just guessing that we're working hard, he's more certain than that. So how are they watching us? Walton takes this job on.

As an aside, I should also say that privately I also ask Walton to see if Niall or Rueben could be a threat to us. I know they've been vetted, but Walton and Subject Six said they couldn't be 100% sure about them and while they seem to be working hard for us, and I've let them in my house, I can't shake the feeling that one of them could be working with the group. As you can probably guess, Walton's thought of this and has already looked again at any links between Niall and Rueben and the terrorist cells most likely to the one's we're dealing with. He's found nothing.

As Walton ramps up his work on trying to find out how they watch us, and who they are, I'm tasked with the Genix question. In the phone-call he basically issues a direct threat to Genix and we all feel bound to tell them. Not just because we think the threat might be genuine, as we all know by now, these terrorist groups like to make threats about anyone and everyone they see as getting in their way, but also because we want to see whether Genix is also fighting the group.

We know Genix have been targeted recently, so could they have been hit by this group? If they came for me because I'd been working with Subject Six, wouldn't it also make sense to try and get to the company who are saying they made him?

Fabian

Benji, I knew you'd come back to me.

Me

Come back? I've never been away.

Fabian

I thought after my revelations, you'd want to at least talk… but I haven't heard from you once. How can I not take your absence as some form of rejection?

I bite my tongue and tell him I've been threatened. Not the detail, not the kids at this stage, but the fact I've been targeted and that they mentioned Genix too. He doesn't seem in the least surprised.

Fabian

As ever, we all have to remain vigilant. You've heard about people trying to attack us?

Me

I did, did they… did they get anything important?

Fabian

Of course not, I know how to protect myself.

Me

And Subject Six? He's ok?

Fabian

What do you think? Of course he is.

Me

So, you've seen him, you're in contact with him?

Fabian

Oh, I see, I get it. You're hurt he's not been in touch with you, aren't you?

Me

Sure, I find it odd.

Fabian

Odd that he's talking to me, his creator, but not you, a reporter? What does he need you for now? He knows the truth and now we're going to move forward.

Me

Will you tell him?

Fabian

Tell him what?

Me

These threats. They took my children, they say they'll do it again.

Fabian

Really?

Me

They mean it and I think he'll want to know.

Fabian

Do you think so?

Me

I know so. He… we were friends, he won't want…

Fabian

Don't you think he's got bigger problems? We're in a very important phase of our plan right now and you think he'd drop that all for some threats to children he doesn't know? I think not.

Me

So that's why he's ignoring our messages?

Fabian

Messages? I guess so. If he's ignoring them that tells its own story, doesn't it?

This is the moment, and not just because it touches me personally, that I start to believe Fabian is lying. His voice doesn't waver, he's speaking logically, but he's forgetting I forged something with Subject Six.

There's no way, as far as I can see, that he'd just cut ties from me, and Walton, no way at all and there's no way he'd leave us hanging like this in this situation. I email Carly to get her take on it too.

CARLY

No, I still haven't heard from the fucker either. If I was fifteen years younger I'd be feeling pretty sorry for myself, let me tell you.

That Fabian is a real douche though, isn't he? I know he charmed us when we saw him, but the more I look at the research he gave me, and the more I compare it with the tests I did on Six, the more I think he's lying. The theory is sound enough in his research, but in practice I just don't see how they could have done what he says - and having seen the results of the tests I did, I'm pretty certain they didn't.

My take now? The guy's lying, seeing as you can't report on Six at the moment, why not report on Genix and prove to everyone he's on a PR drive? Lying through his teeth to try and get headlines and probably get some very lucrative contracts…? Love to W and M

The more I ruminate on Fabian, the more it riles me. That he's convinced the world he's achieved something when I'm virtually certain he hasn't. Like Carly says, how can I prove that?

I call Laura again. She assures me that while a lot of the people she knows are jumping on the Genix bandwagon, there are others who are less convinced, including her. For them, the bigger scoop would be to be able to prove Genix is lying but so far, no-one's got anything. Citing cyber terrorism, apparently Genix's security has been stepped up more than ever. When I call DEBRIS, they say the same thing. That it's becoming impossible to get close to Fabian or anyone else at the company.

They're on lockdown. Something to keep safe, or secrets to hide?

TRYING TO FIND SUBJECT SIX

Me

I'm recording, do you mind?

Mina

No, come in. You look stressed.

Me

I am. Kids in bed? What you doing?

At this point, Mina shows me her laptop. It being a Kylie day I presumed she'd been doing some work - she's got a new TV production coming up - but now I see she's been working on a map.

Mina

These are all the supposed sightings of Subject Six since you last heard from him.

Me

Wow, how come…

Mina

We need him, don't we? He's the solution to this.

Me

Well, yes… but…

Mina

I can't cope sitting back, knowing that people might take them again.

Me

They won't. We've got Walton, Niall…

Mina

You can't guarantee that, only Subject Six can.

Me

You're not suggesting he gives himself up?

Mina

No way. I'm suggesting he kicks their fucking asses. Look, see these places, I think I have a pattern…

Mina shows me what she's found. There are a lot of claimed sightings, unconfirmed reports that Subject Six has been seen. Some as bizarre as he turned up in the middle of the Baja desert to help fix a puncture on a motorbike and side-car, to as run-of-the-mill as buying a loaf of bread in a grocery shop in Boston. Mina knows they're not real, and ones she can dismiss straight away never make it on the map, but every report she can find online (and there are loads and loads) get looked at.

Now Mina's job, as a TV documentary maker, has always involved a lot of research. She's a pro at sifting through online nonsense and getting to the nub of a story, of tracking down people she might need to film, of spotting a chancer versus a credible contributor. But I can't help but look at what she's done and see nothing but conspiracy theories and hoaxes. For years when people have seen something weird in the sky they've blamed it on UFOs, now if they see something not easily explainable one of their first thoughts is Subject Six.

Mina

You think I'm stupid.

Me

No, but…

Mina

Don't look at me like that, Benji, I hate it when you look at me like that.

Me

Like what?

Mina

Patronising, giving me the 'little woman' look.

Me

I'm not doing that.

Mina

You fucking are! What's so bad with wanting to get this fixed? He got us into this mess, he can get us out of it!

Me

It's not quite as easy as that.

Mina

I know that! Jeez.

Me

Look, Mina.

Mina

Fuck Benji, this…

Me

This is hard, I know, but we have to stay calm. Walton and I, we have a plan, I think it's a …

Mina

I don't want your plans, they're half-assed and you know it!

Me

I'm doing my best. You just need to…

Mina

Need!

Me

…to try and believe we can get through this. We're going to tell them to meet us at Subject Six's house and we're… what? What?

Mina

You just don't get it, do you? You don't know what I want! After all these years.

The kids are in bed, I think Walton and the other are downstairs, and I do not want to be arguing. I'm too tired, too in need of solace for this, but I also know how it's inevitable. With all the stress we're under, with how tense we are about the kids, with how little time we've actually had to talk together properly recently.

I look at her and try to draw up some strength, or more precisely, some wisdom. Some magic thinking that can make this better for us, between us. Instead all I feel is devastatingly empty. Like there's nothing I can do, or say, to make things better.

How have we got here? She's right, where is Subject Six? Why's he left us? Where is he when we most need him? You can't just ride to the rescue and then disappear when you're needed!

Me

What do you want? Tell me!

Mina

I don't want solutions… I want you to acknowledge how I feel, I want you to understand why I've spent hours over the last few days trawling the internet for a shred of fucking hope!

WE NEED A SUPERHERO

The following day, we leave home. We need to get to Subject Six's retreat because that's where we're going to set the meeting up. Up until the final moments Mina and I aren't sure whether to take the kids or not. Or whether they're best to stay here with some of Walton's men keeping guard. Staying in London makes it easier to keep them away from the action; but not being with us means they'll be too far away to get to easily if it all goes wrong on Sunday.

In the end, they come with us. We figure Subject Six's estate has a few empty workers cottages far enough away for them to stay in while the meeting happens. Walton is in charge of how to get there. He's devised a route which means we can all make sure we're not followed. It involves the changing of cars in car parks and a huge network of people - only having Subject Six's bank account makes it possible.

I'd like to say there's something cool and fun about all the moves we're pulling off. This is Bond and Bourne territory after all. A little part of me hopes that in the future, if it all works out, we might look back on the journey as being exciting and cool. The truth is, it's awful.

The kids are irritable because we keep moving and they can't settle. They pick up on our fear, our edginess. My mind feels like it has a thousand things to do and I don't feel in control of even the simplest of tasks. Walton has given me a map to read. Places we'll be dropped off, picked up. The listlessness that's clouding my vision means I keep losing my place, can't hold a postcode in my mind for longer than ten seconds.

It's infuriating. Every time I manage to calm down and focus, I do something else to wind myself up and flush with pent-up rage. I've just told Mina to take a wrong turn when Walton calls. My instinct is not to pick-up, to focus on helping Mina get back on route. But it's Walton, so I have to take it.

Me

Walton.

Walton

Two things, one good, one bad.

Me

Bad first.

Walton

We have a leak.

Me

What? Who?

Walton

Let me tell you the good first. Enosh. He's back.

Me

You're kidding, what the fuck... what the...

Walton

He answered one of my messages, he's going to meet us there.

Huge news. As I'm sure you can tell. I wish I had the recording of the whole call but as I erupt in relief and cel-ebration I put Mina off, she misjudges a corner and we leave the road. No-one is hurt, the car is fine, but we end up on the grass verge. Hugging, crying in relief.

After that, for the last leg of the journey, the atmosphere lifts. We still have to be on it, of course, because we need to make sure we're not followed. When we tell the group where to meet us, we need it to be a surprise. We don't want them to have the time to prepare for it by being able to scope out the place and put people in position. We have to get to Subject Six's without them knowing where we are then tell them where to come.

The fact we're going to see Subject Six changes the complexion of everything. Without getting too distracted I keep running through what this means in my head. I want to share my thoughts. with Mina, but with the kids in the back it's impossible.

Reason to be cheerful, number 1: now, we won't be lying to the group. We'll be adhering to their demands so surely that's going to make the meeting better and less of a risk - which can only be good for us as a family.

Walton

Why did I lie? I knew it was a risk and it's not like I didn't think about it. I thought about it a lot. As much as I used to when I was in Iraq and we were going out on an op. In fact, that's exactly what we were doing, wasn't it? Going out on an op. And in the end, to make the op more likely to succeed I decided that I needed to lie to you about Subject Six. I stand by that decision, I really do.

Reason to be cheerful, number 2: of course, I know that the group don't want to meet Subject Six just to shake his hand, or to warn him off, they're going to go for him - which puts him at risk. Except it doesn't, does it? Even on his own I'd back him against these fuckers and with

Walton's help too? Well, it's as close to a sure thing as you can get. Subject Six is essentially going to be able to put a stop to this group in an instant, because they've massively underestimated him.

Reasons to be cheerful, 3, 4 and 5: and finally, I think as we near the estate, I'm going to be able to see a guy I've become to feel is a friend and I'm going to be able to tear him a new one for leaving us in the lurch at the same time. Not to mention I'll be able to interview him about what he's been doing, and my book needs a serious update on how he's feeling about Genix, his genesis and everything else in between.

Walton

No, it wasn't easy to deceive you, but we weren't in an easy situation. The pressure was getting to all of us and in fact I made the final decision the night before we set off, when I heard you and Mina arguing. I was coming out of the shower and I could hear you two shouting and then when there was a moment of quiet, as I was by the door of the bedroom your kids were in I heard one of them tell the other, not to worry, about mummy and daddy, it would be alright, they still loved each other, and that it was all about the men in the car and nothing to do with them.

That, that helped me decide.

By the time we turn off the road and through the gates of Subject Six's estate - the first time I've ever been on this route without a blindfold - the relief in Mina and me is surging through us. She even rests her hand on my thigh as we trundle through the tree-lined path. Our eyes meeting, both smiling. The kids start singing, sensing the change in mood of us both.

Even when I catch sight of one of Walton's guys patrolling the grounds with a gun slung over his shoulder, the chill doesn't stab too deep. Normally, bringing Mina and the kids into such a perilous situation would, of course, have killed me, and it's far from ideal, but I feel better than at any time over the last dreadful week. Things are lifting. When we see the house, the kids get really excited. It's sunny, a blue sky framing the scene, the house stony and majestic. Walton didn't say when we'd see Subject Six and my heart jumps a moment, is he here already? Has he already taken charge again like we need him too?

Walton

Primarily, the biggest reason I decided to lie was to calm you. When I went out on ops in Iraq, and I'm sorry to harp on about it, I know it must be tiresome, but when I went out in Iraq the one thing that put me on my guard was nervous guys. Through training and conditioning you try to get every soldier to be able to function without thinking, to be composed, or better yet an automaton - programmed to do what needs to be done, to be able to act and react in the best way possible every time. Obviously, you can't always do that, you're going to get guys who crack. Whether from their first op, or over time as their nerves crumble. With you and Mina, I was highly aware that you'd never been trained, that we would be facing down these terrorist fucks with two, well, amateurs and I thought you could do with all the help you could get.

Telling you Subject Six was coming, was back, was my way of doing that and the moment you stepped out of the car at his estate I saw it had worked. Both you and Mina looked more relaxed, more comfortable. And that's what I knew we needed. If you'd had met the group knowing

Even though it's disappointing that Walton doesn't know exactly when Subject Six is going to join us, I still feel more sure of myself. Walton shows Mina and me the message he's sent. It leaves us in no doubt that by the time we meet the terrorists at midday tomorrow, he'll be here. Mina takes the kids off to settle in at one of the cottages, with a couple of guards accompanying them. I go with Walton as he checks in with the guards around the perimeter to make sure that we haven't been followed.

It's not that I'm doing anything. Not really, although I know in the back of my mind it's important I'm here to watch the story unfold from the frontline rather than being with the kids. What I'm really there for is so that I'm near Walton for when they ring. They've told me they'll call today to get the details for where we'll be meeting tomorrow and Walton wants to be around when they call in case they throw any curveballs.

The only moment that shakes me is when Niall and Ruben arrive. As we watch them pull-up in the driveway from the CCTV centre in the main house, Walton clears the room and then tells me more about the bad news he told me about on the phone.

Walton

Listen, I've already said not to tell anyone that Enosh is coming because I want to make sure everyone stays on red alert and that extends to Ruben and Niall too.

Me

Really? Aren't they more integral than…

Walton

I think one of them is telling someone about us. They're the leak.

Me

To who?

Walton

I can't go into details now, they're coming up. Just don't talk about Enosh in front of them. Look, I have it under control… trust me.

I want to press him more but that's when they walk in. I feel myself reeling, but the fact he carries on as normal gives me confidence he knows what he's doing. I'm too busy to reel off all the people one of them could be talking to and as I get swept up in preparing for tomorrow I find myself doing exactly what Walton's told me to do: trusting him.

WHAT IT'S LIKE PREPARING FOR A SHOWDOWN

Mina

I didn't hear you come to bed that night, I did hear you get up in the morning. And when you came back to bed, having opened the curtains, bringing the morning light in, the first thing I felt was an oppressive, smothering fear. You'd messaged me the night before saying the group had been told where to meet us and everything was set and it had been almost impossible for me to sleep, my mind was racing so much, but obviously, I managed.

As I cuddled up to you, and you looked me in the eye and told me it would be alright, I wanted to believe you so much, and I could see you were trying to believe it so much that, in the end, we both kind of did believe it.

The two guards Walton had assigned to us, both women, both formal but kind, were in the kitchen when we went down. I felt self-conscious with you because they were there. We were both feeding off a nervous energy and I wanted it to be over, for the moment to happen and yet I was desperate to be with you as long as possible because I didn't want you to walk off.

I arrive in the command centre and hear the news that Walton's team who are monitoring the main routes out of London think they've seen the Nissan Almera from the day of the kidnapping on the motorway.

Then I get a message from DEBRIS:

Nicholas Singh

FABIAN IS ON MOVE. OUR SOURCE SAYS HEADING NORTH WITH LARGE TEAM

Me

WHAT DO YOU MEAN BY LARGE TEAM?

Nicholas Singh

LET ME CHECK…

HE THINKS SOME KIND OF EXPERIMENT. CONVOY OF FOUR TRUCKS. LEFT EARLY

As I'm messaging Nicholas from DEBRIS, Walton answers my question. Subject Six isn't here yet.

I feel a lurching in my stomach. When is he going to get here? But there's no time for procrastination and doubt. Walton manoeuvres me out of the room.

Walton

Benji, listen, I was right about one thing. It's Niall who has been selling us out. And now I know to who.

Me

How? Who?

Walton

Your friend just told us.

Me

Genix?

Walton

I knew it could have been them, they were on the long-list but I didn't find anything otherwise he would never have been with us so long. Fuck, they planted

him deep... they covered his tracks I mean his legend was... fuck, I messed up...

Me

Are you sure? If it was so tough. How did you find out?

Walton

I told him about Enosh, not Rueben. I figured if we saw a response from someone, the government, a journalist, or, as we can see now Genix, then Niall was leaking and if we didn't then the leak was Rueben.

Me

How could he do this to us? He's been staying in my house! He knows my kids are at...

Walton

Hey, Benj, calm down. That's not going to help.

Me

He's betrayed us!

Walton

He has, but no harm's been done. Yet.

Me

Yet!

Walton

And let's keep it that way.

Me

How?

Walton

Use him to our advantage. He doesn't know we've found him out.

Me

So, we could tell him Six isn't coming here, and then he'd tell them and Genix will turn back?

As we're talking, Niall comes into room. I want to hit him. To grab him by the collar and drag him out of the room, the house, send him on his way. I really do. But I don't. Obviously, because he's much bigger than me and Walton's told me not to.

He tells us that we have men tracking who we think the terrorists are and the convoy we think is from Genix. They're on the same motorway. Genix are about an hour behind. I fight back the fear that threatens to smother me, take a deep breath and clench my fists, bite down on my chewing gum a lot harder. Yes, Subject Six is a force, but with Genix and the terror cell, it's beginning to ask a lot of him, and of us. Niall's put everything in jeopardy.

What is Fabian planning? To get Subject Six?

Once Niall's gone, Walton and I walk outside to make sure no-one can hear us.

Walton

I think telling him there's no Enosh is too simple. Knowing Genix, they're on their way here, they know where the place is, they'd probably come and look around anyway.

Me

True, ok, what are we going to do?

Walton

No idea at the moment.

Me

Subject Six might know. When will we know what his plans are? When's he arriving?

Walton

I don't know. But he said he will be. Listen, I've got to get back inside. I need the whole estate properly watched. We go ahead as planned. We prepped for this meet without Enosh and now we do it.

Walton walks off. Standing in the courtyard I see a couple of his guys sat in a 4x4 having a smoke. I haven't been a smoker for a long time, but right now I can see the appeal. I know these are army and good soldiers at that, seeing as Walton's brought them in specifically, but even they seem tense. Their voices low, poker faces on. Taking deep, deliberate tokes.

I don't recognise either of them, which strikes me as odd as I approach. It doesn't make me uneasy, Walton says he's got 30 guys here today so it makes sense I haven't seen them, but it's strange that maybe my life, my family's life, is in the hands of people I don't know. But then, I guess, isn't that always the way? You never see the anti-terrorist teams in London, all you hear about is afterwards, when they've picked the fuckers up before the attacks or taken them down during them.

What's happening today is way more acute, a much more personal version of that. We all think the terrorists are out to get us, as individuals. We run through nightmare scenarios of what would happen if we found ourselves in the middle of an attack. Would we run, shit our pants, save the day, get blown apart, have time to send a message to the people we love?

And now, in an hour or so, I am going to be in the middle of an attack. Which is why I need a smoke.

I'm about to light, when I pause. Where is Subject Six? Where the fuck is he? I want him to just arrive. To turn up. To fall onto the goddamn ground in front of me and take control and make all this better.

I hear footsteps to my right. From around the corner. I know I've heard those footsteps before.

"Daddy!"

"Dads!"

"Benj! Smoking! What the hell!"

There goes the end of my smoke, which I know is only a good thing. The kids are happy, excited to be out and it's infectious and yet, at the same time, it fills me with an even more consuming nervousness and fear I can't shake.

I know we're tracking the group and Genix, but what happens if we get it wrong? If we're surprised and suddenly they're here and the kids are out?

Mina, though, knocks me back as soon as I suggest they go back inside. There's no way she can have the kids in the cottage all day, not when they know what's outside. And as long as Walton says it's safe to be out, then she says she's going to let them out.

I accept this, even though I can't throw myself fully into the games they want me to play, climbing trees, finding sticks, pushing each other over into the mud. Mina and I settle down onto a fallen tree and encourage them to map out a race-track into the mud. She leans her head against my shoulder. Her hair is freshly washed, I take in the familiar fragrance of her shampoo, and I can't remember the last time I washed. Which makes me, suddenly, long for normality.

We talk quietly. I deliberately don't record it. It feels like a long time since we've done that. Even though now, as I put this book together it would be handy for me to have that recording, I don't really regret it. I think we both just need to try and reach some calm, maybe even some closure, before the storm.

Mina seems to know what to say at moments like this, a trait she gets from her Dad, asks me if I regret taking on the story. Whether I'd have been happier actually taking on the job of writing the Brian Parr football biography and staying clear of Subject Six. Or whether being more active, writing about something that's maybe making a difference is more satisfying, despite the trials it's brought.

I start by making obvious points. By apologising for putting the kids at risk, by stating I hate the fact they've been brought into something that… but Mina cuts me off. Telling me that I'm on the record, many, many, many times saying how I never intended to put the kids in harm's way. Seeing as that is not in doubt, she presses me on how do I feel? Has sacrificing the personal comfort my job normally brings been worth it? If the book goes as planned, and helps people learn the truth about Subject Six and what he's done, and if that serves as an example to all of us, and exposes corruption and gets everyone wanting to work together against the 1% Subject Six targeted, and all the other bad shit he's taken on, will it be worth it?

I begin by saying of course. That, obviously, I want to help make a difference. Or perhaps in keeping with what I've seen with Subject Six, I want to show people how difficult it is to try and change things even if you are a goddamn superhero. That the reality of the world today, or maybe always, is that the people who need to change are the ones in power, which makes it tough to stop them. Then, on top of that, we live in a society that seems to love to shoot down, sometimes literally, the few people trying to change things. You try and disrupt the norm, and it's not just the people you want to stop or expose that will come after you, everyone will - because for some obscure, perverse reason we're so scared of change that even those offering to help the masses get swallowed up, churned around and spat out.

And it's this inherent difficulty in making a difference that does make me second guess myself. Putting my head above the parapet, even in the small way of becoming identified with Subject Six, has got me and my family in a lot of serious bother. Which makes me, or part of me, wish I hadn't got involved, and wants it to be over as soon as possible. So that everything can go back to how it was. Because while I'm glad I think my book can help, there's no guarantee that it will and at the moment there's nobody thanking me for doing what I've done. It's not like I'm just after accolades, but isn't it just reality for someone who's risking everything to want some kind of positive affirmation to show it's been worth it?

Mina's been watching me as I've rambled. I come to a pause just as the kids start scrapping over which car they get to race around the track. Once I've settled them down, both happy with the vehicles they've got, I realise I've not really engaged with Mina, all I've done is unload. I obviously needed to do it, but I want to know her take on it too. Because I know that through her TV shows, she's often tried to make programmes that will make her proud at what she's created. Her Dad's a doctor, someone who literally tries every day to make people better and she'd like to do that if she could. But people don't want shows that try to do that. People want popcorn entertainment, they want escapism.

She's told me, in an exasperated way, that 'worthy' is a word that people seem to hate in TV. A show about global warming: 'worthy'. A show about how social mobility is ruining the chances of millions: 'worthy'. Now some shows might try to look at these issues, but only in a small way - because if there's a show about rich and poor people meeting, it's there to show poshos shouting at scroungers, really, it doesn't get any deeper. In a way, that's fine. TV is entertainment and Mina is the first to understand that. If that's what people want, give it to them; it's maybe not noble, but it is reality. So how is she feeling about this story, about what I hope will become a strong book? Is she glad we've found ourselves in the middle of this story, despite the downsides?

She begins by pointing out that she thinks, sadly, seeing as we have kids, that the world is never going to be perfect. It's fucked, it always has been, and it always will be. One person can't change everything for the better. Regenerating flesh or not. But if people try to be the best citizen (and she uses the word 'citizen' pointedly) then surely that will make things less fucked. Now and in the future.

I press her on the word citizen. Why did she use that? What is the difference between a person and a citizen? At first she laughs, telling me I sound like a pretentious twat. Then, she begins to...

...but she doesn't finish. Because that's when the first bomb goes off.

THE ATTACK AT SUBJECT SIX'S RETREAT

The explosion is far enough away that even though I feel the ground shake, my ears aren't ringing. Instead they're full of the screams of the kids. I leap up from the log, crouching down and wrap them up in my arms.

After this initial burst of instinct, I have no idea what's next. Mina's up and one step ahead of me. Screaming at us to get back to the cottage, back to the guards who are looking after them. Another explosion. Making me shrink, squeezing onto the kids who are clinging to me with every muscle in their little bodies.

Overhead I hear a helicopter. I duck. Wincing. Anticipating fire.

Luckily there is none. As I glance up I see it's Subject Six's chopper. And as I hear Walton's guards barking instructions I realise the defence is up and running.

My leg is wet from one of the kids. I put everything I've got into tensing my body so I have enough strength to run with them both. Around the back of the house we go. Some gunfire comes from behind us. But not much and far away.

Then I hear shouting, coming from ahead of us. Mina stops, looks panicked, trapped. Only for a moment because the noises are from our guards. They have guns drawn. Telling us to follow them. Mina nods, takes one of the kids. Ruffles their hair, kisses their forehead.

Once we get to the cottage I know I'm going to have to turn back. Head away from safety. To leave them. I'm

the one who's set up the meeting with the group, I have to
be there. Holding the little body tightly on my hip, I don't
want to let go. Everything is telling me to stay but of
course I can't. Mina and I get a quick kiss, a moment to
see each other. Then they're gone. Doors locked.

Walton

*By the time you arrived back at the house we had things
under control, basically. Don't look at me like that, we
did. Sure, their grenades had surprised us, but it worked
in our favour. They did it, I guess, to try and front up, to
show us they weren't to be messed with, they didn't want
to look like they were amateurs. Fronting up, like a Gorilla puffing out their chest… but in the end, all it did
was get us into action-mode earlier. What they should
have done is waited.*

*If they'd let us think they weren't a threat and then hit
us, that might have been harder for us to deal with…
instead, those two grenades just made sure all my guys
were ready and waiting. Their fingers 2mm closer to the
trigger, a split-second closer to shooting than they would
have been before.*

Rueben and Walton are running the show when I get
to them. The HQ room is full of the sound of people
checking-in, receiving orders, keeping a watch on the area
around the estate.

I notice instantly that Niall isn't anywhere to be seen.
Rueben visibly bristles when I mention it, I notice the
knuckles on his right hand are red, swollen and decide not
to dwell on it.

Walton

*I was pretty happy with the state of play by the time we
went outside to welcome them. Welcome, is that the*

word? Anyway, everyone was well hidden. Anyone driving up to the house might suspect us of having other people with us, but they wouldn't be able to see anyone and I was certain they'd have no idea just how many people we had within 40m of the driveway. It was locked-down.

During my army career I'd taken part in a few face-to-faces with hostiles, hostage exchanges, prisoner exchanges, and the money Enosh had given us meant this was the best prepared meet I'd ever been involved in. In terms of the experience of the guys and the hardware we had at our disposal. He'd told me not to take any chances and, as much as was humanly possible, we hadn't.

After I'd sent the chopper up, because I thought we might be under full scale attack, I suddenly realised that I might have given the game away. They'd told you on the phone that they wanted you and Enosh and no-one else, so how would they feel if they found out you were being backed-up by a chopper? That's when I made the call to tell the pilot to put down at the far end of the estate; hoping it would look like they'd just been flying by rather than out on a mission.

If needed, the chopper would be able to get back to the house within minutes, so I figured that was the best plan. Rather than running the risk of scaring them off by making them aware of just how heavily equipped we were.

The guys in the helicopter report back. They tell Walton that the grenades came from a car that's now waiting in a layby a mile or so away. Best guess is they're the advance party and soon the whole group is going to arrive. Walton demands an update on where Genix are and then turns to me.

He hands me a gun. This time, it's loaded. We get ten minutes to practise. He drills me on pulling it out from the back of my trousers and getting it ready to shoot. Like before, it feels heavy, clunky, alien in my hand. I know I need to shape up, but I can't shake the feeling that I need more than ten minutes to master shooting guns. Not the right attitude, I know, but I can't switch off the thought that this is not what I'm meant to be doing.

Walton

How were you with the gun? Shocking. Absolutely fucking shocking. I knew you would be, that's why I hadn't started you the day before. I figured you'd only get fixated on it and worry about how bad you were. I thought 'short crash course and then go', that was the way to go.

The one good thing about my anxiety over the gun, is how completely it takes my mind off what's coming. Who's coming. One moment I'm practising drawing the gun, the next Rueben appears and says they've entered the gates. Time to go down into the main square.

COMING FACE TO FACE WITH THE ENEMIES OF SUBJECT SIX

Walton gets me to lead. He wants the group to see me as in control. As well as sorting out our plan this week, Walton's also been training me in negotiation and interrogation techniques. Trying to ensure I'll hold it together under pressure. I run through the lessons in my head as the cars come into sight, I clench my fists, fighting hard to stay present, not to drift, not to let terror take me away.

Me

How did I look to you?

Walton

Like you were being led out to your execution.

Me

I wasn't that bad, was I?

Walton

I didn't say that was bad, I said it was how you were. The fact you were there at all was enough.

Subject Six

Agreed. You looked like shit, Benji, but when I saw you were there... well, I was impressed.

Me

Well, thank you, Six, how wonderful to have impressed you.

This is from a conversation I had with Walton and Subject Six a few days later. I wanted to get the events down on record from the people who saw them. I don't have a recording of the showdown itself, for reasons we'll come to.

Me

To me, there seemed to be a lot of cars, all of them full.

Walton

I was wearing an earpiece; the first count came in at 17 of them in five cars. The second put the number as high as 20.

Me

How did that make you feel?

Walton

That's what I expected, what I'd planned for. I mean the whole time I was putting myself in their place. It's unlikely they'd organise a meeting with Enosh just to have a chat, a chinwag, you know what I mean? They were either planning to kill him, or if they believed the headlines and he couldn't be killed, capture him. So, if that was their plan, I knew they were going to come with numbers. And from my research and contacts in the secret service, I knew that any group or cell in the UK, could probably muster about 20, but not many more, not without creating a lot of chatter

Me

Which they didn't, right? I mean from what we know, this all happened off radar...

Subject Six

Yes, amazingly, seeing how noisy and how amateur these people often are. That's what I first noticed, when I looked into them…

Me

Which was when? And what did you notice?

This talk is happening in the hospital. It's the first time I've had a chance to talk to him and while I've been trying to fill in the blanks, I'm still trying to catch up with his story.

Subject Six

As soon as I got Walton's SOS call about your kids, and started to look into what he'd told me, I noticed that whoever it was had been able to plan something big without anyone picking up on it. Which was odd.

Me

How did you know that?

Subject Six

Sources, contacts, our own monitoring of the monitors…

Me

Which you don't want to go into detail about?

Subject Six

Correct. Suffice to say, the UK intelligence services are the best in the world, my tech is better, and yet suddenly there's a group who can stay clear of us… it was, it was worrying.

Me

And did you think that, Walton? You never mentioned how odd it was this threat was off radar?

Walton

It was on my mind, but not something that could ga-zump the rest of my plans. I had to deal with what was in front of me... however they were doing it was un-known, it could have been some new tech, chance, or something more sinister, but we didn't have time to second guess.

Me

Ok, so back to the cars coming towards us, Walton. Me shitting myself about the gun by my arse, you happy enough to see you'd guessed the numbers right, was there anything else on your mind?

Walton

The biggest unknown was Genix. That was a last mi-nute change of plan I didn't have the time to properly prepare for. They were the curveball I had to try and stay prepared for.

Me

My mind was on when Six was going to turn up. That's all I could think about...when the fuck was he going to fly in and save the day?

Walton

Well, I wasn't thinking about that.

Me

What were you thinking?

Walton

Honestly, whether you might shoot yourself if you went for the gun.

Walton's pleased with his joke, Subject Six joins in with the laughter. I let them have their fun then get back to the moment.

Me

**So, when they got out. And walked up to me, how did
you feel then?**

Walton

**Confident. More confident than I'd been before,
which, as it turns out and as you know, was maybe a
mistake.**

Me

Why confident then?

Walton

**I could see they were unsure. Which made me think
you'd deal with them well.**

Me

And did I?

Walton

You tell me.

Subject Six

Yeah, Benj, how did it feel?

As I stand there, Walton behind me to the right, Rueben to my left, I watch and try not to flinch as the cars
unload and they slam their car doors behind them. In a
way, my main aim is to play for time, wait for Subject Six
to arrive. So how hard will that be? What are these guys
like? Jacked-up and nervous, or calm and professional?

They look way more rag-tag than Walton's men -
dressed in jeans, T-shirts, hoodies, coats, but they have a
steel and purpose to them all the same. I can tell the main
guy instantly, not because of how he looks, because, actually, he's one of the smallest, one of the least intimidat-
ing physically, but because his mannerisms and the way
he walks matches the voice I've heard on the phone. He

walks to the front of the group. Stands slightly sideways. Chewing gum.

"Where is he?" he demands, "You said he'd be here."

"You said there would be no weapons, so what were those explosions?" I counter.

"Your man, there," he says, pointing at Walton, "He has a gun, so let's be done with pretence and let's get to the point. We get to see Subject Six, you get left alone."

"What do you want with him?"

"The chance to explain."

"Explain what?"

"He claims he acts for the greater good, no agendas, yes?" he asks and waits for me to nod, "Well, we figure if we can tell him why we're doing what we're doing he'll see the truth."

"To what end?"

"They say he's the weapon that can be used to wipe us off the face of the world - that's propaganda and lies, if he listens and understands then he'll refuse to do their bidding. And if the world sees him decide we are not just something to be wiped out, that we should be listened to, that our motives have substance, then they too can begin to…"

"Bullshit," Walton challenges, "You're here to kill him. Plain and simple."

Me

So, what made you say that?

Subject Six

It certainly shocked the hell out of me.

Walton

Genix. That was just after I heard they'd been spotted, circling the perimeter. Niall had obviously told them a secret way in.

Me

But why rile the group? I had it under control.

Walton

I needed to bring things to a head. I felt if we could neutralise them by the time Genix arrived we'd be in a stronger position.

Walton's intervention escalates things immediately. We're all familiar with people saying important, serious moments happen in slow motion, aren't we? Well this is the complete opposite. Before I've even processed the idea that now is the time to draw my weapon, I'm surrounded by guns.

Walton and Rueben have stepped forwards, joining me in a line as we face down the guns being aimed at us. You can sense the tension, feel the pressure. Not all of the group have guns, maybe half. More than the two we have pointing at them.

The main guy has stepped forward but isn't carrying.

"Benji, Benji, this man you have, what does he think he can do on his own? Let's stop playing games, where is Subject Six?"

"You haven't answered the question," I pursue, "What are you…?"

"Enough, is enough," he spits, "Either I see him now, or I tell my men to search this place and root out your wife and children. When they have guns to their heads I hardly think you'll be…"

He doesn't finish his sentence. On all sides, Walton's men reveal themselves.

Subject Six

I would have made the same call as you then, Walton, you nailed it.

Walton

The guy needed to see our force. He was getting too cocky.

Me

How did you do it? I didn't hear a thing.

Walton

A hand gesture, nothing else.

Subject Six

Then boom, suddenly they were surrounded. Text-book.

This sudden appearance of Walton's men throws the group completely. I take it in too. Not all of Walton's soldiers come out, but most. And now the sides look evenly matched. Does it make me feel safer? Perhaps for a moment, but when I focus back on their leader, and see how twitchy he's become, I wonder if we've overplayed our hand.

"Look," I say, hands up, trying to calm the situation, "We all need to try and..."

"What is this? What did I tell you?"

"You think we're just going to give him to you?" Walton barks.

"I think you should have listened."

"You're good at threats, I give you that, but can you do anything else? We have you out-manoeuvred and you know it."

The guy looks at Walton, looks back at me.

"So what's your plan," he asks, "Kill us all? Because I doubt you'll do that, you're not in Iraq now, war crimes are harder to hide here. And if you don't, and you let us go without seeing..."

He's interrupted, everything's interrupted by the sound of 4x4s. People moving in. Walton grabs me by the shoulder and drags me back. Genix, it can only be Genix.

Subject Six

They did arrive much sooner than you could have guessed.

Walton

I gave Niall too much leeway, the moment I suspected him I should have locked him down.

Subject Six

Mmm, maybe, but you had to be sure it was him who was leaking. Keeping him close, monitoring him, I think I would have tried that too.

Walton

For all the good it did us.

Subject Six

True. But hey, it's not a science, Walton, you went with what you had in front of you, isn't that right, Benji?

Me

There's no way we could have done anything better... we were just in a big, fucking bind.

Walton pulls me back further, and there, front and centre I see Fabian Tree. And the fucker is beaming. But within an instant my focus flips. It's not Fabian's face leering at me that gets me. It's not the fact that there's as many of Genix as there are of us that scares me.

It's the fact that Fabian's sitting next to Mina.

Mina and the kids. And as he steps out of the car, he pushes them in front of him. This is too much. Too much.

Mina screams, the kids start crying as soon as they see me. I want to run, to gather them up, but Walton's grip is firm and digging into my shoulder, "Where the fuck is he, Walton?" I shout, "Why's he not here yet!"

"Yes, Walton, where is he? That's who we're all here for," crows Fabian.

Fabian stares us down, for a few seconds, then turns his attention to the group of terrorists. I have no idea how this will unfold; it runs through my mind that this could work out well for us. If Genix and Fabian are going to deal with this group it could buy us more time - if Subject Six is ever going to turn up!

Fabian and the leader step towards each other. There's a pause. Walton lets go of my shoulder, moving his gun into position. It feels like something's going to give, crack, break.

"Mo," Fabian says, "Well done, you did it."

I have no idea what I'm seeing. Fabian and the leader shake hands.

"Of course I did it, what do you take us for?"

"Manners, Mo, please, we're in public."

Fabian smiles at us, glaring, "Surprised? You shouldn't be. When I want something, I do everything in my power to get it. Hence this... Mo, bring the wife."

WHAT TO DO WHEN YOUR FAMILY IS ON THE LINE

Subject Six

Honestly? That didn't surprise me.

Walton

Well, thanks for letting us know, because it freaked the hell out of me.

Me

I... I was utterly bowled over. Them working together?

Subject Six

Fabian's not a man with morals, with ethics, he's about money. He was making money hand over fist by spreading fear in the Middle East and he'd put everything on the line when he said I was working with him... so he needed to get me, didn't he?

Me

But at the time we didn't know for sure whether you were with him or not!

Subject Six

Of course I wasn't. Walton knew that!

Walton

I did, but still, I'd looked at every angle and Fabian using them to force us into a meeting... that was not one I'd thought of.

Subject Six

They needed funding, he wanted me and a way of getting to me without accountability. He's a clever cunt, I'll give him that. Cruel too. What he did to Mina was unforgivable.

Mina's pushed forward by a white, skinhead. Mo grabs her and forces her to her knees in front of Fabian. Things have got very out of control, very quickly. Mina's head is being forced down by Mo. I want to catch her eye. I'm desperate, itching for this to be over.

"Ok, where is he? Bring him here, or as you can see, Mo, will do something you're going to regret, Benji. So, bring him out."

"He's not here," I managed to croak.

"Bullshit, I was told he was. On good authority," Fabian counters, "In fact, where is Niall? What have you done to my mole? I'm surprised you found him out actually; it took you so long I thought you were never going to catch up. You haven't hurt him have you? I would so like to thank him."

"Let her go," I tell him, "Subject Six isn't…"

"Now, now, now," Fabian says, wagging his finger, "Stop lying. Bring him to me."

"How can I when…?"

"It's not just Niall's information we have," Fabian says, "I'm not such a fool to play my hand like this on one ex-Army, ex-alcoholic's word. I've been monitoring you and your team and I know you've been in contact with him."

"That's not true. I haven't spoken to him for ages. We don't know where he is!"

At this Mina screams, Mo's gripping her neck even tighter. He looks wound up, angry. Both the kids seem

rooted to the spot. Their red, swollen eyes flicking between me and Mina.

"I don't mean you, Benji, calm down," Fabian leers,
"I mean Walton. I've had some spyware on you for a
while and he's been in contact with Cryoman. Haven't
you?"

Walton

**I knew it was possible that once I left the firewalls we'd
set up in the mansion HQ it might be easier for me to
be hacked, and I was right.**

Me

So, what were you doing?

Walton

**I used my laptop to send messages to Six, and then cre-
ated a false server that would make it look like it I was
receiving messages back from somewhere else…**

Subject Six

Clever.

Walton

**The messages were encrypted, so no-one could read
them but once Fabian had word from Niall that Subject Six had been in touch, he must have decided the
person messaging was Subject Six and that's why he
put so much firepower into the mission to the mansion.**

"Yes, Walton," Fabian says, "Poker face all you want,
but you can't…"

"Do you think," I carry on, "That if he was here he'd
just stand back and watch you do this? He'd take you all
at once."

For a moment Fabian is thrown. He hasn't thought
about this. He stamps his feet. Now, it doesn't please me,

because I don't want him to be desperate because that could be dangerous, but for the first time I see that while he's the one wielding power here, he's not in control. He is desperate. He's come up here expecting to find Subject Six, expecting, I guess, to use Mina and me and the kids as bargaining chips to get Subject Six to go with him, and it's not going to plan.

"Mo, make yourself useful. Search the house, the grounds."

Mo looks at Fabian. A steel in his eyes.

"How do you think people are going to take the news, Mo…?" I begin.

"Shut it, Benji, I'm warning…"

"…when they find out you've done a deal with Genix? Do you know how many people their weapons have killed?"

"…you!"

"He's offered you something, hasn't he? But what good's that going to be when your fellow countrymen…"

Fabian raises his gun. Fires at me.

The world kicks up. Throws my feet into the air.

My stomach screams in pain. I'm wearing body armour but I'm in agony. More shots ring out. I smash the floor. Winded. A siren screaming in my head. I try to scramble up.

Mo is standing over Fabian. He shoots him. Gun fire is everywhere. Walton is next to me on the ground, bleeding. I try to get up. Expecting to be too weak, for my wound to stop me. But I'm up, I'm running. Mina, the kids.

Mo turns, raises his gun. My gun is in my hand. I fire. Do I hit? Mo goes down. Then I have Mina's hand. I drag her up. We sweep up the kids. Dive behind a truck.

Mina's shaking, I'm trembling. I double-check where I got shot. No blood, just shattered plastic and microchips from where the bullet hit my voice recorder.

Genix trucks are backing out. Mo's men are trying to reverse away. Walton's guys are running in, shouting, taking control.

He must be here now. Subject Six. This is his doing. He's saved us.

A DEBRIEF WITH A SUPERHERO

Subject Six

You know, he's not going to make it. He knows it too.

Me

I know.

Subject Six

**Don't feel guilty. Walton's a born soldier. The mission
was a success.**

Me

He took the bullet protecting me, if I'd…

Subject Six

Don't make this about you.

Me

It's hard not to.

Subject Six

**Just don't. He doesn't want that. It was his job to pro-
tect you, to get you and everyone else out of that situation and he did it. End of. Sure, he'd like not to be in
that bed, paralysed, suffering from internal bleeding,
about to die. But that's the brutal truth and he knows
it.**

Me

Fuck, do you have to put it like that?

Subject Six

Take a moment, take a moment.

That's exactly what I do. Sitting in outside the hospital, watching ill-looking patients force themselves to smoke, I pull myself together. Walton's been as forthright about his prognosis as Subject Six is being, but it doesn't help. I still can't shake the guilt, the flashbacks that won't go away.

On my phone, I see Mina has taken some pictures from the hotel pool she's at with the kids. I'm joining her later and they look to be loving it. Neither has been sleeping properly, there've been wet beds and night terror screaming, but the specialists we've spoken to think they're doing ok and it will pass. Hopefully.

Subject Six

Feeling better?

Me

I guess, I'm not used to it.

Subject Six

I wasn't either. When I started doing this, taking on these missions it took me some time to get used to shoving the bad moments deep down somewhere…

Me

Sounds healthy.

Subject Six

Mmm, maybe, maybe not.

Me

So, let's walk and talk?

Subject Six

Sure. Right. What do you want to know?

Me

Where the fuck were you?

Subject Six

Yes, that.

Me

That.

Subject Six

Where do you think I was?

Me

Don't play games.

Subject Six

I'm not. You obviously thought about it a lot while I was gone. The messages I was getting from Walton told me that at least.

Me

Your family. I think you were with your family.

Subject Six

Partly, yes. Once I got forced into the centre of the war against terror I realised the best way to protect them was to be with them. So, I got them.

Me

How did that go?

Subject Six

Great guns. You know what?

Me

What?

Subject Six

It was Oscar who told me where I needed to go next.

Me

He's a bright kid.

Subject Six

Cleverest guy I know. I think, maybe, cleverest guy ever.

Me

Don't we all think that about our kids?

Subject Six

Do you? Do you really think yours are the cleverest people you've met?

Me

Well, put like that… so what did Oscar say?

Subject Six

He told me that the only place I could come from was the future.

I don't react to this. I take it in.

Me

And do you?

Subject Six

Do I what?

Me

Come from the future?

Subject Six

I need to find out.

Me

So you haven't nailed it then? All that time away and nothing. I thought you must have been finding out the truth about yourself. I thought you'd…

Subject Six

Look, I tried. I went underground to infiltrate Genix after Fabian sent me that message and soon found out Fabian was lying, that he was using it for publicity, to make money by creating even more unrest in the Middle East… from both sides, the West and the governments… that was why he said what he said about me.

Me

Can you prove that?

Subject Six

I can. I found a recording of a Skype between him and the weapons companies he owned where they devised the strategy. The moment he said he'd use Cryomen to come for the terrorist camps, he made huge profits by selling arms to them so they could defend themselves. Then, when he leaked that information to the UK and US, they tooled up too. Genix and his companies made loads, and imagine what they could have made if I'd believed him and allowed his lie to become truth… that he's invented me.

Me

Why didn't you say this at the time? Carly and me put hours into this and you already knew? Why didn't you come out and…?

Subject Six

I didn't already know anything. We were working at the same time, I just had to keep on the downlow after the furore around me broke, after the Imam spoke out.

Me

Ok, fine, but if you have the evidence, we need to get that out there. The press are turning Fabian into a deity, a hero killed by terrorists, his son and daughter are seen as the heirs to his throne, the people who will help Genix roll-out Cryomen across the world to protect us.

Subject Six

Maybe.

Me

Maybe? Definitely! The people deserve…

Subject Six

Listen, when I was in Genix, I opened up their systems way more than Walton and I ever had before. Right now all their data and information is transmitting back to Rueben. If we don't rock the boat, we'd be able to monitor them. Keeping enemies close and all that.

Me

No, you're all about transparency and exposure, that's what…

Subject Six

Am I? In some cases, but with Genix? If it's not them making money from war, someone else will be… being able to watch them could be what we need.

I stand up. This doesn't feel right.

Subject Six

What's wrong, Benji? Why so mad?

Me

How do you do it? How do you change the world! If you can't, then no-one can.

Subject Six

I wouldn't say that. When I got Walton's message about the terrorists and your kids I was on a mission that my Genix investigation had put me onto. Coming back would have blown it. Messaging you would have blown my cover and I thought I might be able to get to you in time once it was settled. If not, I knew I could trust him, and you. I hacked into the cameras at the mansion and watched it all unfold. The grand showdown.

Me

There was nothing grand about it.

Subject Six

The big showdown then. I watched it, watched it all and I saw you nail it. Without me there.

Me

Nail it, Walton's dying!

Subject Six

We all die. It's not about that.

Me

What is it about?

Subject Six

It's about making sure you succeed before you check out. And you proved you can, and Walton did.

Me

That feels... that feels too simplistic.

Subject Six

Of course, but doesn't everything when you try to put it into words? What, why are you looking at me like that?

Me

Where were you, Enosh? Where were you?

Subject Six

I saw you, looking for me, once you'd got your family, you thought I'd arrived, didn't you? Is that why you're angry, because I didn't turn up?

Me

I'm not angry.

Subject Six

What are you?

Me

Desperate.

Subject Six

Desperate for what?

Me

Answers.

He doesn't speak. He stands there, looking at me, hands in the air. Then Rueben calls. Then he leaves. And that's all the debrief I get. So I get in my car and I drive to Mina and the kids.

Two days later I'm back in the hospital as Walton dies. Subject Six isn't at the funeral. Rueben is and he gives me a phone when we shake hands. Very cloak and dagger. Which, I have to admit, I find thrilling even though it's been a total relief for the past week to feel free of Mo and Genix and all of that.

On the drive home the phone rings. Mina answers and puts it on speaker.

Subject Six

I'm not calling with answers, is that going to bother you?

Me

What are you calling for then?

Subject Six

To tell you to get the book done, get it out there. You're right about Genix, we need to expose them. Show the world they didn't make me... you can do that. All these rumours about how I was Genix, how I have terrorist ties, how I'm now in prison, how I'm now training Jihadists in Syria, I want it stopped.

Me

I can do that.

Subject Six

I know you can. And you can do it properly. An article can get brushed aside, a book's-worth of proof can't.

Me

What are you going to do?

Subject Six

What I am doing.

Mina

Which is what? God, Six, don't be so fucking cryptic.

Subject Six

Ha! Hi Mina. Sure, well, you know, I'm continuing with missions.

Me

Really? But I haven't heard anything...

Subject Six

That's how I want it now, as much as possible. It's how I wanted it to begin with...

Mina

Is that what you were doing that day? When you should have been with us?

Subject Six

Should? Well I don't know about that, but yes. I'd been looking at Genix, spying on Fabian and I saw he was doing a big deal with Mo's backers on the day of your meeting. I hoped to go out there, shut it down and then answer Walton's cry for help. But it didn't go as planned, not quite... so I didn't make it to you.

Mina

But did it work out?

Subject Six

I stopped the shipment. Got the terrorist weapon suppliers and Western company arrested, in the end, so yes. And Benji, the mission I left you for last week when we were at the hospital, that went well too.

Me

So that's what you're going to do?

Subject Six

There's nothing else I want to do.

Me

What about what you said about the future?

Subject Six

We'll see about that.

Mina

Jeez, Six, you're so fucking evasive, why don't you...

The line goes dead.

The following day I begin work on the book. As I write, that's the last time I heard from Subject Six. But I have no doubt he's still out there.

I warned you at the beginning I don't have the answers. Although maybe that's not quite true. If you ask where did Subject Six come from? The real answer is that we don't know. Yet.